Twist

TOM GRASS

PEGASUS CRIME

NEW YORK LONDON

TWIST

Pegasus Crime is an imprint of
Pegasus Books, Ltd.
148 West 37th Street, 13th Floor
New York, NY 10018

First Pegasus Books cloth edition February 2021

Library of Congress Cataloging-in-Publication Data is available.

ISBN: 978-1-64313-661-5

10 9 8 7 6 5 4 3 2 1

Printed in the United States of America
Distributed by Simon & Schuster
www.pegasusbooks.com

For everyone who could do better.

PROLOGUE

FBoss said you made your own luck but that was just a lie. You could be on top of your game and still have bad shit happen like a fat gallery owner called Maurice bum rushing you and emptying half a can of mace in your face.

Two weeks. I'll come to get you myself.

Two weeks had crawled by. He still couldn't figure it out. Why leave him half blind, out in the cold, when they could just as easily have stuck him in a lock-up somewhere? In Harry's mind it was all too much nonsense.

Now at least the waiting was over as he walked up the incline to where the overpass rose up about fifty metres at the peak of its parabola. He was exposed. It wasn't the kind of place where you walked but the only vehicles were trade vehicles, their drivers too busy sucking in super-heated coffee and hitting their deadlines to clock a skinny boy standing out in the wind on the hard shoulder.

Harry brought his hand up to his face. The swelling had gone down but his eyes were still itchy. Red enough that the bums in the park were still hitting him up for a blunt.

Ninja thief maced in art house raid.

He wondered if FBoss had seen the funny side. Probably not. The CCTV footage on the evening news would have strangled any sense of humour he'd had left. Now, fourteen days on, Harry had seen the footage so many times that it had become his memory. When he tried to remember the moments that preceded the ambush he couldn't. All he could picture were the grainy black and white images of a black-suited male figure groping his way out of the gallery entrance then stopping, tearing off a black balaclava and throwing up.

He'd been tempted to go back and set fire to the place but he'd remembered something Dodge had told him. Something about revenge being a cold dish and he'd thought better of it. All that mattered was staying out of the can. The thing would run out of steam before too long and, when it did, FBoss would pull him out of whichever cellar or attic they were going to stick him in and drive him to the docks and onto a ship bound for a faraway shore.

He consoled himself that the worst part was almost over. Climbing hoardings and drainpipes at night to nest where the crazies couldn't reach him. Avoiding direct contact with people until he felt like a leper, a deformed creature, creeping in the shadows, sleeping beneath bushes at night in public gardens and the City's parks.

One night, probably the seventh, he'd broken into a work-man's hut in a railway cutting and slept inside black bin bags. It was cold in the hut when he'd woken up. The door had opened in the night and was banging in the wind. He'd felt a presence then, something that had been coming for a long time, and he'd felt a pressure in his chest and wondered when he would feel safe again.

A dull red glow was rising in the fog bank to the east. It blanketed most of the City in a sulphurous mist. Harry's eyes were naturally drawn to where the Shard sliced up through the murk and he remembered Dodge, the bug-eyed stoner, telling him there was a giant camera on the top that the spooks called 'The Eye of Sauron'. Harry was looking forward to seeing Dodge most of all.

During the recce he had counted nine streetlights up the incline to the drop-off. He tried hard to picture the stack of tyres beneath him in the whiteness, but could not. Forcing himself to swallow his fear, he stepped up to the hard edge. It was now or never. FBoss wouldn't hang about and there would be no second encounter.

He hit the top tier hard and the momentum pitched him forwards. He cartwheeled out into thin air and felt himself turn a complete circle before his shoulder made impact with the stack. It punched the air from his lungs but he managed to roll, turning his body so that he hit the next tier flat on his back. The loss of downward velocity allowed him to reach out a hand and snatch the rim of a tyre and pivot himself into an upright position and land, like a gymnast coming off the bars.

The fog was thicker on the ground. Car wrecks were stacked six or seven high, crushed and broken like rows of bad teeth. FBoss had said they were laid out like a wheel. Seven spokes that led to a hub at the centre. The hub where he would be waiting now.

Police hunt Boy Ninja …

A metallic clang rang out and Harry started as a fox burst from the stack to his right. He watched it bolt then skid as it saw him then skitter to a stop on the wet tarmac two metres in front of him. It looked up at him nonplussed then turned tail and slipped silently back into the fog.

Two more clangs followed and Harry felt a wave of excitement as he walked faster, deeper into the stacks. It felt like coming home. The prodigal son walking back up a long driveway to the only family he had ever known. Everything would be forgiven and forgotten in a single smile. No words would be needed. There would be more work. Not here maybe but somewhere …

He smelt the smoke before he saw the colour of the fog change to a dark grey that shrouded the figure of a man who stood warming his hands by a fire.

'FBoss?'

The wood smoke surprised him. He smelt it before he saw it, black against the fog. It hid the figure more completely, like a cloak, so that the body beneath was ill-defined. A hunched man who stood, silhouetted by the flames that leapt from a rusty steel drum.

'FBoss?'

Harry smiled. To think he'd doubted him. FBoss was here. True to his word. Bang on time. Even as Harry had run, hounded by the police sirens approaching the gallery, he'd felt the buzz in his pocket. He'd prised open his eyes to read the text. That was two weeks ago and now here he was, just like he'd promised. Harry was getting out. On a boat or on a plane, it hardly mattered. In a few days he'd be somewhere hot with a fat wad in his pocket watching the Premiership on TV and dipping into the pot that FBoss kept safe for a rainy day.

'FBoss, it's me. H-Bomb. Harry.'

Steam was rising from the hunchback's coat. Harry rubbed his eyes and squinted. The smoke was black. He edged closer towards the fire. It looked inviting after so many nights sleeping rough. The wind lifted the fog and Harry's heart skipped a beat. It was FBoss's green coat but he wasn't in it.

Where the coat's collar met the shoulders the wool was drawn tight. The arms rode up an inch too short so that the man's wrists and black leather gloves were visible. Harry fought against blind panic, the voice in his ear again as fear writhed like a snake in his stomach. Then the voice started screaming and Harry fought to block out a truth he could not accept.

They had decided to kill him.

He took a few steps back, reeling as his senses quickened, his ears picking up the crackling of the flames and the sap squealing and fizzing in the blazing wood and a steady sound, like an animal, panting. Harry turned to see it trot out of the fog towards him. It was sleek, squat and muscled. Dog and man, the betrayal was now complete. He exploded off his quads and reached the bonnet of a wreck as the dog lunged. He snatched a ledge of crushed metal above him and looked down as the dog lurched up, baring its fangs.

There was a muffled crack. A dead sound and a concussion in the metal close to his head. He scrabbled up to the top of the stack and lay flat. The fog obscured the shooter. He rolled and dropped off the far edge and ran towards the gates and heard the dog tracking him on the far side.

He reached the gates, slipped through and slammed the bolt shut behind him. He took off up the track at a sprint towards the dual carriageway. The man would have a car. He had to get off the road.

He crossed the scrubby verge and hurled himself at the fence. The barbed wire on the top caught his jacket and it tore as he jumped, grabbed the branch of a tree, and dropped into stinging nettles that were taller than he was. They stung his face and his hands as he rushed through them towards the low rumble of a large diesel engine.

He slowed to a walk as he entered the lay-by where a tall man wearing a turban was taking a piss against the front wheel of a lorry.

'It's all right. It's mine,' the man said. Then, without turning to look at Harry, added, 'Do you need a lift?'

The lorry pulled off the North Circular three quarters of an hour later in Neasden. Rush hour was a first for Harry. He got off to the north of the road and watched the commuters crossing a footbridge. He dropped his jacket in a bin and made for the crowd. He noticed a short, bald man eating a bacon sandwich as he walked to join a bus queue that had become a ruck. Harry caught a flash of a girl in a red hood in the queue ahead of him and his heart froze but when she turned he saw that she had a round, plain face and a fake handbag.

Harry took a sharp angle for the bus and his hand darted into the bin by the stand and pulled out a plastic bag. He let the girl with the fake handbag get on the bus first and smiled at her as he disembowelled it with his craft knife, catching its contents neatly in the plastic bag as they fell.

He turned and took a cut away from the street down a cul-de-sac and ducked into a covered walkway to count his take. There were three twenties in the purse: a good feed and his ticket back to Gravesend. He still had friends there. One or two of his old mates worked down the docks. They might be able to hook him up. Get him working passage on a ship out of there.

He went further down the alleyway, making for the light at its far end. It was dark and there was broken glass on the floor. It was pooled at intervals where someone had systematically smashed all the lights, one after another.

'Hello, H-Bomb.'

Harry froze and turned to look back the way he had come. He saw a red dot light up against one wall and illuminate the gimlet eyes he had hoped to avoid. He shrank back towards the entrance fingering his mobile in his pocket. Jason Bourne always used a pay-as-you-go. There was a reason for that. He pulled it out of his pocket and stared down at it.

'It was a test,' the voice added. 'We needed to know. I hope you understand.'

'Fuck off!' Harry said.

'You run away, Bullseye thinks you're a deer. I fired the shot to stop him. It's all he understands.'

Harry watched Sikes step away from the wall.

'Why are you wearing his coat?' Harry asked.

'Ask him yourself. He's waiting for you. If you want to see him, that is.'

Harry froze. He didn't know how he felt about FBoss now, or the rest of the crew. They were the only family he'd ever known. He'd trusted them and now they wanted him dead.

'The Feds are onto you, Harry. We had to know,' Sikes went on.

'Fuck off!' Harry bawled at him then smashed the phone against the wall. It fell to the floor and as he ground it into the concrete he took his knife in his hand, watching the dog as it closed on him. He turned. There was only one way out.

There was a litter bin in the corner and on the wall above it was a satellite dish. He lengthened his stride, picking up his knees like a triple jumper. He pushed up off the top of the bin and caught the antennae with his right hand, following with his left, and pulled himself up as the dog turned tight circles beneath him. A wolf whistle sounded shrill behind him as he reached the stairwell and began to climb.

A fire door opened onto the roof. The fog had lifted and he could see there was a ladder at the far end of the roof. He slid down it to a platform some ten feet long. It led nowhere. There was a fifty-foot drop on all sides. When he turned he saw that the dog had reached the top of the ladder. It was peering down at him, touching the top rung with its paw.

Harry jogged to the far edge and dropped down flat to look over. There was no drainpipe. No easy way down. He got up to his knees and then the next conscious thought he had, that something like a brick had hit him between the shoulder blades, seemed dislocated, like he'd missed a bit. Then he tasted blood in his mouth and he saw that some of it was spattered down the front of his T-shirt.

He pushed himself back up onto all fours and coughed flecks of blood onto the concrete. Then he saw the brick lying a couple of feet to his right and he heard a rasping sound and became scared when he realised it was coming from inside him, and then a sensation arose that felt like air was being blown into a burst balloon.

The wind was moving faster now. Wisps of fog were lifting, spiralling into columns rising hundreds of feet into the air. Looking west he could see the towers of Wembley Stadium and he remembered the bet. Dodge's wager when he'd put up a grand for the runner who would go from one tower to the next along the giant twisting white tube that connected them.

Harry struggled to get up. He could hear footsteps coming down the steel rungs of the ladder. He wasn't going to take it on his knees. Not like a dog on his knees. He focused and managed to get up onto his feet. The effort made him cough and he put his hand to his mouth, staring at the blood that ran down the lines of his palms and dripped down onto the concrete floor.

He could see now that it could be done. That there was a way to take Dodge's money because there was no single white tube but many tubes all woven in together like threads in a piece of rope. Once you got up there then you could walk on one and use the next one up as a handrail. Nothing simpler. He spat the blood from his mouth and pushed himself forwards. He was going to take Dodge for a grand and use the money to get out and start again. Somewhere they didn't know his name.

He took two steps towards the edge. Two steps closer to the white tubes until he could imagine he was there. With the paintwork shining beneath his feet. It was a good day to climb and he could almost hear the Dutch fans chanting something van Oranje. He could see the orange and white players on the pitch and the guards looking nervously up and he wondered if anyone was going to risk it by climbing up the railings to the tower and following him out here.

There was always one, he thought. Some guy that wanted to be a hero. He could hear the commentators down below. It would be on national TV once they got the cameras focused in on him. They'd be asking if he was a jumper. Or just an exhibitionist, some kind of streaker perhaps that no one sane would want to tackle by following up the vertical ladder

But, rest assured, they would be waiting at the far end. Watching and hoping you lost your nerve, but he wouldn't.

He'd walk out to the middle, bold as brass, pull his cacks down and moony the crowd. The players would stop when they realised the cheering wasn't for them. They'd look up and watch him open-mouthed as he took off again, moving through the white tubes like a chimpanzee swinging through the trees. The same one the papers would say the next day. The same Boy Ninja from the White Cube heist.

But then there was a click behind him and he turned. He was not alone. He had never been alone. As the clouds broke he watched sunlight dance on a short steel blade, swallowed a mouthful of blood then stepped out towards the towers, determined to take Dodge's money.

1

She tried to avoid the past if she could help it, returning only when the present required it, to help calibrate the severity of a current crisis or to understand if what happened back then was making her overreact or behave weirdly now. Of course, she knew it didn't do to dwell. The past was gone. She preferred to believe in the future. To train hard and do what she was told and place faith in the gang and the idea that this life was finite. That there would be a jackpot and it would put an end to this insanity and wipe the slate clean so she could begin again.

But she was back in the past now. Searching for an answer to a question she had been asked after the first time, which she knew held the key to understanding her present predicament. Events that had begun on the floor of the room she shared with three other girls in the foster home the day two strangers had come to meet her, the manager standing in the doorway as she watched the faces of the other girls, hoping they would not hate her because she had been chosen and they had not.

She skirted the fence line behind the old hotel then crossed the parkland and jogged through the underpass that led to the Tube station. There were trees in the park, their natural colours still visible in the half light. They smelt nothing like the 'magic tree' which had been hanging from the rear-view mirror of her foster parents' Volvo estate the day they had come to collect her. She could still see the eyes of the man in the mirror as he'd driven back to the red-bricked semi-detached house in Highgate for the first time.

The woman said her favourite aunt had had red hair like hers, but the man, who was older and had a strange lump on his nose, had just smiled and told her that they had visited her school and spoken to her teachers. Who had told them the same thing, that she was a natural athlete and terribly clever and could be anything she wanted to be if she got over her 'little chaos'.

She hadn't actively disliked the woman, just the man who lied all the time. But she hadn't hated him all that much. Not as much as the one who was paid to care for her but who only visited once a month, spoke to her like she should be grateful to have foster parents and always left without saying if or when he would come back.

She sat on the underground looking at all the worn-out winter faces and told herself things were better now. That nothing could be worse than those first three weeks. Like actors rehearsing their roles for a play called 'family'. Knowing at once that she could not love them and creeping downstairs to listen at the kitchen door as the woman cried to the man that they were not 'bonding' and listening to him reply as if he were reading from a text book that she had problems trusting adults and that it would take time.

About an hour had passed since rush hour and people were still making their way home. She stepped out of the underground station and realised she hadn't registered a single face during the journey. She was like that when she was upset. She went foraging in the past. Looking for clues, rerunning every path she had taken, following them as they branched, asking herself if it was always inevitable that she would end up in the mess she was in today.

And the woman's face was here with her now, standing over her shoulder as her trainers touched lightly on the frozen pavement, telling her that she had to 'sit' a test which was a practice for the exam she had to take so that she could get a scholarship. And so too was the psychologist who came once a week for what she called 'socialisation', providing her with the skills that would allow her to fit into her special school, not once suggesting that it might be a good idea if she actually just played with other children her own age.

But there was no escaping the past. Not even in the crowd. Her senses quickened and she closed in on her targets, watching pupils dilate as credit cards appeared from wallets, shining brightly beneath shop lights, the day after B-Day, as the bankers broke into their bonuses, topping up their high-maintenance girlfriends like mobile phones in high-end boutiques and three-star Michelin restaurants.

She could see the girls who had got what they wanted and those that had not by the expressions on their faces. They reminded her of the girls at the school after she'd passed the exam. Girls who learnt early how to make things go their way, all staring at her as the man walked with her to the Headmistress's office to register on the first day. It was all part of the annual ritual. First the men pretended to be thoroughly dissatisfied with their five-figure bonuses and then it was their girlfriends' turn.

She walked further down Bond Street and crossed where it met Jermyn Street. It was a good spot to watch the wallets on legs but she was tired, had slept badly, so she bought an espresso and half-filled it with sugar and sat watching the beady eyes of the stockbroker in the boutique across the road. And he was watching the shop girl as she climbed a ladder to reach for the sparkling silver slippers that seemed to float with all the other pairs of thousand-pound shoes in the high glass ceiling of the shop.

She crossed the road and pushed her way in between the half a dozen couples who were hogging the floor, doing the bonus-day dance. She felt her pulse quicken as it always did when she was in the presence of easy money, which she felt coming most strongly off a man in a black suit who she knew was alone and who was watching her from behind his wire-rimmed spectacles.

He was stood in the corner of the room with one of the shop girls. The girl was holding up a white, snakeskin cowboy boot and when he turned to admire it she saw two strands of loose fibre sticking up out of his right rear trouser pocket. He was good-looking in a bookish kind of way and she thought he might be forty-five or -six and self-made, perhaps the brains behind a 'lucky' hedge fund. He turned and looked directly at her as she circled in front of him.

'Cowboy boots always come out small. They pinch the toes if you're not careful,' she said, watching his eyes blink twice then look back at the boot.

'That's what worries me,' he replied, 'she's got webbed feet. Like a frog. Kind of broad at the front.'

His accent was lost somewhere in the mid-Atlantic but there was still a drawl to it that reminded her of cowboy movies.

'But if you get it right she'll love you forever,' she said, standing on the tips of her toes and stretching up to touch the heel of a low-flying green slipper, trying to picture the man's girlfriend because he would certainly have one, imagining she was most likely English and attracted to a geek who went against type.

She pretended to go on shopping and never once looked at him again until his back was turned and he was walking out of the shop. Then she followed him out onto the street and round the corner and down into the underground, keeping track of his sandy mop as he stood in the middle of the carriage. Then, after he'd changed trains and was bound south-west on the Piccadilly line, she stepped up close to him and watched him smile.

'Are you following me?' he asked.

She feigned outrage and allowed the braking train to press her against him as they entered the darkness of the tunnel, feeling the fool's hand in the small of her back as they entered a final bend, exploring the space between his thighs and the muscles of his lower back as she ran her hands along the top of his belt.

And then she fell, hooking his right leg with her own so that he joined her, his back pressed hard against the glass partition, masking the sensation of her two fingers pinching the two stray strands of cotton in his back pocket.

She felt him try to push them both upright but she stuck her breasts into his chest and pulled the wallet vertically out, slipping it inside her inner mackintosh pocket as the lights of the station lit up the carriage and the train slowed and the door opened and the crowd carried her backwards. She watched his face as she let the flood take her. A picture of misery and longing as her feet touched the platform and the exit sign beckoned her away along a tunnel, up the escalator and out onto the frozen street where she broke into a slow jog.

She ran a while until she reached Covent Garden where Batesy had hacked her membership of a basement kick-boxing club. She nodded to the girl behind the counter then headed down the steps and took a shower. The wallet held about two hundred dollars in bills and just shy of three hundred and fifty pounds in cash. There was also a platinum Amex card, a bank card, a local driver's licence and a stack of ten business cards which concealed one last card, a single, translucent card with no type on it.

She washed the wallet in the shower with the shampoo as it ran from her hair and stuck it in a post box outside the studio. The postman would read the address in the bank cards and they or the police would post it there. He'd be glad to get his cards back and surprised to find that no attempt had been made to use them. At the same time he'd be alarmed that the most valuable card of all had been taken; the card with nothing on it.

She felt her phone ring in her pocket. It was FBoss. He was talking about Harry. His voice was feeble and he sounded like he was genuinely cut up about it all. He was saying that it was important that they all pulled together but she was not listening to him. Instead she was drifting back into the past to the playground and her nemesis, the prefect who had her backed into a corner, after she had passed the exam and won the only scholarship in the school for especially clever girls.

I knew the day you arrived that you were different. Everyone in your dorm knows and the teachers all know. The ugly man and woman who brought you are not your real parents. They don't really care for you and they will abandon you, just like your own mother abandoned you. Because you are a liar and a thief and I knew it just by looking at you.

Her pulse was racing and her breathing was shallow. She had tried to outrun the past by stealing from the present but it was no use. She wondered again if her path had been marked from the outset; if it had always been that way and that now it was time to go home, to the life she had truly, always belonged to.

'I'm coming,' she heard herself say as she held the translucent card up to the light.

2

No guide should have to put up with this kind of abuse, let alone the most highly qualified guide in London's Tate Britain. But such was Trimble's fate this cold January afternoon.

The Fine Art Undergraduates were a walk in the park. They wanted to know how, not why or when, and the act of actually trying to create art made them appreciate it in a way this group of middle-aged amateur art historians from Tunbridge Wells never would.

They were pedants who concerned themselves only with where the artists 'fitted in' so that everything had to be placed chronologically, so that nothing was valuable, in and of itself, unless it was clearly labelled 'late this' or 'early that'. For them art wasn't supposed to *move* you. It was a platform on which they competed, falling over each other to ask him questions that only a world expert or a fool would attempt to answer.

And this particular group had excelled themselves. The cherry was now officially on top of the perfect shit of a week. It wasn't their fault Trimble had recently emerged from a catatonic depression, but he felt like they had somehow sensed the abyss he had just crawled from, and had seized upon his weakness like a flock of psychic vultures, taking it in turns to peck at him before swarming in to tear him apart.

The ferocity of their initial assault had shocked him. Unanswerable questions ranging from the obscure to the wholly irrelevant had rained down on him for the first forty-five minutes leaving his palms sweating and his nerves shredded, watching their mouths open, their gums receding over yellow fangs as they smiled and he parried, apologised, turning questions into questions, tumbling on through the charnel house of the late Middle Ages.

He watched as a lady in a peach-coloured cardigan stepped forwards and smiled at him before unleashing hell.

'I'm afraid you'll have to ask my colleague Harvey about what Lowry liked to eat for breakfast. He's quite the expert,' he replied.

He felt tired. On his feet all day, rudely used by cretins to the point where he wanted only to sit down in one of the white chairs in the cafeteria and weep into his Earl Grey, but instead he had to stand and suffer this abuse, turning just in time to mount a defence against the ring leader, the Queen Bitch in a grey cardigan whose nostrils flared, thick black nasal hair bristling, as she spoke.

'Isn't the real problem with Blake that we struggle to isolate him because he doesn't belong to any system or movement, and as a result he doesn't get looked at in a broader context?'

'I don't give a fuck what his broader context is,' Trimble wanted to say. 'Just look! Look at the face of the devil as he tumbles down from the gates of heaven pursued by Gabriel's sword of burning white fire!'

But it was no use. After the two-month leave of absence it was more than his job was worth.

He needed some kind of a distraction. A fire drill or some catalyst that would allow him to accelerate from the killing fields of the Romantic era into the relative safety of World War One.

'Of course, Blake was a true original,' he said, raising his right arm in a dramatic circular sweep, using it to part the ladies and make his run up the gallery, careful to avoid his reflection in the coal-black habits of Millais's grave-digging nuns and not stopping until he had reached the queer piece, provenance unknown, on which he was the gallery's undisputed expert.

They were a pair, identical, Elizabethan, and sat side by side, bolt upright in bed, cradling a pair of identical, red-swaddled, grub-like babies.

'Ladies, please allow me to introduce the Cholmondeley Ladies,' he said, smiling at Queen Bitch as he pushed the boat out into waters unknown. 'Now who can tell me who the artist was?'

He watched, waiting for one of them to try and fail. But none spoke and then, just as he was about to begin his party piece, a small shrewish lady in a pink jacket stepped back from the group, pointed at the polished walnut bench in the middle of the gallery and screamed.

Pushing through the gaggle he saw the source of the excitement. A pair of dirty white Adidas sticking out from under the near end of the bench, by far the most beautiful thing he'd seen all day.

'Do something!' Queen Bitch shrieked.

But Trimble already was, walking with all the confidence he could muster towards the figure of the man lying face down beneath a dirty black trench coat. Dead or alive, sane or insane, it hardly mattered. He was Trimble's ticket, a blessed escape from the Bitch and all her kind.

He reached the bench and looked down. Poor devil, he thought, it was hard to blame the 'sleepers' as they were known. It had to be two or three below at night. Too cold to sleep outside so they ended up pacing all night just to stay alive and then staggered in, exhausted when the gallery opened at nine and either locked themselves in the men's lavatory or passed out here, beneath the benches in the main concourse.

He edged closer and saw a bare arm stretched out across the floor. It was stained with red, white and brown paint and pockmarked with tiny black pinpricks which spiralled round his arm to disappear from sight.

Was the story the guard had told him true? About a sleeper who'd pulled a needle to protect himself? True or false, it had certainly made a profound impression on him. Enough to make him wonder if this man was not just an addict but infected and was ready, playing dead, with a needle teeming with an incurable flesh-eating virus ready to stick in the first person who dared to disturb his narcotic slumber?

He edged closer and used his foot to lift the right arm high enough so that he could see beneath it. He was no hero. He just wanted the tour to end, to go home and put the kettle on and crawl into bed.

T ... W ... I ....

He was no hero, he just wanted the tour to end, to go home and put the kettle on and crawl into bed.

Trimble let the arm drop to the floor, then watched as the man began to stir. He saw a chin, mouth and nose emerge from beneath the mop of greasy hair and the sinews of the exposed arm twitch involuntarily as the man opened his eyes. They were pale blue, clear and focused, and they were sat in the face of a boy, no more than eighteen years old, who had woken with a start and was staring up at him through the walnut slats of the bench.

And now Trimble had to pause for thought because, quite unexpectedly, he had a dilemma on his hands. Should he deal with the interloper himself, or wait for the guards to get hold of him, knowing that if they caught sight of the tattoo on his forearm they would most certainly hand him over to the police?

He looked up, listening to the sound of steel-toed boots booming in the gallery next door, then down at the pale, unwashed boy with the stained hands who was scrabbling sideways, clearly realising for himself the peril he was now in. For this was the boy they were after. The one who each night for the past two nights had stood all night in the freezing cold painstakingly spraying a giant, picture-perfect version of William Blake's *The Simoniac Pope* on the gallery's rear wall.

Yes, thought Trimble, there was no doubt about it. Here lay Twist, the only graffiti artist dumb enough to tag his own forearm.

3

Red turned the transparent card in her hand. She had a feeling she had seen one like it before. No name, no address, no logo. Just clear plastic she could see her fingertips through. If there was a chip inside it then it was transparent too. She held it up to her eye and stared through it at the young policeman across the street who was alternating between his walkie-talkie and his Big Mac.

'You fat bastard!' she shouted, blasting him with her cheesiest smile then laughing as he went to take a bite out of his walkie-talkie.

They weren't all bad but quite a few of them were stupid. At least Big Mac had a sense of humour.

She picked up her mobile and called Batesy, who used to work for his uncle in Hatton Garden. He knew about shit like this. About security holographs and high-tech stuff. She'd seen him use a special magnifying glass with a UV light to check to see if a stone was a blood diamond. Calling him seemed like as sensible a next move as any.

He wasn't answering but she let it ring. He was crazy about her and she knew he would call her back, especially now, at six o'clock on a Thursday, when the bars were beginning to fill.

She crossed Oxford Street and walked down Wardour Street to the junction of Old Compton Street. She didn't mind the bars here. She got a lot less hassle from the boys in them than the ones in the City at this time of year.

She walked into a pub called the Ship and the men at the bar didn't even look at her. It was dark on the stairs but they were empty so she walked down them holding the handrail to steady herself. She pushed open the black swing door and went into the dance room. It was pitch black so she used her phone to find the light switch and watched her teeth turn blue.

She pulled the card from her pocket and held it up to the light. It looked very different now. A single word was written across the front in plain font. It read:

LUNA

She asked a girl she knew who worked in a sex shop. The girl was not going to help her until she put a bottle of something called Super X on the counter and refused the change for a twenty. Then she smiled and pointed next door.

'The DJ next door fixes shit for rich people,' she said. 'Ask him.'

Next door was a neon-lit bar. The door was open so Red went in. She could see a shadow in the corner of the room, gesticulating behind a Plexiglas window as his other hand worked what had to be a turntable. He couldn't mix a pudding, let alone a track, but he had enough self-confidence to pass it off. He was stood up in the booth with his headphones on, pointing at imaginary dancers in the empty bar, and as she walked in he pointed at her, turning his palm skyward and lifting it in a series of jerky movements, calling upon her to move to the beat that only he could hear. She lifted her right fist half-heartedly and walked across the empty floor and stuck the card through the semicircular hole in the Perspex.

He shook his head and kept shaking it, even when she held the card up to the fluorescent tubes above his head. And it was only when he looked down and saw the twenty pound note that he smiled and nodded, as if to say, hit me again.

Knowing the location felt somehow like money in the bank, so she took a cab, which cost her twenty on top of the forty she'd dropped finding the address. It was just off Gloucester Road and the description checked out with the address. It was a white faux Regency building with recessed triple-glazed windows whose white wooden screens made it impossible to see in from the street.

She stepped up to a large black front door and saw a crescent moon in the glass above the door. She pulled the chain and a bell rang somewhere in the interior, then she waited for someone to come to the door. But nobody came and she felt uneasy, aware that she was alone, outside some kind of secret club for men that the pimp had been reluctant to tell her about.

She stood looking up at the white walls of the house. She imagined the scene inside. Probably a dimly lit corridor and a cloakroom like a strip club. She knew places like that from the east. There were always doormen in the hallway and a dimly lit basement bar with a few tables and chairs, mirrors and poles on low stages.

She checked her pockets. The money was almost gone but at least she was warm. The stop in the Selfridges sale had made sure of that. A winter coat to replace the mackintosh. Red, full length, with a belt fastened tight at the waist. And she had left the Green Flash trainers in a changing room and traded up for a pair of black Italian heels. She pulled the chain again and heard the same bell ringing in the hallway. At least she looked the part.

She walked back down the steps and stared up at the house and the crescent moon in the glass. Perhaps the pimp DJ had got it wrong. Perhaps the house's occupants had moved on or found God. But she didn't believe it and she waited, thinking that at half past ten at night someone was bound to come or go eventually.

And her patience bore fruit half an hour later. A midnight-blue Mercedes purred to a standstill thirty yards further down the road and she watched an early middle-aged Asian man step out, cross the street, turn left, pass in front of her then turn right and climb the steps, two at a time, as if he was in a hurry.

'My boyfriend left something,' she started from the foot of the steps behind him. 'He's in the middle of an important business dinner so he asked me to pick it up for him.'

The man turned and smiled but looked surprised when she produced the card. When she climbed the steps he took it from her, studied it then turned and wiped it in a vertical then horizontal motion across the door's surface. A pale glow illuminated his face and she looked up and saw a beam of light coming from a tiny hole in the top right-hand corner of the porch. Then there was a click and a whirring sound as the mechanism within the door engaged and heavy bolts slid back and the door opened.

The Asian man stepped across the threshold and placed his back to the wall, holding out the card to her as she stepped past him into a dark candlelit hallway. She had modified her expectations when she'd seen the Mercedes, but the deep crimson carpet and the original oil paintings on the walls still took her by surprise.

She heard the door close and the bolts slide back into their housings. She felt the man's presence behind her as she slipped off her red overcoat to reveal her dress. It was Dior, basic black, and she had stolen it by isolating the paint capsule in the tamper-proof tag with a special tool that FBoss had given her for Christmas.

'Thank you,' she said as the man took her coat.

'It goes with your hair,' he commented.

She followed his gaze to the floor and she saw it was true. The carpet was the same auburn red as her hair. She stepped forwards and touched his forearm and he turned and led her up to the first-floor landing in silence.

'You must have a unique relationship,' he said as they climbed.

'My boyfriend is very open-minded,' she replied.

When they reached the first landing they were met by a pair of large black doors with brass handles.

'Go through these doors and you'll find yourself in a waiting room,' he said, handing her the coat. 'Ring the bell and then ask for Luna. She will help you find what you are looking for.'

She watched him stiffen and without replying he motioned with his hand to the double doors behind her.

'Have a pleasant evening,' he said.

Then she watched him turn and begin to climb again. Two steps at a time once more, springing up on the balls of his feet like a man half his age, disappearing around the next half-landing. She was left uninvited and unaccompanied in a large house which a pimp pretending to be a DJ had told her not to visit alone.

She pulled on the doors and they felt heavy in her hands. She leant against one and pushed, listening to the sucking sound as it opened to reveal a pair of thick crimson curtains. She reached to push the curtains back but something stopped her and she just stood there in the darkness as the door closed behind her, hands raised, fingertips barely touching the thick velvet in front of her.

She felt a vibration against her and she pulled out the phone and looked at the screen. It was a message from Batesy. Four letters on the screen ...

GTFO

It was the code that had reached Harry too late. Too late for him to get the fuck out of the White Cube.

She hit speed dial then switched to Wassup so she could text while he talked.

B. I can't talk but I can listen, she typed, listening to the click as he picked up the line at the other end.

'That card you've got. It's bad news. Ditch it and don't go there.'

Why? she texted back.

'I'm not alone here,' came the reply. '... And I don't know where you are. We never spoke.'

The line went dead and all she was left with was the pulse of blood in her veins and the card which was cold in her hand.

She put the phone back in her coat pocket and reached up to touch the curtains. They were quarter-inch-thick fire curtains that theatres used to make silent scene changes but she imagined them being used for something different. She felt pressure mounting at her temples, the edge of panic as she imagined someone with large muscular hands using the curtains to silence her.

4

Shipwrecked sailors clinging to a rock, a bronze muscleman wrestling a constrictor and a dog with mad eyes flashed past him, the questions tumbling and jostling for position as he ran. How long had he been asleep for? And why had the gallery guide told him about the window?

A guard appeared, filling the doorway in front of him, and with the shock he found himself yelling: 'Aaaaaarrgggh!'

Fifteen, ten, five feet and closing, still screaming until he saw the man flinch and turn to look back for support. That was his mistake as Twist sidestepped in the opposite direction, boosting off the door frame into the space beyond.

'It's him! The little shit! Stop him!'

The words were high-pitched and nasal, snapping at his heels as the footsteps came booming behind them. He reached the high portico and took the corner in a skid into a group of French students who stood unwashed and reeking at the top of the stairs.

'*Putain! Merde!*'

He silenced their cries by vaulting up onto the flat, polished stone of the wide banister, sliding down beneath their teacher who flapped at him with her guide book. As he gained momentum, bursting between the queue for the cloakroom and ticket sales, a question came to him. The guide in the gallery had mentioned a window in a toilet but hadn't said which one … the Ladies or the Gents? Or both?

Stop! Think! What do they expect you to do?

He heard the words of his new best friend in his ear.

Now do the opposite!

He slowed, took a deep breath, pulled up his hood and pushed open the door. A middle-aged woman, possibly Italian, was stood, leaning over the washbasin, puckering her lips. Twist slipped past her to the cubicles. There were two of them but he saw the light reflected on the ceiling was brighter on the right side. He pushed the door open and looked up at a tiny pane of frosted glass.

It was sealed shut. He was trapped.

'Check the Gents!' He heard the guards outside.

He stepped up onto the toilet seat and examined the window. Even if he could kick out the glass, it would be a miracle if he could squeeze through.

Resting his hands and elbows on the tops of the cubicle walls, he lifted his knees to his chest, drawing his legs back like a spring. Bam!

He felt the impact in his spine. He took a deep breath then kicked once more. Again it held firm.

'*Che cosa fai?*' the woman screeched.

Twist hammered again, once, twice, each time focusing his heels at the centre of the glass. As he drew back for the fourth strike he heard the door open and the Italian woman screaming for help. He kicked again, the toilet walls juddering as the guards burst into the room. The metal frame gave out a fraction as the big guard, whose voice he recognised from the gallery, began pounding on the cubicle door.

'The police are already here, son. They're waiting for you outside.'

Bam! Bam! Bam! His legs became a steam press until finally he felt the metal frame give and cold air on his ankles and stomach as he wormed his way out. Thoughts rushed into his mind now that he had stopped moving. He saw his tattoo. It was the same as his tag. The tag that he'd sprayed on the back wall of the gallery …

He was suspended now, halfway in, halfway out of the window, arms flailing inside the cubicle, pinioned by his chest.

'Kick it in!' a guard screamed, and Twist struggled like a contortionist, raking his armpits against the window frames and turning his head sideways, legs scrabbling in thin air on the far side of the wall.

As he saw the screws on the lock strain and pop he stopped wriggling and instead took a shallow breath then exhaled, steadily, feeling his diaphragm contract as the weight of his body took him and he slid out from the window.

The roof was wet. When he rolled onto his back he could see the big red face of the guard, head and one shoulder stuck in the window. There were no police but there was a wall, some twenty feet high, and at its foot was a garden square, red-brick houses dominated by a Victorian church that stood alone in its centre. And a drainpipe, the piping plastic but with fixtures that held. Within seconds he was climbing down and had his feet on the ground again and found them leading him across the road towards the rose garden and the sanctuary of the church.

5

She pushed back the curtain and it opened to reveal a small, wood-panelled room with a thick green rug and a wood fire burning in a large open fireplace at the far end.

A single black leather armchair on the left of the room sat facing a black door on the wall to her right. She walked over to the door and tried the handle but it was locked. She glanced around, looking for a clue, fingering the card in her pocket as she heard a key turn in the lock and she stood back, fists bunched in her pockets as a tiny, middle-aged woman appeared in the doorway, smiling as if she had been expecting her.

The woman's face bore the hallmarks of having been surgically altered, the skin stretched tight across strong, prominent cheekbones so that a frown would be indistinguishable from her smile as she looked back at Red, eyes quizzical beneath arched pencil lines and the red and gold patterned silk scarf she wore upon her head.

The effect was disorientating and somewhat sinister. She was larger than life. Somewhere between a fairy godmother and a fortune teller, her face masking her intentions as she turned the tables on Red, who felt naked under her intense gaze.

'Can I help you, my dear?' the woman asked.

'My boyfriend left something, he asked me to come and pick it up for him,' Red replied, watching the woman think about her statement then nod her head, appearing to accept it.

'His name is Richard Bruce. He's American. He's stuck in a business dinner. He asked me to collect his coat on the way home from work.'

The woman didn't nod this time but the thin skin on her cheeks drew tighter as her smile widened into a rictus grin.

'I'm afraid I cannot recall that name, my dear,' she said.

'But he gave me his card. Here.' Red held it out to her.

'I'm afraid we have very strict rules governing entrance, Miss …'

'Kennedy. Miss Ja … net Kennedy.'

The woman stared back at her.

'Well, Miss Kennedy,' she said, stepping closer to her, watching her face, 'it's dark outside but you must be forgiven for not seeing the sign because there isn't one, because we like to protect our members' right to anonymity. And even if your Mr Bruce were a member, I'm afraid I would not be able to fulfil his request because we don't allow women to enter unaccompanied by a member. So I'm terribly sorry for your trouble and I can assure you I will contact him directly, but all I can offer you now is a lift home. There is a car waiting outside. It's a ghastly night and we wouldn't want you to get lost in the dark now, would we?'

Red watched the woman turn and push back the curtain. She was stronger than she looked and she moved well, stepping lightly as she escorted Red to the front door and what felt like a lucky escape. Red thanked her at the door and skipped down the steps into the sleet, turning when she got to the bottom to look back once at the smiling plastic-faced woman on the top step.

She pulled the collars of her coat up to protect her face as the frozen rain lashed her exposed calves and saw the rear window of the Mercedes open and the driver's black leather glove beckon her into the warm interior.

It was tempting, very tempting, but she had learnt long ago never to accept lifts from strangers, especially men who worked for places like this.

'Thank you, kind sir, but I think I'll walk,' she said, suddenly aware of a blond, pinch-faced man in a black ski jacket standing blocking her way, his left hand pointing towards the back door of the car which was opened on cue by a bearded man wearing a Russian wolfskin hat.

'Get into the back of the car, bitch,' the bearded man said.

She smiled and nodded back at him, pretending not to have heard him as she dipped into a crouch, making as if she was going to get in, then taking two fast steps forwards and stepping up onto the back rear bumper, using her hands to boost herself up onto the roof. Then she felt a vice-like grip tighten on her ankle, pull her off her feet and drag her kicking and punching from the roof to the pavement.

She gripped the top of the door but the man was too strong. He was bigger than the man in the ski jacket and she could feel the strength in his massive hands as he prised her fingers off the door frame, pinioned her arms to her chest and pushed her inside.

As the car pulled out into the road she straightened up off the back seat and looked back at the house, but the porch was empty and the woman had gone.

6

Twist vaulted the eight-foot flint wall at the rear of the church and fell into brambles. He liked to look before he leapt but the guards had spilled out of the gallery like wasps from a nest, their torches searching the darker recesses of the square.

Like most decisions made hanging upside down, his decision to hide in the church grounds had been made quickly. He was relieved that he'd fought the temptation to run. By now the local patrols would have been alerted and every CCTV camera within a half-mile radius would be being scrutinised by surveillance teams, keen to be the first to catch sight of the Tate Britain vandal.

His eyes adjusted slowly to the darkness. The internal wall he had seen from above separated the garden of the church's annexe from the main church grounds and he was relieved to see there was no door in it. His best hope was that the guards fell back on protocol and stop to knock on the church's main door before scaling the walls and clambering in after him.

He crept forwards on all fours, hugging the shadows, aiming for a narrow gap between an old shed and the side wall of the annexe. He found an overgrown path, its paving stones green and wet beneath his knees. They led him to the shed door where he stood and slipped silently into the foot-wide gap beside it.

The glass of the window was dirty but not so dirty that he could not make out a faint orange glow inside. He spat on the tip of his index finger and rubbed it, clockwise against the glass, then placed his eye to the circle and peered in. The room inside was murky but not entirely without light. A thin sliver of amber spread fanlike from beneath the door of what appeared to be the larder. He scanned it quickly, conjuring a mental picture of the annexe's occupant as he traversed the rows of tins, pulses and condiments stacked neatly on clean wooden shelves. It was conventional convenience food. Pasta sauce was as exotic as it got. He imagined a small man, a vicar, some seventy years old with a bald head, wire spectacles and the appetite of a sparrow.

He reviewed his position. Any moment now a guard would knock on the front door of the church and rouse the old boy who would most likely invite the guard in to search the grounds. This left Twist with three options. He could bolt now and run the gauntlet with the guards and the police patrols, stay where he was or find a new hiding place.

Opting for option three he edged back towards the garden. It was barren. Thorny tendrils sprung from rose bushes frozen into submission and offering little in the way of cover. Looking beyond them into the dark corners of the garden gave him more hope. The prevailing wind from the river had blown the leaves of the elm trees that stood like sentinels around the church grounds.

He crept out and dashed across to the pile of leaves. It rose to some four feet where it met the corner walls and spread out into the garden some six or seven feet, far enough to cover his entire body even at full stretch. He plunged his hands into the mound, palms up like tiny shovels and grimaced as they sliced into dense, ice-cold mulch.

Withdrawing them, he turned and fell backwards onto the pile of leaves using his hands to scoop those at the top of the pile on top of himself, wriggling down into the wet, cold mound until only his face was visible. He peered up at the wall of the annexe as a white torchlight scanned it from left to right, hopelessly restricted by the wall of the church grounds.

He lowered his gaze as a light went on in the room at the rear of the annexe and he felt his hand reach instinctively for the knife in his pocket. It fitted snugly in his palm but the voice inside him telling him to bury it in the leaves was cut short by a sight that surprised him.

The vicar was older than he'd imagined, but he was alone. Twist waited, watching to see if a guard appeared but none did. Instead the old churchman opened the back door and stepped out into the garden. He was eighty-five if he was a day, his hair a thick white thatch framed by the black of his vicar's shirt.

He advanced into the garden supported by a walking stick and brandishing a small red torch at chest height as if he were about to poke a fire with it. Just as Twist was about to sink down into the leaves he saw the old man turn and shine the torch into the space beside the shed. Confident that no one was behind him he advanced down the path towards the centre of the garden, not ten feet from where Twist was using tiny sideways movements of his head to draw leaves across his face.

'I don't think your friends from the gallery appreciated my lecture on sanctuary,' the old man said, 'so I won't repeat it, but please, do come out from under those leaves and join me inside for a restorative cup of tea.'

7

Red had regained consciousness about an hour previously with no recollection of how she came to be lying on a dirty mattress in the corner of a small dark room with no windows beneath its low ceiling.

Her eyes had adjusted quickly to the gloom, making full use of the thin ribbon of light beneath the door. For a while she'd tried to piece together the events that had brought her here but could only get as far as the men strong-arming her into the Mercedes, the bear-like one swearing in what sounded like Russian when she had bitten his hand.

After that her mind was as bare and empty as the cell she was in. There were no furnishings and only a single light bulb hanging from the ceiling in the middle of the room. It didn't give off much light but she thought maybe she could use the metal inside the light fitting to try to pick the lock.

Doubling up the stained mattress to stand on, she reached up and twisted the bulb but found it would not budge. Running her fingers up its neck to where the glass joined the metal she found two tiny bumps where it had been spot-welded to the fitting, and when she cupped the bulb and lifted it in her hand her suspicion was confirmed. The frosted glass was too thick and it was concealing something compact and dense in the middle of the ring of LEDs. Something like a camera.

She stared up at the black dome, picturing the two men watching her and whoever else they kept imprisoned down here in their dungeon. She sat back down on the mattress and remembered the rules FBoss had imposed after Harry had failed to turn up.

Go out and play, but keep a low profile. No risks and no thieving. If you need money just ask me … at least until the heat dies down.

She wished he was here with her now. No cage could hold him. He always had a plan and he could talk his way out of anything. So why had she done exactly the opposite of what he'd told her, wandering out on a frozen January afternoon, to embark on a one-woman crime wave which had culminated in a failed attempt to rob a high-class brothel presumably run by the Russian mob?

She had no illusions about what lay in store for her. About what those two animals would do to her once they got word from their boss. They wouldn't wait for confirmation of her identity. They would shred her existing ID and brand her as their own and there was nothing she could do to stop them.

She had fallen through the cracks into an alternative world in which the power of her captors was absolute. There was no human kindness in them. They were as dead-eyed and indifferent to the suffering they caused as abattoir workers. They just worked the machine that their boss had designed. The one that lured poor young women with the promise of a better life, trafficked and broke them, then put them to work selling their bodies to pay debts that escalated at impossible rates of interest.

There was only one card she could play now and it scared her. It would mean breaking the one rule that mattered most. The pact of silence, the bond of trust that once broken might sever her link to the only family she had ever known.

She heard the key turn in the lock and watched as the one she had come to think of as 'the bear' filled the door frame and stepped into the room, fingers like sausages beginning to work on the buckle of his belt. She couldn't see the other one. They had probably drawn straws and the other one would be sulking, sipping his coffee, watching his partner get first dibs on a screen somewhere.

She stood up and straightened her shoulders uttering a silent prayer that he knew some English.

'You are making a mistake,' she said. 'I already belong to someone known to you.'

He said nothing, but looked once up at the light bulb before stepping towards her, forcing her back into the corner of the room.

'Give me my phone,' she began again. 'I will prove it to you. Give it to me.'

She felt the terror mount as he ignored her. Probably he spoke English just fine but it was easier if he pretended not to. To shut out the last-minute pleas of 'you don't have to do this' that he must have heard many times before.

She felt his hand reach out towards her and touch her hair where it lay on her right shoulder. His grip was gentle and he looked at her hair with curiosity like he had never seen red hair before. Then there was a voice from the doorway, something in Russian, a string of words that were quietly spoken and commanding and she felt the weight of his paw lift from her shoulder as he turned to see the other man standing in the doorway.

He was nodding and she saw that he was holding her mobile phone in his right hand, offering it to her.

'What name?' he said.

'Sikes,' she replied. 'Bill Sikes ... William Sikes, a thief.'

'Si ... kes?' the man repeated his name, snapping it into two distinct syllables.

'He works for Fagin, FBoss.' Spoon-feeding them each syllable she continued, '*Fay ... gin ... ess ... cue*. A master thief. Paintings, pictures ... not just any old shit.'

For the best part of five seconds the blond stocky one stood looking at Sikes on the mobile phone and then he turned to the Bear and shook his head.

'No!' she shouted as the Bear advanced on her again. 'No. You have heard of us. We did Hauser and Wirth in Piccadilly and the Lisson in Marylebone and the Blain in Mayfair. And the last one was all over the news ... the ...'

The Bear reached her and picked her up with one hand, choking her words as he pinned her to the wall. She struggled, gripping his forearm with her hands, fighting to remain conscious, telling herself she had been here before and to wait until the man was on top of her before ...

'Stop!' the blond one said, entering the room from behind them and rattling off a sentence in Russian that contained the words 'Ninjas' and 'White Cube' before extending her mobile to her.

'Call Si-kes,' he said, motioning for the Bear to let her down.

She quick-dialled but there was no answer. She tried again, picturing him at the gym, his mobile phone vibrating silently in his duffel bag in the corner, wrapping the bandages round his big, scarred fists before stepping into the ring to hurt someone.

'Hello.'

He finally picked up and his voice took her by surprise.

'It's me,' she said. 'I'm in trouble. It's serious. Listen. Some Russians took me. They have me in a basement. They want confirmation …'

She paused for a moment, struggling to finish the sentence, listening to him breathing.

'They want confirmation …' she tried again.

She could not finish the sentence. She knew she had crossed the line and she knew what the remaining words would cost her and the debt she would owe Sikes forever.

She looked up into the blond Russian's emotionless eyes.

'They want confirmation that I belong to you.'

8

Twist looked down at the inky black water of the canal and wondered if his mate Martin was still fishing it. He remembered meeting Martin for the first time down by the canal. He'd pulled out the holding net and shown him a fish that he said was a trout. It had been about three inches long and had spines up the ridge of its back and later, when Martin had fried it in butter, a black diesel-like liquid had oozed out of it.

Martin claimed that they were a special kind of urban sub-species of the freshwater variant. They were blind and navigated the hidden rivers that ran deep beneath London using sonar when the Thames was in spate. Twist smiled to himself as he ran, remembering Martin's hand swimming through the ancient subterranean tributaries that kinked and ox-bowed deep underground to the pools where they spawned in perpetual darkness. He laughed to himself thinking about Martin, stoned as a trout down by the canal bank, and he wished his only real friend was with him now.

'Define "real",' Alan, Twist's social worker, had asked him the day before he and Martin had gone before the magistrate for tagging 'crash' up a forty-eight sheet M&S lingerie ad that had been jamming the A40 just before the Hanger Lane roundabout.

'Someone who is there for you when you need them most,' Twist had replied, watching as Alan had nodded, sympathetically, and listened as Twist had told him it had been his idea, not Martin's to hit the poster.

Which was the opposite of what Alan had told the judge the next day before going on to explain that Martin's psychological profile revealed sociopathic tendencies which had impacted negatively on his 'client' who had formed 'unhealthy attachments' since childhood.

Twist had also taken the DSM1V, the mental health assessment they gave all repeat juvenile offenders and it hadn't said anything about wanting to hang out with arseholes. So when his time to take the stand had come he'd told the magistrate the truth. That he always had the ideas and Martin just went along with it. And that there wasn't anyone in the world alive today who'd had his back more than Martin and there wasn't anyone he could think of that put himself out more for other people, even sometimes for strangers he'd hardly met.

But the old man in the wig hadn't budged. He'd just nodded condescendingly and asked Twist if he had any actual evidence that he wanted to share with the court; he said he hadn't, which had given Alan his chance to stand up and drop the bombshell that had blown his head apart.

He revealed how Twist's need for attachment stemmed from the fact of his abandonment, shortly after his birth, on the doorstep of a block of flats in London's exclusive

Holland Park. Bubble-wrapped for protection against the cold, he'd been found in the bottom of a Harvey Nichols bag by a Colombian cleaner who had taken him into her arms and out of the cold, and wept when efforts to trace a receipt found in the bottom of the bag to his birth mother had ended in failure.

Twist could not remember exactly what had happened next in the courtroom. Only that he'd managed to punch Alan hard in the back of the head and the sensation of having his face pushed into floorboards as the magistrate had called for order.

A year had passed since the trial. Six months inside Beltham for criminal damage and six months on the run, living out of skips and off the two quid caricatures he sketched for tourists in Leicester Square; trying to find out from friends what had happened to Martin, hearing rumours that he'd been sectioned and stuck in a loony bin near his nan's house in Broadstairs.

Twist hadn't said a word to Alan since the day he'd punched him but still the little shit persisted. Every Monday morning, first thing, without fail, Twist got an email. The message was always the same. That he was sorry. That he knew he'd overstepped the mark trying to get Twist a reduced sentence and promising that if they met off the record he would do two things to make amends.

Firstly, they could go and see Martin together. Secondly, and only if Twist thought it was a good idea, and after they'd discussed it, Alan would find the money to pay a professional tracing service to track his birth mother …

Twist hadn't responded to any of the emails. He didn't trust Alan further than he could throw him but once the idea was in his head he'd found it hard to exorcise. At first he'd tried to shut it out but recently, living alone in the tower block, he'd started to dwell on the offer again, lying awake at night trying to picture her face and coming up with theories as to why she'd had to abandon him.

Alan said there were a couple of charities that specialised in tracking the birth relatives of orphans who were not registered on a contact register or with an adoption agency which, given that Twist had been brought up in foster homes, would be the best way to go.

And what at first had sounded like a long shot, designed to sucker him into meeting Alan, had come to seem possible. The doctors had been able to estimate the time of his birth to within a twenty-four-hour window and while there was a high chance his mother would have given birth in a hospital she would definitely not have reappeared for a mandatory six-week postnatal check.

So, as Alan had explained countless times in his Monday-morning emails, it was possible to eliminate the lion's share of the two thousand babies born in the UK who shared his birthday. From this long list the trackers could then eliminate the names of all the mothers of babies that had been given up for adoption.

The short list that remained would, Alan guessed, hold no more than ten names, women who could be easily tracked using the Electoral Roll and the Register of Births and Deaths. So unless Twist's mother had given birth outside a hospital, died or left the country, there was a high chance of finding her.

The temperature was falling fast now and he could see that a thin glaze of ice had formed on the canal in the shadows where the towers blocked out the winter sun. In a week, maybe two, the ice would thicken and the annual ritual would begin. Boys from the estates would gather in gangs on the footbridge and drop breeze blocks, weighted traffic cones and shopping trolleys onto the ice to test it before stepping out to try to cross it.

The cold was a problem but darkness had never bothered him. He'd got used to it when he was tagging. The three guys he ran with from the estates would sit in Snark's mum's garage smoking dank then pack and go out. They would always have a target. The spot they were going to hit. Sometimes they would even have a plan. A way in and an exit route, the four of them working together, taking it in turns to tag the spot while the others stood watch. But they rarely had any message to get across. Leastways, nothing more profound than 'X was here'.

Not like the activists Twist had begun to follow later on. Zealots who didn't seem to care if they got pressure hosed after chaining themselves to a Japanese whaler or arrested after abseiling down the clock face of Big Ben dressed as Batman. But that had become annoying. Being stuck with dead-heads while he was sketching in his notebooks the whole time until it had come to seem like wasted effort, monkeying up drainpipes, running from blokes who'd lose their jobs if they didn't catch the punks who'd hit the warehouse or the District Line train they'd been contracted to protect.

Apart from Martin, who was a dreamer like Twist, the others in Snark's crew could have been surfers or base jumpers. They got high and had nothing to say for themselves. Twist was dyslexic but it hadn't stopped him learning to read. By force of will he had kept himself up to speed with reading and writing so that he could cram his head with ideas. And so what if he couldn't spell his name. He could look at a face for sixty seconds and reproduce a perfect likeness in under three minutes.

And as his stack of notebooks had grown in height so had his dissatisfaction with Snark, who had a mean streak and who Twist came to believe might even be jealous.

In Beltham, Twist had worked in the lending library. The range was shit but the little librarian who ran it let him read his Kindle. There were also a lot of over-sized coffee-table books donated by art galleries and museums. And that was how Twist had started copying art.

A week after he'd been working in the library he'd been beckoned into the stockroom at the back. The librarian had kicked a dusty red plastic storage container full of charcoal and oil paints across the room to Twist, who had spent twelve hours a day, Monday to Saturday, for the next five months, 'taking stock' of Velasquez, Michelangelo, Picasso and Vermeer. He watched podcasts on techniques in his bunk at night and told himself that one day, when he got out, he would visit the art galleries and see the pictures and, just like he did with faces, recreate them from memory on the walls and tunnels and trains of London.

9

The Bear stopped at a closed door off a stairwell which read *Fire Escape*. Through it Red could hear techno, slowed down so that it sounded like the death throes of some great beast. Opening the door, the Bear ushered Red inside. She was temporarily blinded by red laser bursts but had a sense of a vast blackness, or a massive, square room which was completely empty as though they had stepped out into space. Then Red heard the blond one close the door behind her and she became aware of movement in the darkness as a strobe light flashed like sheet lightning and Red caught her first glimpse of the second level of hell.

To her right on a red divan, a young woman was cradling an old man's head between her legs while a fat man in a top hat drank from a bottle of vodka on an adjoining leather armchair, head thrown back as two girls stroked his chest. The Bear grabbed Red by the wrist and pulled her across the floor, careful not to tread on the carnal malefactors who writhed and contorted on the shagpile carpet beneath their feet, their faces grotesque masks of pleasure and pain, lit intermittently by the dancing strobes.

Sparks flashed in the darkness some sixty feet away and she caught sight of a stick-thin brunette with a white-painted face biting on a latex bit, her back arching as a man in a white surgeon's mask applied two wires to her skeletal buttocks.

There was a voice in the speakers. It was deep and distorted so that Red could not understand what it was saying but it was somehow commanding as if the people in the room had no choice but to obey it. She stumbled over someone's leg and looked down to see a woman on her knees as two men held her arms and a third tightened what looked like a garden hose around her neck until her eyes bulged and the skin of her cheeks flooded with blood.

A hand reached out and snatched at her ankle as the Bear opened a second steel door in the wall on the far side of the room. They began to climb up a narrow winding stairwell lined with padlocked doors and mirrors, then stopped at a red wooden door at the top.

The Bear looked to his blond colleague, who nodded, and the big man knocked three times and waited, listening at the door.

'Enter,' said a Russian voice from within and the Bear turned the handle and stepped inside, standing by the end of the door, watching Red as she walked in, blinking in the strange light that danced like water across the white marble floor.

The Bear pushed her forwards and as she walked she saw the source of the light came from illuminated glass water pipes which ran parallel to the corridor-like room before opening out into a round chamber dimly lit by spotlights in the roof.

She saw something move in one of the tubes and it made her start, which elicited a laugh from a man with black eyes. He was sat behind a desk in the middle of the chamber beneath a white dome that reminded Red of a church or a cathedral. As she got closer to the man, the chamber opened up and she caught sight of a second man – Sikes – standing off to the left of the desk. Then a flash of movement in the glass tube to her left caught her eye and she saw a squid propel itself along the inside of the tube.

The man behind the desk leant back and smiled, opening his hands like a priest drawing a couple together to take their marriage vows. He looked at Sikes, then at Red. He had a long face, high cheekbones drawn tight across his skin which was chalk white. His eyes were thin slits and she could not see inside them but she could tell that they were reading her, scanning her face for micro-signals that would give him a clue to her relationship with Sikes.

'Rodchenko says you owe him money,' Bill said, turning to her, his face a mask.

She turned and felt a wave of relief flood through her as Sikes's lynx-like eyes met her own. She was burning up inside. The fear almost overwhelming her capacity to think straight but here he stood, as cool and as confident as ever, as if, in a strange way, he was at home here, among his own kind.

'… Says that if you go poking your nose in you have to pay the price,' Bill went on.

There was a cracking sound and Red looked up and saw the Russian unlock his fingers and place them down on the desk.

'What price do I have to pay?' Red asked, looking between Bill and Rodchenko, knowing instinctively that some kind of a deal had already been struck.

'*We*,' Sikes went on. 'What price do *we* have to pay?'

Rodchenko leant forwards and looked Red up and down. She felt his eyes crawl up her legs, exploring the shadows between them, her hips and the curve where her waist narrowed before pausing below her breasts, nodding at her to unfold her arms. She let her hands fall at her sides and saw Rodchenko smile, then look at Sikes who was staring at the wall behind the Russian, giving nothing away.

'Can I just say, Mr Rodchenko,' Bill said, turning at last to look straight at the Russian mob boss, 'what an honour it would be to work for you.'

Red felt her stomach knot inside. Sometimes Bill overstepped the mark but the Russian let what could have been interpreted as impertinence slide. Instead he sat back in his chair, drawing both hands back across the desk until they reached the catalogue he had been holding. He turned and pushed it towards them so they had no choice but to look down at the six pictures arranged sequentially, left to right, like the storyboard of a film.

Red took three steps closer. The pictures looked old. Maybe two or three hundred years old and they were spread out like a cartoon strip. She caught sight of a fresh-faced young girl, about her age, wearing a white bonnet and standing next to a hideous old crone. She looked at the second plate and saw the same girl caught in bed with a young lover by an older male in a wig, which explained her presence in what looked like a brothel in the third, her imprisonment, treatment for syphilis and finally her funeral in what looked like a madhouse full of lecherous vicars and working girls blighted by pox.

'Do you like this story?' Rodchenko said, smiling like a wolf across the table at Red.

She tried to brighten but could feel the muscles in her face tense up, making it impossible to smile back.

'They were painted by a man called Hogarth and up until recently only copies existed. Three of the originals were lost, supposedly in a fire in the 1750s, but they have now surfaced and are in the hands of a dealer called Losberne in Mayfair.'

Rodchenko paused briefly, waving his hand behind him where the ambient light in the glass tubes changed colour with the passing of a squid. It was alien, otherworldly as it propelled itself along, reminding Red of things she had seen in jars filled with formaldehyde.

'You'll never be able to shift them,' Sikes said.

Rodchenko looked slightly perplexed, then broke into a smile that became a laugh as though Sikes had made a joke.

'Who says I want to sell them?' he began. 'They will be a gift. My boss likes pictures that tell stories. Do you know this one?'

Red watched as Rodchenko stood up and unbuttoned his shirt. His skin was pale and hairless on his broad chest and there was a picture there, tattooed into the flesh of his left pectoral. It was a picture of the Madonna and Child. Red watched Rodchenko's eyes meet Bill's to see if he understood the meaning of the iconic image and Bill nodded.

'It means I have been a thief since I was a child,' Rodchenko said, turning his eyes towards Red as his fingers worked the last button back into place.

Red felt like she was falling. She tried to breathe but Rodchenko's stare was somehow suffocating and as her brain raced to recall where she'd seen tattoos like his before, she felt tiny pinpricks creep up her spine, crossing the nape of her neck and spreading wide across the base of her skull as if a million tiny tattoo artists had somehow been set to work by their dark master, who stood weighing her fear from behind his desk on the far side of the room.

She'd heard so many stories from Fagin about the criminal types that he had met but one stood in front of her now. A rake-thin, pale-skinned sixty-six-year-old ex-con from his circus years who had been known only by his stage name, 'Stalag 17', who made his living by staggering out into the round roaring drunk, balancing lit Molotov cocktails on his arms which he would then catch and threaten to hurl into the crowd.

Fagin had described the fire-breathing dragon coiled up on Stalag 17's right pectoral, spewing flames across his chest at St Michael as the archangel ran it through with his glimmering lance. But most of all, Red recalled Fagin's retelling of the man's story. Of his imprisonment in Stalin's gulag and his initiation as a *vor v zakone*, a 'thief in law' bound by an eighteen-point code of conduct, following which he had forsaken his own family, denounced all women and agreed to help all other thieves on pain of mutilation or death if he violated the code.

'You will steal the three paintings that have been found,' Rodchenko began. 'You must infiltrate the Losberne gallery and steal them from him. Meanwhile, I will pay a visit to the private collector who has the existing three paintings and find out when and where he will put them up for auction. You will know the location of the auction when I do, but it will only be revealed to the elite of the art world twenty-four hours before the event. You will infiltrate the auction and steal the paintings.'

Red looked at Bill, whose face finally registered emotion. She saw to her horror that his eyes were smiling. As though the request amused him.

'Just so I'm clear,' he said, 'you want us to first steal three paintings from the vault of a Mayfair gallery and then, with news of the theft buzzing in the ears of every art buyer, dealer and detective in London, hit a major auction house to steal the remaining three?'

Red saw Rodchenko smile.

'Exactly,' he said.

'And what happens if Fagin says no?' Red asked, stepping forwards. 'He only ever takes jobs from one man.'

She watched Rodchenko nod his head to the Bear behind him, who smiled and nodded back. Red's mind raced.

'How am I going to sell this to my boss?' Bill asked.

'The paintings as a set of originals are valued at sixty million,' Rodchenko went on. 'We will advance the costs of the job and give you a ten per cent fee upon delivery.'

'And what if our boss refuses to work with you?' Red asked.

'Then I'm afraid you will experience first-hand ...' Rodchenko smiled at Red as he turned the catalogue on the table so she could look at the sequence of pictures again that showed the downward spiral of degradation, disease and death of a girl her own age almost three hundred years ago. 'Yet another case of life imitating art.'

10

Working double time in the library, washing dishes, scrubbing floors and running in the governor's infamous cross-country team had all stacked up in Twist's favour. He'd qualified for day parole and been driven, on his request, to plant trees outside a local old people's home on the outskirts of the governor's village in Hampshire.

He'd hated running for the governor in Beltham. Out on the gravel track in a singlet and shorts running 12 by 400m repeats while the boss man stood barking into a loud hailer from the centre of the field. But that day on parole, when he'd ditched his spade and legged it across the gardens of the old people's home, the training had been put to good use. He'd quickly outpaced the screws, running through a Christmas tree farm before climbing up a steep escarpment, through a beech wood and never once looking back until he had a quarter of a mile on his pursuers.

And he was still running now. Into the estate and up the cracked asphalt walkway past the allotment that a consortium of Newham's OAPs had got off the developers who'd seen it as a convenient way to appease the local planning committee. Twist had to hand it to the old folks. They had perfected a kind of subsistence farming not seen since the last world war. He wondered if any of them were asleep now in the shed they'd built behind a stand of bamboo. He knew they got fucked up in there on gin and sometimes slept it off on an old mattress in the corner.

The towers of E12 loomed from the darkness in the middle distance. There were no lights among the condemned blocks of Newham's derelict council estate but the crunch of shattered safety glass always told him he was close. He never felt quite safe until he was inside the lift shaft, climbing the rope to the sixth floor which was the only floor that could not be accessed by the stairs and had not been scarred by successive waves of vandals, junkies and tramps who came in to light their fires, cook up and shelter from the rain.

He slowed as he approached the fire escape at the rear of the block and looked up at the work that marked his break from Snark. He called it 'The Matador' and it was a work in progress. Just as he'd promised himself inside Beltham, he'd begun copying famous paintings from memory and he was guilty of stealing this one from Picasso.

It showed a man fighting a bull. The man wore a matador's cap and had two swords raised above his head pointing downwards at a raging bull whose horns were coming up at him from below. It was a simple painting, more like a sketch that Picasso had completed in charcoal, but it had struck a chord in Twist.

He'd found the picture originally in a book in Newham public library. Unable to take out the book without a library

card he'd stared at it until it was stuck, then taken it back
to the tower wondering where he was going to put it. The
tower had been an obvious choice. It was pale grey and had
been pounded by the elements until it was off-white. The
buildings were around a hundred feet tall but were strangely
narrow and the side walls had no windows. To Twist's mind
they'd become the pages of a giant sketchbook as he'd gone
about burning wood to make the dustbins full of powdered
charcoal he'd needed to recreate Picasso's masterwork.

Working at night, swinging from a rope fastened securely
to the winch that had once drawn the tower block's lift,
Twist had struggled to overcome the nagging sensation that
someone who didn't want him to succeed was watching.

As he fastened a karabiner to the ring on the winch that
held the cables and pulled his belay out he found it hard to
believe that it was nearly finished. It bore such a close resem-
blance to the original despite only working from powers of
recall, returning each day to the library to commit another
part of the painting to his memory.

Looping the rope onto his right foot he began to ratchet
himself up the lift shaft to the engine room at the top. Assuming
none of the junkies or one of Ake Bumbola's crew could free
climb the stainless steel walls of the lift shaft he would be safe
inside the room he had come to think of as his own.

He lay down on the dirty mattress he had hauled hand over
fist up the shaft, attached to the rope. He had mixed feelings about the Matador. It was his best work and he wanted
people to see it but not the wrong people. If they caught
him now he would not be sent back to juvenile court. He
would go before Newham Crown Court and wind up with
a stretch in adult prison.

He opened his bag and reached for the book the vicar had given him, *Lives of the Great Artists*, the title embossed in gold leaf on the front cover. It looked seriously old. It could almost be from the time of its author, Vasari, an artist who'd lived in the days of Da Vinci and Michelangelo and written about their life and times without envy or flattery.

'Few are called and fewer are chosen,' the old man had whispered to him, handing him the old book after Twist had shown him his sketch books in which he had made his initial studies of The Matador. He had seen the old man's bushy eyebrows arch in surprise when he'd opened the book and seen the quality of the initial drawings and the scale of the challenge he had set himself in reproducing it.

Twist reached for the side of the mattress and felt for the corners of a car battery. He hooked a wire loop around the positive so he could light up his room and stare at the walls. He'd painted pre-Raphaelite nymphs on them that reminded him of some of the angels in the stained-glass windows of the church and his mind drifted back to the vicar warning him that he had until sunrise to shelter with him before police would return with a warrant that no amount of medieval litigation could protect him from.

There were no get out of jail free cards for parole breakers. The prosecution would brand him a vandal and treat the jury to an estimated cost of his so called 'street art' to the taxpayer, money that would better have been spent on sick children or war veterans than on sandblasting the walls and trains that he had defaced.

He opened the pages of the old book, moving from front to back, from one illustration to the next. To his surprise, many of the images were of saints, tortured in horrible and grisly ways, and he thought about the great artists who had painted them and wondered if the world had been more violent then. He flicked on, staring at the portraits of their cruel-mouthed patrons, the Borgias and the Medicis scheming in their city states and stacking their silver ducats in their counting houses.

He closed his eyes, breathed in and held the breath, letting the air out slowly, letting his mind relax. Half opening them he stared up at the cracked paint on the ceiling and wondered what real prison was like and if three square meals a day and running hot water might not be so bad. But then he felt his body sink and he became aware that he was floating as if on water, flat on his back in the canal, watching a fishing line twitch above him, and listening to Martin telling him to wake up and get out; the magistrate was climbing his tower on eight spider-like legs and was chewing up The Matador piece by piece and would soon cast a web around Twist's room that he would never escape from again.

11

He stood at the end of the platform, shoulders hunched, wearing the green collars of his overcoat up to mask his face which was a mess of anxiety. The events following the White Cube debacle had wrought havoc with his sleep patterns, which were erratic at the best of times, and most mornings he'd woken up on the sofa nursing a flask of *tuică*, the moonshine he distilled in iron casks on the roof. Christ alone knew what it was doing to him. His blood pressure was up to one hundred and eighty. If he couldn't find a replacement for Harry soon his head was going to explode.

And rush hour didn't help. It was an absurd time to go anywhere on the underground, let alone from Bank to Mile End at half past five on a Monday afternoon on an old fool's errand, but the boy called Snark had convinced him.

He knew a boy who was not only a tagger but also a street artist. 'We used to run together but he got above himself ...' Snark had whispered conspiratorially to Fagin when he'd called him to tell Fagin about 'the tagger formerly known as

Twist'. A young man who was, in Snark's opinion, 'a mental assburgers case' on account of his being able to look at a famous painting and reproduce it from memory on any wall using spray cans.

Fagin never trusted a man without a motive and Snark was clearly riven with envy, however unlikely his diagnosis of Twist's high-functioning autism. It was possible that the wannabe artist might have a photographic memory but there was no way that a boy with severe autism could have escaped from Beltham Young Offender Institute or, for that matter, been sent there in the first place.

But he was excited. Excited enough to put on his old green overcoat and a wide-brimmed waxed hat and walk out into the wind and the rain in search of a former child prodigy who, again if Snark was to be believed, could both recall shapes, colours, tones, proportions and the very essence of a scene and copy it from memory after a single sitting *and* outrun prison guards to escape from borstal.

To find such a freak when Fagin needed him most felt more than serendipitous. It felt as if his destiny might finally have woken, got up off its arse and come knocking on the door of the derelict hotel in the reclaimed marshland that lay between Beckton's sewage and gas works. It had been his headquarters for the past fifteen years and he had not enjoyed the location, the hotel keeling slowly to one side as it subsided gradually beneath the water table. And so he was on his way to meet Snark on the mean streets of Newham to see for his own eyes the miracle of a boy who might be the key to the plan that might, finally resurrect their flagging fortunes.

And Christ knows they needed it. Morale in the gang had sunk to an all-time low. Dodge, Batesy and Cribb were monosyllabic and Red had exploded then disappeared for forty-eight hours. Only Sikes was motivated, appearing early the morning after Red had finally reappeared to bang Fagin awake where he'd fallen asleep, face down on his desk, to inform him of 'the score to end all scores'.

Fagin could see that Sikes was back. It didn't matter any more that he was lame. He had brought the money and that, in simple terms, meant that now he was *the* money. Fagin reflected on this power shift but there was nothing that could be done about it now when the demands of the task ahead were more pressing. In the eyes of the gang it would simply not be enough to replace Harry. In Red's eyes nothing would fill the gap he had left behind and it was her sense of loss and betrayal that bothered Fagin most of all.

For it was Red who reeled them in and so felt the most guilt when trouble found the boys. Red who had hooked Dodge and Batesy and Harry, in turn, leading them back, dazzled by her beauty and her skill only to be met by a skinny old, hook-nosed gypsy with a straggly red beard.

Nor would it do to simply fill it with an exact replica of Harry either. A traceur who was as quick-witted and nimble as Harry would answer only part of this job's description but not the part that Fagin now saw as vital to the mission's success, a role that in spite of Snark's protestations might very well prove impossible to fill.

For the person Fagin sought was refined and by their nature private. An individual who, if they continued to exist outside fairy tales and films, must by the nature of their crime move unnoticed in elevated circles, attend parties at galleries and museums, and stand on the sidelines at the glittering auction houses before returning to their garrets and outhouses to exercise their spectacular gift for emulation.

Quick-witted, gymnastic two-bit vandals might be ten a penny on Snark's streets but Fagin very much doubted if the toerag could bring him what the big score demanded; a master-forger who could not only break, enter, run and hide with the best of them but also skew auction prices and blight the walls of galleries.

And the clock was ticking. If Snark could not bring the talent then Fagin would have to look elsewhere and how would he hook such a catch without the girl? Half mother, half sister to all the boys in the gang who might be the only way to draw such a talent into their company and so, staring in horror at his grizzled appearance in the window of the train as the struts of the tunnel flashed by, he asked himself the hard questions again.

Why had he left Harry out in the cold for fourteen days after the White Cube? Why hadn't he gone himself rather than sending Sikes?

He recalled his hands palms up on his desk as Dodge had appeared in the doorway and joined Red, putting his arm round her to comfort her and how, in that moment, he'd seen something like weakness in her for the first time. That when he'd risen, wringing his hands together, asking for her forgiveness, he'd seen a shadow fall across her eyes.

Did she want to tear the gang apart now? To throw it all away after they had worked so hard to get a score like the one that Sikes had brought them?

And before she'd walked out on him she'd turned and looked back at him from the doorway. Although there was still fire in her eyes there had also been fear and Fagin had realised at once that it was not just her guilt over Harry that was troubling her.

Looking up from a double page *Metro* spread on celebrity handbags he thought again about his friend Grigoi's surprise reappearance three years ago. So many years had passed since he'd last seen the thickset boy with the mono-brow standing in a snowdrift looking back at their village as Ceauşescu's police had corralled their friends and families into coaches and open lorries like sheep.

It had never occurred to Fagin that he would see him again or be in a position to offer him such lucrative contract work, supplying one of the cartels that in turn supplied a closed online black art market that fed the appetites of the global elites.

He stepped off the Tube at Bank station and switched back through an exit tunnel to beat the crowd as he changed from the Docklands Light Railway to the Central Line. He looked down the platform at the city workers who were elbowing their way to the front. Sleek was the word he would have chosen to describe them in a police line-up. Neat in their pinstripes as he visited each of their faces in turn, assessing their net worth with far more acuity than their regulators. Then, as the train screeched to a halt, something gold caught the light beaming from inside the carriage and his eyes alighted on the wrist of a tall man with a dome-shaped bald head. It was a gold Rolex. Older than its owner, Fagin guessed, as he stepped up onto the train, careful not to lose sight of the man's shining skull.

The air grew fetid as the train entered the darkness of the tunnels and he squirmed his way between the heaving, stinking bodies, feeling wallets and purses protruding from back pockets crying out to be taken.

'I can't breathe … excuse me, sir, I'm choking,' he gasped, moving forwards with his head down as people moved apart until he'd reached the middle of the carriage where he found himself trapped and held fast where the commuters stood thickest and could not budge to let a sick man through.

He imagined Harry in a similar situation. Most likely he would be operating alone, preferring not to trust finding his way wherever people congregated and were distracted by sex or drugs or movement. Getting more confident, less inhibited as his success grew until one day he would overstep the mark or form an alliance and they would catch him and match him to the boy last seen clawing at his burning eyes outside the White Cube.

He slid the fingers of his right hand from the pocket of his jacket and imagined them as eels slithering through the solid mass of bodies which swayed off-centre as the train banked, exerting pressure on his target's back so that he never felt the sharpened fingernail slice through the cotton holding the button of his trousers in place.

The wallet was heavy as he rifled the notes and the cards from it then dropped it in the forest of legs behind him, catching a glimpse of the Rolex still on the man's wrist as he gripped the handrail above him. The train slowed, screeching to a stop in the next station and Fagin held himself back as the people shuffled around him, recalling a time when such an opportunity would have seen him snatch it and run. A time when he was as cocksure and fleet-footed as his boys were now, disappearing into the crowd leaving the man floundering shouting 'thief' as the watch switched hands before reaching the street above.

Youth versus experience, short versus long cons, opportunism versus well-laid plans, the lessons of a lifetime tumbling over one another as the train doors opened and he stepped off, lowering his head and disappearing into the crowd, scurrying up the tunnel marked exit to an elevator which opened into the bitter cold of the street outside.

Too cold to steal a gold watch, to dig a grave or run through the forest at night while the vampire Ceaușescu corralled your people like cattle in barren state farms hundreds of miles from their ancestral homes. He thrust his hands deep into his pockets and recalled those nights alone on the mountain after the secret police came. Emerging from whichever snow hole or abandoned barn he'd lain up in during the day to watch the sun set, remembering which peak or which point on which ridge it had sunk behind and beginning his run.

Bitter memories flooded his mind and disorientated him as he made his way along the grey, frozen street past a Chicken Cottage and a Costcutter, seeing the faces of the peasants who had betrayed his family and his father's blazing eyes as the police held him, shouting at him to run and never look back. Westwards with the wind in his face with the ghosts of his friends and family at his back, calling him still, their voices shrill from open drains and alleys, whispering that he was Roma not Romanian and that he must trust no one and learn to spot the false friends who would turn him over to the Securitate.

He crossed the road at the traffic lights and stepped into what remained of a landscaped area, thick privet bushes growing in a children's playground at the edge of the condemned estate.

'Cornelius?' A boy's voice, nasal and almost hoarse, came from behind him.

He turned and saw a squat figure in a black hooded parka raise his right hand and press his index finger down on the nozzle of a can of glossy black paint and make his mark on a green metal circuit box.

'SN … ARK?' Fagin read aloud.

The boy grinned at the recognition and revealed stained teeth shunted into place by metal braces.

'Which tower is it?' Fagin asked, watching as the boy swung the can and nodded with his head.

'Show me.'

The boy set off at a brisk pace towards the point where the wire fence protecting the site met a six-foot wall which backed onto the high street. He watched him reach his hand inside a hole in the fence and unhook the wire to open a gap wide enough to step through and low enough to be sheltered from the street above.

He felt his chest constrict as he followed Snark, who broke into a slow jog several times until he reached the penultimate tower in the row where he stopped, locked his palms together and offered Fagin a leg-up so he could get a better view.

'Tell me he ain't heading for a fall,' Snark sniggered.

Fagin planted his foot on Snark's hands and reached the top of the wall, pulling himself up until he could see the nearest tower block and the image of the giant man plunging to his death down its nearest face.

Fagin stroked his beard and wondered if it was possible to go bald on your chin then he looked down at Snark whose sharp features were hidden by his parka's faux-fur fringe.

'Are you sure it's him?' Fagin asked.

'Yeh,' said Snark. 'It's him.'

Fagin twisted his beard in his right hand and motioned Snark to lead him to the boy's bolthole with his left. He had already played through what he would say to the boy if they ran into him. It was taxing always having to be the brains of the outfit. Having to think two steps ahead. So this time he hadn't bothered, reassuring himself instead that there was always a deal to be done.

Snark stopped and fixed his ferrety eyes on Fagin.

'You need him, don't you?' he said. 'You want me to help you persuade him?'

Fagin stopped tugging his beard and stared blankly at Snark without compassion, watching as the youth took a step back half clenching his fists as Fagin drew his long thin hands from the deep pockets of his coat and extended them palms down towards Snark, like a magician dispelling any suspicion of foul play.

He watched Snark's eyes follow his right hand as he slipped it inside the left breast pocket of his dirty green overcoat.

'Who sent you?' Fagin asked.

'Dodge,' Snark replied. 'We used to run together. He said you was a man down and did I still tag with the boy that did real art. I always look out for my old mates …'

Fagin watched Snark flinch as he withdrew his hand swiftly from his jacket pocket and hit him between the eyes with a crumpled fifty pound note.

'Of course you do, Master Snark,' Fagin replied, as Snark crouched down and unravelled the note and held it up to the light. 'Now, do exactly as I tell you.'

12

He woke up to the sound of hammering on the quarter-inch steel roof. He knew it wasn't rain because it was louder and more percussive, but he didn't click that it was hail again until he had belayed down the elevator shaft and stepped outside. Hands deep inside the pockets of his overcoat he started walking across a carpet of frost, enjoying the crunching the marble-sized frost balls made beneath his feet.

It was well below zero and there were patches of ice where the ground water had frozen in the night. It was no weather to be out working or smashing your BMX on the estate's overgrown concrete half-pipe. He'd heard the yell before he saw them there. A boy in a cock hat screaming as he shot fifteen feet up off the near end of the tube followed by his short-arse mate who was on foot aping his friend's manoeuvres like he was on a bike too.

Twist wanted to get closer to get a better look at them but he was nervous. Maybe he was just being paranoid after the shit at the gallery but something about them didn't feel right. He kept low as he skirted the allotment and came up slowly behind the grassy knoll that abutted the skate park. He could see them both clearly now. The one on the BMX was wearing an old-fashioned hat, crushed and raffish, at an angle shading his face. He was balancing on the pedals of his BMX as the other ran up and down the half-pipe using his speed to push off the tops and kick his imaginary back wheel in the air.

Twist stood up and walked towards them, keen to get a better look at the show, but as he approached the one on the BMX seemed to sense him and he turned, doffed his hat then hopped the bike about face and dropped silently off the edge.

'You're Twist, innit?' a voice started behind him. 'Fierce.'

Twist spun round, surprised that the runty one had somehow got round behind him.

'What is?' Twist asked, guessing he meant the BMX bandit's moves.

But the boy shook his head and pointed at the concrete floor of the kidney-shaped tube, forcing Twist to take a few steps forwards, squinting in the darkness to make out anything as the one in the hat exploded up the near edge of the pipe, turned a complete corkscrew in the air and landed the bike perfectly, the mags spinning down into the bowl, his right hand trailing low to the right side of the bike, his index finger outstretched, pointing at a series of jet black tags on the concrete floor.

'You been busy, innit?' the runty one said as Twist reached the edge of the bowl and looked down at a string of over twenty of his own tags that curved like a daisy chain around the smooth surface of the bowl.

His head was a blizzard of questions that needed answers, because the tags were nothing to do with him. He'd given all that up. He'd been told he had talent. Not just for climbing places other taggers were too scared to hit, but real talent. So he'd gone straight and taught himself as much as he could, read as many art books as he could find in the library. But there was a lot that he couldn't learn without being taught. Art school. That was his dream, and now someone was fucking with it. Putting up his old tags like a sign around his neck that read: *Twist. Sociopath. Parole breaker. Beat him. Lock him up. Eat him alive.*

He looked up at the two clowns who were still hard at it. But how had they found him and how did they know his name was Twist? It was just too much of a coincidence. Two strangers materialise out of nowhere then match you to your tag.

He glanced around. There was no visible surface that didn't have his name on it. The walls, the litter bins, even on one of the burnt-out cars that littered the weed-ridden border where the estate met the wall.

He took a deep breath and held his left wrist in his right hand then counted one thousand, two thousand, three thousand, reciting the words calmly until the fire in his head died down. It was a trick they taught all young offenders at Beltham. They called it impulse control. And it worked because he was 'responding' not 'reacting' to the runty one who was goading him by staring open-mouthed at him while the other one pedalled in circles around him giving him lip.

'Twist?' the one on the BMX said. 'Never heard of him.'

'Oh?' replied the runt, picking up the double act. 'Isn't he the one that broke parole, the one what Bumbola, the Fat Man, is looking for in connection with the vandalising of his ve-hicle?'

Twist turned, watching the one on the BMX. It was clear he was the alpha dog. Not big or physically menacing but there was something behind his eyes that scared Twist, an intelligence, a low cunning that had set alarm bells ringing.

'Dunno,' Twist said. 'I'm not from round here.'

He watched the one on the BMX balance this statement then sit down in the saddle and turn and pedal furiously back to the tube, his knees rising up above chest height like he was riding a kid's bike.

Twist made eye contact with the runt as he backed away from him. The cheeky little shit was still staring at him mouth open. He wanted to go over and shove his fist down his throat but he knew a fight would get him nowhere. It would be two on one and they would be armed. Responding not reacting, he turned and started to wrestle with the doom they'd just laid on him. Roughnecks on BMXs he could handle but six foot four, three hundred pound Nigerian career criminals were best left well alone.

He knew the Fat Man on sight. His real name, the one printed on the ID he wore on the front of his ribbed commando jumper, was Ake Bumbola. Twist saw him talking into his mobile each night, parked up by the only entrance of the estate. With his peaked black-and-white cap and his gut he resembled Idi Amin.

When the estate had been condemned Bumbola had volunteered to patrol it. He had forged documents stamped by a friend who worked as a cleaner in the Nigerian High Commission. They showed that he'd been one of thirty police officers in Abuja trained by an NGO who had employed retired members of London City Police's Serious Fraud Unit before sectarian violence had broken out and forced him

to seek asylum in the UK. His papers had stacked up with
Newham's Council. They had been hard-pressed finding
anyone willing to police the abandoned estate after dark.

With the contract signed he had wasted no time. His business model was like a Venus flytrap. When he'd first arrived
on the estate, Twist had been wary. He'd watched from his
roof as Bumbola had opened the eastern gate at sundown each
night, watching the girls appear in ones or twos, taking up
their positions beneath the shadow of the plywood hoardings
that shielded them from the main road above.

The hookers paid protection but the real revenue came from
their johns who arrived in their cars after work. Bumbola's
security waited until a car started rocking before they went
over. A tap on the window from a man in a white peaked
hat followed by a camera flash were normally enough to get
a john's attention. Then the fun really began. The charge was
trespassing but the inference was clear. If they didn't pay the
two hundred quid on-the-spot fine then the car licence plate
would be reported to the police.

The security officer would then hand them a receipt with
a code on it and the address of an encrypted local authority
website. By visiting the website they could delete their licence
plate number from the database before it was sent to the
police on the last day of each month.

But the fun really began when the john got home and
inputted his code as instructed. Sure enough, his name would
appear alongside their licence plate but clicking delete would
not remove it. Instead it would bring up the photograph
of them caught in flagrante along with an offer of a four
hundred pound 'season ticket' for 'Bumbola Night Car Park'
and 'Bumbola Self Storage'.

Twist had heard the rumble of the generator on the roof of the tower block nearest the gate that housed 'Bumbola Self Storage' unit. Word was there was a mattress in every unit except one which had been done up as a bar. Each night he'd seen a low red glow shine through the cracks at the edges of the windows that shone off the patent leather shoes of Bumbola's guards who ensured the season ticket holders' cars didn't get scratched while they enjoyed what Bumbola called 'complete self-security' inside.

Twist turned towards the tower, but the nightmare was just beginning. If the Fat Man was coming for him he would find him in no time because as he could now see, there was a chain of tags leading like a paper chase from each corner of the estate to his tower.

'Stop! I will beat you!'

Twist froze for a second then ran, clocking Bumbola's giant head leaning out of the window of his white van, screaming at him as the driver swerved left and right avoiding the detritus strewn between his tower and the next to reach him.

Twist raced across the open space trying to make it to his lift shaft but the driver cut him off. There was a screeching sound and he watched as the white van skidded then spun one hundred and eighty degrees, blocking his path and revealing his tag sprayed up its left side.

The rear doors burst open releasing a pair of men in black and gold striped Adidas tracksuits who wasted no time separating to either side of the doorway to the tower trying to encircle him. Bumbola hobbled out of the van, pointing his finger at Twist as he advanced across the broken paving stones towards him.

'Catch him! Beat him!'

Then the van started to reverse. The rear doors were still open and Twist turned and ran for the north face of the towers where the first of the high rises had been demolished and where the mounds of twisted girders and rubble might give him an advantage.

He jumped down into the clay trenches where the JCBs had clawed up the foundations of the broken buildings and ran along into the maze using his hands as well as his feet to clamber out onto terra firma before running up a scree slope, white concrete dust billowing up around him, stinging his eyes but obscuring his location to the men below.

He didn't pause to look when the mound dropped off to nothing, where it had been clawed away by a digger to form a vertical twelve-foot cliff. But he landed well then jumped and caught hold of a twisted girder, the first in a tangled web of rusting metal, bent pipes and broken walls.

He looked back at the mound behind him and saw one of the thugs searching for him from the top. He was covered from head to toe in fine white powder which lit up blue as Twist heard the signature double whoop of a police car that must be closing fast following the figures of the men behind him.

He scrambled across the last of the rubble into the tall weeds that had sprung up on its far side and sprinted through the vegetation, feeling the fibres snatch the fabric of his jeans as a grey unmarked police car drew level to his right, then skidded to a stop.

He turned but could not see the Nigerians. Perhaps they had retreated at the first sign of the police. Perhaps they had called the police. It was pointless speculating. He had to reach the canal and to do that he had to get out of the estate. He saw a string of girders spiralling up over the rubble and wreckage of the next tower block in the row. He jumped and caught it with his hands, pulled himself up, ran monkey-like along it until he had cleared the rubble and was close enough to the ground to let go.

It had given him a lead of maybe fifty yards and he used it to cut hard right towards the underpass that was his best chance of crossing the canal if the cops hadn't got there first. Garage doors flew past him then he hurdled the low fence weaving through a playground on the south side of the canal as he saw Bumbola's van cut down off the road towards the entrance to the underpass.

He was too preoccupied at first by the plain-clothes cop with the telescopic cosh in the tunnel mouth to see the kid on the BMX cut down the steep incline to his right. But BMX boy struggled to follow him as he ran back up to street level, under a railing and dropped off a ledge to the towpath below, heading for the red railway bridge in the darkness ahead.

The rivets were hard through the soles of his trainers and the metal was cold to the touch as he gripped the diagonal that rose up to the flat top of the bridge. He looked back at the towpath and saw the first of the two policemen looking up, shaking his head as he watched him climb.

The cast iron plates were about a foot wide and covered in frost. He slid his foot on the icy surface, pulling his feet to the metal with his hands as he made his slow ascent. The canal ice was already some twenty feet below him and he wondered if it would break if he fell. He looked back at the cops but to his surprise they were looking beyond him to the bridge strut that ran parallel to the one he was on and the boy on the BMX who was cycling along its flat top as the Runt scrambled down the far side.

They were running across the flat roof of an apartment block some three storeys up. His companions refused to relinquish the pace. Their movements were precise, controlled bursts of power more like machines than men.

'What are you doing? It's me they want!' he shouted after them, watching as they dropped out of sight onto a lower roof.

It was obvious they didn't need to be there, just as they hadn't needed to be in the estate alerting him to the fact that his tag had been sprayed in deliberate snaking lines that all converged on his bolthole in the tower. And perversely, even though they would be charged with aiding and abetting him, he could see that they were enjoying themselves. Like running along the precipitous ridges of rooftops was a big game to them.

'Jump!'

It was the one in the hat, the one who had been riding the BMX across the bridge. He must have sensed that Twist was not with them. His voice was loud and urgent from the roof below as Twist stepped back and jumped, losing his footing and landing on his coccyx and winding himself.

'Get up,' the boy shouted, pointing skyward. 'We've got company.'

A steady thrum of rotor blades was clearly audible now, coming low across the rooftops up from the estuary. He watched as the boys sprinted towards the far edge of the roof then skidded to a stop. There was a gap between the roof they were on and the next roof. It was about fifteen foot lower but some twenty feet away. He scanned the roof for another way down, feeling vibrations in his feet and knees then looked back and saw the pair of them sprint for the edge and jump.

He jogged back on the balls of his feet. Beltham had been full of joyriders who'd tried to escape from thermal cameras in fast cars but he'd never met anyone who'd outrun a chopper on foot. He took a step forward then rocked back twice on his lead foot then ran, lifting his head and pumping his arms, building speed, hitting the two-brick-deep wall which rose up to mark the edge of the roof.

The scream died in his mouth as the ground disappeared beneath his feet which pedalled in the air in front of him. The far roof rushed up at him, then came the impact as his legs slid out from under him and he skidded to a stop feeling the asphalt bite.

'Son of a bitch!' he screamed as much from the pain as the adrenalin, as the one in the hat appeared by his side offering him his hand.

'It's Dodge actually,' he said, as Twist took it and felt himself being dragged across the roof to a ventilation shaft where the little one was sat panting.

'Meet Batesy,' Dodge shouted, trying to make himself heard over the sound of the helicopter which was banking after its first pass and coming back to look again. Twist winced with the pain. His back felt like it had been flayed and his ankle was swelling but Dodge didn't care. He was pointing to a circular yellow tube, three feet in diameter, that was bolted to steel scaffolding about thirty feet to their right.

He shook his head but they weren't going to take no for an answer. The little one had got round the back of him again and he felt Batesy's arms pinning his own to his sides as Dodge reached out and grabbed both his feet.

'Get the fuck off me!' he screamed at them, twisting and trying to kick out as they slid him head first into the mouth of the tube.

It reminded him of a water slide at a leisure centre except that it was almost vertical and there would be a skip full of rubble at the bottom to break his fall not a pool full of warm, chlorinated water.

'Don't worry about the helicopter,' said Dodge. 'The fall will probably kill you.'

Twist felt Batesy's hands release him and the acceleration seize him immediately. There was no point fighting gravity as he dropped vertically for thirty feet, arms at his sides, then feeling his shoulders touch the sides, then his back until he was sliding down the tube at an angle of forty-five degrees at a speed somewhat in excess of one hundred and twenty miles an hour. Then the incline flattened and the tube kinked to the right then corkscrewed a half turn then flattened again as the bright dot at the end grew bigger. Now he was flying through the air above a skip filled with cardboard to bounce, slide, spin then tumble across a grass verge before juddering to a complete stop, face down in a flower bed. He lay for a moment, stunned, listening for the helicopter but hearing nothing but shrieks and thuds as Dodge, then Batesy, bounced then tumbled across the grass like sacks of potatoes.

There were stars dancing above him as he felt himself being dragged to shelter beneath a tree at the edge of what he could now see was a football pitch. Twist wanted to punch out at his tormentors but he was in too much pain. His ribs hurt and the pain intensified when Dodge's infectious laugh caught him and Batesy until all three of them were lying on their sides, cackling like hyenas.

Twist felt the anger in him subside. Whoever these two clowns were they had led him to safety. What these two had done for him was so crazy that it didn't stack up. Was it simply a coincidence that they'd been there, waiting for him back at the estate? Or had they planned it and if so to what end?

He struggled to his feet following Dodge's lead and took half a dozen tentative steps forwards. His legs still worked despite the swelling in his left ankle but his back was a mess, grazed on the roof then scraped as he'd slid down the tube and bounced across the half-frozen grass.

He looked up and saw that Dodge was texting on his mobile phone.

'Do you want to go to prison?' Dodge asked, aware he was watching him.

'No,' Twist replied.

'And you've got no home to go to now. Am I right?'

Twist had to nod.

'Glad we're clear,' Dodge said, looking up as he slotted the mobile back into a zip-up breast pocket. 'Because someone will be here any minute to pick you up and then we're going to take you somewhere safe. Fix up your cuts and bruises and give you some hot food.'

'You set me up, didn't you?' Twist asked.

'You believe what you want to believe,' the boy replied. 'But if I were you I'd take all the charity you can get.'

And Twist knew that he was right. He was in no condition to start playing detective and if he walked now he might never know who they were or why they had helped him escape. But the simple fact remained: without them he would have been caught and spent his eighteenth birthday packing his bag for an extended stay in the big house.

So even though he didn't trust either of them as far as he could throw them, right now they were the only friends he had. He watched Dodge turn from where he had been leaning against the tree stretching out his calf muscle. He saw the boy's eyes search the feeder road that led into the estate and widen in alarm.

'Come on,' Dodge said, 'the Feds have come back.'

13

Where did you go?
I was upset.
You were fond of him.
We all were.
Like a big sister.
You said you would go.
How could I?
What do you mean?
It was hard to reach him there.
But why send Bill?
I trust Bill.
Do you trust me?
Of course I do.
Prove it.
How?
Go and fetch the new boy.
She'd seen the look of despair in Fagin's eyes when Bill had
come back alone. And while Bill had just stood there and

shrugged and lit another cigarette, Fagin had stared at the floor unable to meet her gaze or answer the question that had been on all the boys' lips.

Why did you send Bill to fetch Harry when you promised him you would go yourself?

Fagin, the man she had come to look upon as her father was sly, criminal and ruthless when he needed to be but he had always been straight with her. Even when he was economical with the truth he would look straight at you and smile, but not this time. There had been something about his manner and Bill's studied indifference that had spooked her and she'd been close to screaming out and voicing her innermost fears – that Harry's failure to return was no accident and that the 'family' that had been his whole world had turned him out, or worse, actively done away with him once his exposure had made him a risk and not an asset.

But the chance of ever finding out what had happened to Harry was receding and she blamed herself for losing her cool that night. Not only had her rage pushed the truth even further from her but the events that had followed, her capture by the Russians, had bound not only her but all of them into a potentially lethal contract. And what scared her most was that Fagin didn't know the half of it.

Bill had been vague in describing to Fagin how he'd met Rodchenko through one of his associates, a man called Andre, at a cross-discipline martial arts title fight at Bethnal Green's York Hall.

Red didn't know how Sikes had linked Andre to Rodchenko, but Fagin was always meticulous and had done his research on the Russian known as Arkady 'The Archangel' Rodchenko with his friend Grigoi who had, up until that point, brought them all their jobs.

Fagin had come back from the meeting smiling. Rodchenko was the real deal and, according to Grigoi, would most likely be looking to secure the paintings for his patron, a man Grigoi knew only by the moniker of Nevsky, which he used to bid in the double-blind private auctions.

Known in certain criminal circles only as 'The Prince', Rodchenko's only master must have chosen his pseudonym in reference to Alexander Nevsky, the Slav Prince and Russian nationalist hero who had saved Russia, leading the Knights of Novgorod to victory over foreign scum in the Battle on the Ice in the mid-thirteenth century. It was an obscure reference but a meaningful one. According to Grigoi, 'The Prince' was well known for his nationalism and for sending three high-ranking triad bosses back to Beijing frozen in blocks of ice.

Red kicked her bike into life and pulled away from the hotel headquarters. As the traffic cleared she bit her lip and ducked into the racing position to escape the drag, feeling her mobile bunch up in her jacket against the bruises on her abdominal wall, the pain bringing back a vivid memory of the Bear crouching by her side, touching her face tenderly seconds after he had driven his fist hard into her solar plexus.

Bill had said nothing of her ordeal to Fagin. How that night, which had begun with Bill returning alone without Harry, had led her out onto the streets losing herself in the adrenalin that came with picking pockets until she'd found herself staring through the clear plastic card that had opened a door into the second circle of hell and bound her as collateral in the deal that Bill had done with Rodchenko to steal the six paintings for the Russian crime syndicate.

She lifted her left foot and felt the third gear bite as the road opened up and the Tower of London receded behind her. She looked down at the speedometer as it topped eighty on the dual carriageway towards the Isle of Dogs and she knew that if she maintained this speed she would be with them in fifteen minutes. Although whether she would find them was now a moot point because the red dot on the satnav taped to her dashboard had stopped flashing.

He who forms a tie is lost ...

She remembered being led out of Rodchenko's room by the Bear and looking back to see Bill step towards the Russian *vor* who was smiling at him, his arms spread wide like a father welcoming home a prodigal son. There was something about the white chamber and the light dancing on the marble tiles from the water in the glass tubes that had reminded her of a church in which a baptism might be performed. But then strong hands gripped her and she was pulled from the room; Bill had never told her what had followed and she had always been afraid to ask. All she really knew was that she owed Bill everything.

She shivered, then squeezed gently with her right hand and took a racing line across the roundabout and down into the tunnel that led to the HSBC tower. The orange lights in the tunnel flashed on the clear visor of her helmet, recalling the hellish strobe lights as the Russians had led her through the black room to meet Rodchenko.

She thought about Bill. Before meeting Rodchenko she would never have gone with him. But now she had no choice. She was grateful to him. For coming when she had needed him most. For making her debt to Rodchenko his own. She would play at being Bill's girl for as long as it took to pay

Rodchenko off. But she knew she would not stay with him. They called him Bulldog and he was violent and unpredictable. He came back withdrawn from each meeting with Rodchenko and had begun to view Fagin and the boys with a cold detachment, as if they were just tools to be used, not the surrogate family that had once saved him from the streets.

The bike burst out of the tunnel and up the ramp to the T-junction and she wondered if the stories about the *vor* code were true. That a man had to be prepared to kill his own family if the *vory* prince asked it of him. She braked hard and felt the pressure in her arms as the chassis of the Honda with the 1000cc Fireblade engine groaned to a stop at the traffic lights. They were red, giving her enough time to lift her visor and gasp in cold air and try to shut down the images flashing in her brain – of the puppet master with the long face and the black eyes who sat behind the desk in his bunker controlling the machine that would rape, traffic and sell her if Fagin's gang failed him.

The lights changed. She pulled back the throttle and turned left inland away from the river to the estate where the red dot had disappeared, hoping that the new boy would be easy to spot and would have no aversion to accepting a ride on the back of a V2 rocket.

14

She slowed down to look up at the police helicopter as it crossed the road in front of her and banked steeply up above the buildings to her right. Away from the last place she'd seen the red dot blinking on the satnav.

She dropped to thirty-five as a police car turned out of a side road and came slowly towards her without give a medical supplies courier on a beat-up Honda a second glance. She turned into the cul-de-sac the police had emerged from and pulled the bike into a U-turn, coming to rest alongside an alleyway that led into the estate. Locking the bike, she stepped off it, and untaped the satnav. She pulled off her helmet but kept on a thin, red balaclava as much to keep out the cold as to shield her from prying eyes.

She walked to the corner of the block where a white plywood map provided the visitor with a guide to the estate. The blocks faced inwards into a landscaped area where trees grew on raised brick-lined banks. Matching the blocks to the shapes on her satnav she started into the estate, reading

Casterbridge, Tolchurch and Weatherbury, the names of each block on a white Newham Council sign on the corner of each building.

A curtain twitched and she saw an eye peer out at her and retreat quickly back into the darkness of the flat. She couldn't see any more police and she consoled herself that even if they did come they would think twice about getting out of their cars.

She glanced down at her mobile, hit speed dial then waited. Ten seconds, twenty seconds and then she heard the siren. It was coming from the far side of the estate. She started to run, making a beeline to the furthest block, then slowed beneath a covered walkway and a wire fence that prevented children from running out onto the railway line. On the far side of this was a row of semi-detached suburban houses and beyond that the crenellated roof of what looked like an old factory.

Hot-stepping across the railway tracks she scrambled up a stack of rotting wooden piles and tore up a trail through brambles on the far side of the railway embankment. When she reached the top she looked further up the tracks and saw a pedestrian tunnel a couple of hundred yards along. The tunnel they must have stopped in.

She looked down at the satnav and was pleased to see them again, close now, perhaps three hundred yards from here, but moving slowly, which could spell trouble. She sprinted along the litter-strewn path, glancing at the fence until she found a rear gate and ran through a tiny back yard, avoiding washing on the line and a geriatric Labrador which lay prostrate on a flagstone patio.

Out on the road the siren was louder, coming from behind the houses on the far side of the road. The dot was closer now, the flashes more frequent and when she turned at the corner of the street she saw an unmarked grey police car parked up diagonally in front of the gate which opened into an industrial estate.

There was movement in the guardhouse to the left of the barrier and she accelerated to a flat sprint.

'Oi!' a voice called but she ignored it, turning left into a long avenue lined on both sides with square single-storey warehouses along which two plain-clothes cops were running, checking right and left until they slowed and turned right into one of the yards.

She sprinted after them and took a right turn into the yard before the one they had taken. Climbing wasn't easy. There was a drainpipe attached to the wall but it was fixed into ageing concrete and the bolts shifted as she pulled herself up it.

Once on the roof she saw a whitewashed perimeter wall and although it was narrow, maybe half a foot, she found she could balance well enough to jog slowly along it behind the policemen's backs as they looked up at the roof of the warehouse furthest from them where Dodge and Batesy were lying on the furthest side.

They had both put on black balaclavas but she could tell them apart by their movements as they crabbed backwards out of sight. She wolf-whistled across and Dodge looked up, raised his hand and pointed at the wall of the warehouse facing him, the one whose roof she was now standing on. Careful to keep out of sight, she began to crawl on the edge furthest from the cops until she had reached the wall above them and could peek out and look down it.

One of the cops was stood in the middle of the avenue. He was pointing what looked like a yellow toy gun up at a spot on the wall below her. She followed his line of sight and saw two figures directly below her, both climbing the drainpipe. The figure at the bottom was gaining on the figure at the top. He was using his feet to push up easily off the brackets that fastened the drainpipe to the wall at three-foot intervals but the one at the top was struggling, groping with his right foot at a point on the pipe where there simply was no bracket.

'Woohoo!' she cried.

But her voice was cut short when she saw the cop flicking the safety off the yellow gun and taking aim at the boy she was supposed to be rescuing.

15

There were a couple of rusty masonry nails where there should have been a bracket. His arms were burning, holding his weight as he looked down and saw the cop below him gaining ground. But what worried him more was the one on the ground, the one aiming the taser pistol at his back.

He turned and looked at the kid called Dodge who was pulling the little one called Batesy up onto the opposite roof.

'Tie yourself on,' Dodge shouted. 'He's going to tase you.'

Twist looked down and saw the cop on the ground priming the taser. It looked like he was figuring out how to use it which meant it was probably one of the new ones that the Met had got skanked on, shelling out fifty per cent more for them than their counterparts in the US. So the upside was that the cop was slow, but the downside was that this new kind had an effective range just short of sixteen feet.

'Tie yourself on,' Dodge shouted again. 'Do it now!'

Twist felt something touch his shoe and he looked down to see the cop straining to reach up and snatch his shoelaces.

He kicked out viciously but didn't connect. Then he looked down and saw the cop sliding down the pipe. There was, after all, a first time for everything.

Twist looked down at his belt. It was the only thing strong enough to hold his weight so, wedging his feet and left hand as far as he could into the gap between the drainpipe and the wall, he undid the buckle, pulled the belt then slid it behind the pipe to fasten it to the other end.

Then he heard a crackling sound and a couple of sharp pinpricks, one in his lower back and the other in his right buttock, followed by a pain so intense that when he opened his mouth to scream, no sound came out. It felt like someone was tearing his muscles apart with a blunt fork. His knees jerked convulsively against the brick wall as superheated pins and needles shredded every nerve ending in his body.

It finished as suddenly as it had begun. The belt had held him perfectly, tightening its grip as he'd jerked ninety degrees to the left down the wall leaving his arms and legs bruised and hanging limp beneath him. He looked down and saw the cop lying flat on his back clutching his right arm. He was surrounded by pieces of terracotta red tile and the yellow taser gun was lying a couple of feet away from his right hand. For a moment Twist couldn't put the pieces together, then there was shouting. It was Dodge.

'Hold on. Help is coming,' he yelled as the little one took aim, frisbeeing a tile at the cop who was still conscious and who was starting to climb the drainpipe.

Twist blinked the tears from his eyes. The pain had been intense but he wasn't in shock and, apart from the bruises and the grazed knuckles on his right hand, he was in no worse a situation than before with the climber still coming up at him, trying to grab his ankle.

Righting himself, he wedged his grazed hand into the gap between the drainpipe and the wall again. It hurt like hell but he had no choice: the belt round his waist didn't have enough slack in it to use it as a climbing harness. He undid the belt and began to climb but felt a searing pain in his lower back and right buttock. He looked down and the bastard cop smiled up at him. He had taken hold of the wires attached to the barbs from the taser and he was yanking on them hard like a maniacal puppeteer.

'Let go and the pain will stop,' the cop said.

Twist felt the blood running down his back and his legs and his head began to swim, the bricks in front of him beginning to distend. But just as he was opening his mouth to surrender he felt something hit his face and fall away to his right. The impact was not hard but enough to draw his attention to the rope which was dangling about a foot from his face and a Mexican wrestler in a red mask who was climbing down it towards him.

He felt a karabiner snap tight on his belt as the person in the mask's hands explored his lower back and found the barb, cutting the wire that held it, then moved lower to cut him free of the wire attached to his buttock. His head was swimming now and he fell backwards and felt himself hanging, suspended from the rope as the cop caught hold of his ankle and the Mexican Wrestler worked fast, upside down to tie a makeshift harness beneath his shoulders then reach down and with a single slash of the knife cut through the belt and buttons that held his trousers on.

The Mexican Wrestler had only said two things the whole time they'd been together and they'd both been commands.

'Swallow this,' had been the first command, offering him a yellow pill which he'd struggled to swallow and then: 'Don't move.'

Which he hadn't despite the excruciating pain, as the wrestler had dug out the barbs with the point of a very sharp-looking knife as Twist thought about the injured cop and the helicopter which must be circling back to find them.

And as the yellow pill kicked in and the pain in his ribs, back and ankle had subsided, the game had begun again, trying to keep up with the person in the mask in an acrobatic version of Simon Says that had led them across the roof, along the top of a narrow white washed wall then down a drainpipe and out into the maze of warehouses, zigzagging and doubling back until they were across the railway tracks, through the council estate and sat astride a beat-up motorbike that had made good their escape.

The ride had been uneventful. Twist strapped to the courier box on the back of the bike behind the wrestler as day had passed into night. People, cars and buildings rushed past in a blur as the bike topped the ton, heading east towards the badlands of the Essex borders. And if he hadn't dreamed it then it must have been real – the sensation of assisted flight, clutching to the back of a flaming meteor which banked to the left and then to the right, threatening to tip you off, roaring when it accelerated, low-pitched at its maximum velocity and high-pitched when it slowed and turned.

And how long they had ridden he could not tell, just that they had arrived in a wasteland with the stars above them and points of light closer to the ground illuminating giant steel balls that hung suspended by chains as thick as a man's neck and houses reduced to rubble and swept up into giant conical piles at the feet of the monstrous machines.

And Twist, slumped forwards, his head lolling on his chest, was now appreciating the ride and the rider who handled the bike with great skill, navigating through the wreckage and climbing a steep, muddy escarpment then dropping off the far side, standing in the saddle and balancing the bike perfectly as the back wheel slid down onto the flat and a dirt road compacted by the ten-ton diggers and thirty-ton lorries that used it.

Until at last the wrestler had pulled to a stop atop a rise and pointed down at headlights flicking on and off about half a mile away in the dusk. A signal answered by the dust exploding up off the rear wheel of the bike as they tore down onto the plain and across it to meet the lights.

And despite the numbness and the exhaustion Twist felt something like fear. Fear of this gang who were not like any gang he had encountered before and the answer they would give when he asked them why they did it. Jumping off buildings and outrunning Feds might be enough for them but Twist had his doubts. So what was their angle? Because they weren't just doing it for fun and if this was the case, what could possibly explain the effort and risk they had made to help him?

A white van accelerated towards them and swung into a tight handbrake turn, spewing up gravel and dust. He watched as the side door slid open and Batesy leaned out, holding on with one hand and beckoning him with the other as the motorcycle skidded to a stop alongside. And there was Dodge, his head round the door frame, grinning like a loon.

'You've met Batesy, haven't you?' Dodge said. 'And in case you were wondering, you can walk away now if you want to. It's your call entirely.'

Twist stood for a moment, feeling the cold wind on his hands and his face. He was exhausted and hungry and he had no money, no family and nowhere to go now that his hideout in the tower had been compromised. So he did the only thing he could do. He staggered forwards and half fell into the strong hands that reached out from the back of the van and laid him down on the side that didn't hurt across the row of seats inside.

And as Batesy slid the door shut behind them, Dodge knelt beside him and turned his head sideways so that they were face to face.

'Sorry, mate,' he said. 'We're definitely not kidnappers but would you mind wearing this?'

Twist looked at the black pillow case in Dodge's hand and shook his head.

'I didn't think so,' Dodge replied.

16

They must have crossed a river at some point. A gentle incline had been followed by a descent that had exactly mirrored it but he couldn't list more than ten London bridges so the exercise had been futile in all but one respect. It had momentarily distracted him from the fact that he was being driven blindfold in the back of a locked van by a gang of wall-climbing anarchists who had clearly been stalking him for some time.

'You can take it off now.'

It was Dodge's voice and it was followed by the sound of the van door sliding open. It surprised Twist when he pulled off his hood how dark it now was and how surreal everything had become. It was as if the day had been condensed and accelerated into an alternative, more intense version of reality. He felt disorientated and confused and now with the adrenalin wearing off, exhausted.

He'd rerun the sequence of events several times in the half-hour journey in the van and try as he might, he couldn't help reaching the same conclusion. He'd been set up. The tags had been put there to signpost where he was hiding in his squat in the tower, but more perniciously still, to provoke Bumbola into all-out war. He could never go back.

And the fact that two strangers had showed up at the exact same time his tag had appeared all over the estate made them the prime suspects, but he still didn't know why they had chosen to fuck his shit up and not someone else's. It felt like they'd singled him out, but why and for what purpose?

It had been a strange day. Like he'd woken up and everything had been upside down, from the tags to the chase to the wrestler running down the wall. It was as if he had stepped through the looking glass and there was no turning back. His world had changed the moment he'd laid eyes on the two jokers in the skate bowl and he began to wonder if anything was going to be the same again.

He opened his eyes wide then squinted, looking out at his surroundings. It was a technique he'd learned off a burglar in Beltham. A way of getting your eyes to adjust faster to the darkness and he'd often used it at night when he'd been out tagging in places where a light would have drawn attention to himself.

It was true what they said, that blind men must feel more acutely with their other senses, but it didn't take extra sensory perception to figure out that he was stepping out of the van into a shin-deep pool of ice-cold mud.

'I don't think we were properly introduced,' Dodge said, holding out his hand to pull Twist out of the muddy trough. Twist found his hand in the darkness and allowed himself to be pulled out of the water-filled rut he'd just stepped into, watching as the van's white door slammed shut and it sped off, its wheels spinning in the slurry.

'How's your ankle?' Dodge asked, noticing that Twist was favouring his right foot.

Twist just shrugged. The left one was worse but the shock of the impacts had left him aching all over, in the joints of his knees, hips and shoulders, to say nothing of the bruises when he had slipped and fallen during the chase.

'I've never seen anyone get tased before,' Dodge went on. 'It was well funny.'

'Ha ha,' Twist replied with all the sarcasm he could muster as they moved off together over the mud on a pathway made out of wooden pallets that wound between mounds of bricks and hastily erected awnings.

Twist felt the bruising in his back and buttocks. The pain was muted. They had given him some kind of pill called Vicodin in the van and it had taken the edge off it. There was just a dull ache remaining and although he didn't feel as spooked now they were away from the Feds, his mind looped back to one question: who was his rescuer, the mysterious Mexican Wrestler who'd turned up in the nick of time?

'Who was the man in the mask?' he asked, as Dodge belly-rolled over a large section of piping.

'Wild outfit right?' Dodge replied, keeping moving so that Twist had to run to catch the rest of his response.

'I think you'll be surprised,' Dodge went on. 'He looks like a real macho guy but I think you're going to like him.'

As the ground rose beneath them up a gentle incline, Twist became aware of a white halo of light from a lantern swinging on a pole in the distance, its light diffused by the rain and the darkness. It was like their beacon, their North

Star, and he followed Dodge as he used it to navigate through the mess of what must be a massive building site, through a hole where the wire fence had been cut into an overgrown garden, chest-high with weeds and stinging nettles, and along a beaten-down path towards a derelict old house at the top of a two hundred metre incline which had once been a lawn.

Dodge trotted ahead, pausing to wait for Twist who could not believe how much energy he had left as he bounded up the curved steps and across a mildew-covered driveway to the front doors of what, judging by the shadows of the letters on the wall above them, had once been a country-house-style hotel.

DANGER! KEEP OUT!

Dodge moved away from the clapboard sign that hung from the handles of the front doors, moving to the right, and for a moment Twist lost sight of him. Then he heard swearing and he rounded the corner to see Dodge sat on his backside looking up at a rusty ladder that was the lowest part of a metal fire escape that rose up four storeys to the top of the hotel.

'Give me a leg up,' Dodge barked, and Twist guessed his weight at around eleven stone as Dodge stepped up into his cupped hands, caught hold of the bottom rung of the ladder and pulled himself up onto the iron platform and began kicking it until it gave and slid down, alighting some four feet from the ground.

Dirty tarpaulins sheltered the metal stairwell and platforms from the elements and from anyone looking up at the hotel from the wasteland outside. It meant that Dodge and his crew could enter and leave without being seen, something Twist imagined might have numerous benefits for people doing whatever it was that they might do.

When they reached the third floor, Twist saw Dodge run his hand down the far edge of a plywood board until there was a click and the board pivoted out on a pair of hinges to reveal a wooden door behind it which Dodge opened with a key.

'The good thing about this place,' Dodge said as he held the door open, ushering Twist inside, 'is that it's listed.'

Twist shrugged. Maybe listed meant it was in the Yellow Pages.

'Means the developers can't knock it down or renovate it without the right papers, which they'll never get without a unanimous vote from the local council, which,' Dodge explained, 'they'll never get because we have a man inside. Which means, so long as we're careful, we can continue to live here, rent free, for as long as we like.'

Twist was just wondering how this place would match up to his engine room in the tower when Dodge pulled the door closed behind them and they were plunged into darkness until Dodge's iPhone switched on and Twist found himself staring down a corridor piled high with blackened furniture that looked like it had been damaged in a fire at least half a century ago.

He followed Dodge along the tunnel until he reached the end of the corridor and pulled a king-size mattress towards him to reveal a small, white, padlocked door which opened onto a narrow staircase and a ladder bridging the mid-section, which appeared to have collapsed.

The stairwell was claustrophobic and mysteriously hot, and the only light came from the dull red glow of LEDs embedded in a keypad that hung down from a tangle of black cables. Twist watched as Dodge punched in a long string of numbers then pulled back a metal grille above him and pushed up a trapdoor, bathing them in what felt like daylight.

And stepping up into that light was like stepping into an alternative reality. For the fire that had gutted the hotel below had not reached the top floor and the red carpet was as thick beneath their feet as it had been beneath the feet of the Edwardians who had dined here one hundred years ago.

And when he looked up Twist got a shock, staring at his own frayed and torn reflection in a full-length gilt-edged mirror in front of him.

'Do you think this place is secure enough?' he asked, clocking the black fisheye lens at the base of the chandelier in the middle of the grand landing.

'Can't be too careful,' Dodge commented as he motioned for Twist to proceed across the landing to a pair of massive double doors, passing a set of portraits of eminent Edwardians that looked to Twist's unschooled eye no less original than the works hanging in the Tate Britain.

But he stood corrected by Dodge.

'All forgeries,' Dodge said. 'Part of Fagin's collection.'

Dodge walked to the far side of the double doors and placed his hand in the mouth of a badly stuffed brown bear which stood on its hind legs like some kind of guardian to the inner sanctum. Twist watched as Dodge rummaged in its throat before turning frustrated back to the doors.

'Oi, wankers!' he shouted through the keyhole. 'The bear's stuck.'

Twist heard a click from the inside as the doors opened a fraction, allowing Dodge to get his body into the gap and prise them apart to reveal the polished oak floor of what must once have been a ballroom or casino, but which now lay empty apart from a bank of oversized white beanbags piled up in the middle of the room in front of a large TV.

Twist could see now that they were not alone. There were several guys who looked like they were practicing acrobatics in one corner, while two others lay sprawled across the bean-bags, lost beneath a haze of smoke. He didn't recognise the film that was playing and the two boys didn't move. They just kept watching the screen and drawing on a three-foot-long water pipe.

'I thought he told you to stay off the camel shit,' Dodge barked but there was no response and Twist heard him tut to himself then run at the nearest beanbag and kick it so hard that the boy sitting on it rolled off onto the floor and lay there, face down, with the business end of the pipe still stuck in the corner of his mouth.

Twist looked around for the source of the pale light. It had been dimmed but he still found himself wondering where it came from, and how it was possible to so accurately mimic daylight, as they crossed the room to a door on the far wall beneath a twisted mass of golden orbs bound together like a string of tiny suns glowing softly inside a building where the sun never shone.

They left the smoke-filled ballroom behind them and entered into a long, green-wallpapered corridor where what Twist assumed must also be forgeries hung inside their wooden frames. He felt a glow of satisfaction as he recognised a Miro, an early Monet and a malignant Bacon, which he stopped to stare at, forgetting for a moment that he was supposed to be following Dodge.

'Where are you living?' Dodge said, projecting his voice from the far end of the corridor. 'He will want to know.'

'I was in Beltham until a month ago when they started letting me out on a tag to attend a youth apprentice scheme.

Before that I was in a squat on Pudding Mill Lane. People used to come for lessons from the squatters. A lot of them were in the circus.'

'Did they teach you anything?' Dodge asked.

Twist nodded.

'You got no family?' Dodge asked, watching Twist shake his head. 'So how did you end up in trouble?'

'Extreme graffiti,' Twist replied, turning to walk down the corridor to join him.

'Is that why the Fat Man was after you then?' Dodge said.

Twist could see Dodge watching his reaction closely. Like it was a test.

'No,' Twist said, meeting Dodge's eye. 'I stopped tagging about six months ago.'

'Why?'

'It got boring.'

'Did they teach you a trade in Beltham?' Dodge asked.

'Apprenticeship was a condition of my parole.'

'What did they give you?'

'Mortuary assistant.'

Twist saw Dodge's lips curl into a smile and, not for the first time, found himself surprised at how much interest the living had in the dead.

'No wonder you ran,' Dodge said, changing tack, Twist reluctant to be drawn into revealing any more about himself to this strange boy who had a knack for getting stuff out of him that was better kept to himself.

Twist turned to study a Da Vinci print of men on horses who were fighting. They had ugly, spiteful faces and not one of them was wearing any clothing.

'I had to.' Twist finally replied to the question after giving it some thought, knowing that he must be careful never to let on that he'd broken parole.

'The embalmer was a perv,' he said, watching Dodge's eyes widen in surprise.

'He tried it on, did he?' Dodge asked.

'Not with me, but …'

He struggled to stifle a laugh. Dodge's face was a picture.

'There was this girl. A pretty one,' Twist began. 'The file said she'd drowned because she was pale and had reeds in her hair when they brought her into the mortuary.'

Dodge was open-mouthed now. Not knowing where this was going.

'The mortician forbade me to go into the mortuary alone. He said it wasn't respectful. That I was to stay in the embalming room on the nights we worked to clear backlogs. Thing is that he used to go up there a lot. And he went up this time. Just as he always went up when there was a girl …'

Twist looked up, watching Dodge battling a wave of revulsion.

'Anyway, so this drowned girl came in so I was put to work putting in eye caps to recreate the natural curvature of her eyes and glued her lips together before he took her up to the morgue. She was done, ready to go, so I thought it was weird that he said he was going up to check on her. I followed him up there and I looked in and then …'

Twist looked at Dodge. His mouth was open, hanging on his every word.

'And then he saw me,' Twist continued. 'He turned round and I could see what he was doing and I wanted to shout "you sick sod", but instead I made a big mistake.'

'What?' Dodge asked, his eyes on stalks.

'I told my parole officer,' Twist said, hanging his head, 'and about a week later I had to report to sick bay for a "psychological assessment". That's when I knew that dirty bastard had turned my story around and claimed that I was making a "pre-emptive strike" at him because in fact, it was him who had caught me …'

'So you had to run,' Dodge said.

'It was that or the funny farm,' Twist went on.

Dodge looked at him for a long minute, sympathy and shock writ large on his face.

'So what's his name?' he finally asked. 'The mortician?'

Twist paused, thinking maybe it wasn't such a good idea telling him, until he knew exactly what kind of outfit he was dealing with.

'Sowerberry,' he said, 'of Tottenham.'

Dodge nodded sagely, as if the addition of Tottenham explained everything, and a silence descended upon the corridor which Twist finally broke.

'So how come you brought me here?' he asked.

'We lost someone recently,' Dodge began, warily, Twist thought. 'And we need to replace him.'

Twist wanted to ask in what way they had 'lost' him but he noticed Dodge's expression change as the little one, Batesy, appeared behind him, holding what looked like a broken circuit board and beckoning Dodge into a room off the corridor, which was dark apart from the flashing of LEDs and silent bar the sound of whirring as fans struggled to keep banks of hard drives and servers from going into meltdown.

Batesy sat down and blew the dust off the circuit board in his hand then pulled down a light attached to a coil which hung suspended from the ceiling. Then he closed his eyes as if visualising a non-existent screen and began to type furiously on a keypad with his left hand.

'Batesy!' Dodge shouted into his ear.

But Batesy kept his eyes shut and just raised his right hand like a concert pianist, holding a note before returning it to the keypad.

'Don't take it personal. He can only communicate in XML,' Dodge said, beckoning Twist out of the room and back along the corridor, stopping by a door three-quarters of the way down on the left.

'Right, you smell and you need some new togs,' Dodge said abruptly, pulling down the door handle which didn't budge.

'Here, give us a hand.' Twist stood alongside Dodge and they pulled together, the door opening a foot, allowing a JJB Sports box to tumble off a stack of other boxes and smack Twist in the face.

'Now I can see why they went under,' Twist said.

'Got a bit carried away,' Dodge quipped back. 'Wait here.'

Twist watched as Dodge clambered into the breach and disappeared into the mountain of boxes, several of which were thrown from within the room through the gap in the door.

And despite the demise of JJB Sports he felt a lot better with a pair of box-fresh Nikes and a couple of tracksuits under his arms.

'You got a shower?' he asked, as Dodge led him back out of the ballroom and turned right down the long carpeted corridor towards a single blue door at the end.

'We've got a two-hundred-gallon marble bathtub,' came the reply. 'But not until he's seen you.'

17

'Is that you, Dodge?'

Dodge's hand had barely touched the handle when a voice came from inside the room. It was soft, nasal and strangely accented and Twist watched his new friend pause before pushing down on the door handle and stepping inside.

The room was not small, about the size of a squash court, and about as high. Right slap bang in the centre was a big desk and behind that a chair upon which a man was sitting, his face and body obscured by an antiques catalogue.

'FBoss,' Dodge said, as if the man who had just invited them in needed now to be reminded of their presence.

Twist watched a hand lift from the catalogue and beckon them forwards through the piles of stuff that filled the room and, rather like he had been doing all day, he found himself following Dodge along a narrow, well-trodden path.

It was as if a giant had filled a skip with stuff, two parts art and antiques, one part garbage and electronic junk, then shaken it like a cocktail and tipped it out into the room. As far as Twist could tell there was no particular order to anything. Paintings, shop mannequins, disembowelled computers, books and obsolete gadgets lay jumbled up on top of one another in various states of disrepair. It was hard at first to know where to look but he still found himself drawn to the rear right corner of the room.

There, a microscope stood on a stainless steel gurney surrounded by glass test tubes in front of which stood an oil painting of a small boy petting a wet dog in front of a roaring fire. But what interested Twist most was not the painting but what was in the glass test tubes. There were pieces of rock, seaweed, tree bark, viscous liquids and a beetle. And the only thing they all had in common was that each had its own quite distinct and entirely unique colour.

Twist looked at the A-frame upon which the unremarkable picture stood. The oil paint had lost its sheen and the little boy petting the King Charles spaniel had been trussed in a starched collar and tight-fitting formal waistcoat. So it surprised Twist to see a dash of fresh paint in the bottom right corner whose dark grey colour perfectly matched a small circle of wet paint on the easel which hung from one of the A-frame's pegs beneath the painting.

'Arthur Jofferry. Scottish painter. Circa 1880. Caught syphilis in a brothel in Jaipur and died in India a year later. That was 1825, I think. His lady wife then caught it and outlived him by a year. Fifty tops at auction. Not much demand for him these days. Not much demand for him in 1826 either. The dirty bugger.'

Twist stopped alongside Dodge, sensing his agitation at being studiously ignored by the man behind the desk.

'Are you the artist?' the man finally asked in an accent lost somewhere between Bethnal Green and Bucharest.

'No,' Twist replied, studying the man's hands as they gripped the edges of the Sotheby's catalogue, noticing the tip of the index finger of the left hand hovering above the cover. It was stained with paint. The same colour as Arthur Jofferry's signature.

'I used to be a tagger,' Twist went on, watching as the catalogue slid slowly downwards revealing four matted grasps of greasy grey hair swept across a bald pate then furtive, dark grey eyes perched upon a nose the like of which Twist had never seen before.

Hooked and badly broken just below the bridge, it belonged on some nightmarish prehistoric bird, not on a man, and Twist found himself fixating on it until the man scraped the metal feet of his chair backwards, and stood staring across the desk at Twist through red-rimmed eyes.

He moved slowly, guiding himself around the edge of the desk, shoulders hunched, eyes occasionally flicking up to meet Twist's then falling, apparently lost in contemplation as if each new glance had further confirmed a negative first impression. It made Twist feel uncomfortable. Like a specimen, a beetle pinned alive beneath the unforgiving gaze of the microscope in the corner of the room. He wanted to ask why they had gone to so much trouble to bring him here if they were just going to prod and probe. But he lost his nerve and he ended up saying nothing.

But it did occur to him that he was still in control. And whatever this strange man offered him in the way of money, clothing, food or board, he would smile, thank him and then politely ask to be escorted back through the garden, across the wasteland and back into the real world where all his troubles would be waiting for him, just as he had left them.

But the man had something. It radiated off him. A peculiar energy that Twist felt drawn to as the man stepped in front of him and offered him his hand which he felt compelled to take. Twist looked into his eyes which shone above the broken ridgeline of his nose, his thin lips stretching into a smile so wide that it threatened to detach the straggly wisps of red hair that he wore on his chin.

'Cornelius Fagin, art collector, at your service,' he said, bending his knees in a curtsy that would not have looked out of place in the court of Elizabeth I.

Twist could not help but laugh as Fagin squeezed his hand with unexpected force and he found himself struggling to break his grip.

'I'm sorry, did I hurt you, my dear? You must look after your hands if you're an artist. They're the most valuable thing you have,' Fagin said.

Twist was just about to make his excuses and leave when the man turned his back on him and began scanning the junk with both hands as if they were a pair of metal detectors.

'Andy Warhol's mother told him as a child that if he wanted to make friends he should invite them up to tea,' he said, his hands circling over a cardboard box behind his desk, then reaching down to pull a white china teapot from it which he passed to Dodge.

'How do you like it?' he asked.

'Builders,' Twist replied, watching Dodge skulk towards the door as Fagin waved him to sit in one of the two cracked leather armchairs facing his desk.

The tea was very strong with a metallic aftertaste. It seemed to have triggered a buzzing sensation that rose up his spine and fizzed in the base of his skull.

'Gunpowder,' Fagin said. 'Admiral Nelson swore by it.'

Apart from feeling slightly more awake Twist had to admit that the pain from his bruises did seem to have subsided, and when Fagin picked up the teapot and rounded the desk to pour him a second cup he could not refuse.

'Tea is a way of life here, no?' Fagin asked.

Twist turned to look at Dodge who was observing him over the rim of his teacup before turning to answer Fagin, only to find him already sat back behind his desk. The old man reached down and emerged with a poster-sized sheet of plywood, turning it to reveal a mediocre-quality print of Banksy's infamous kissing policemen.

'Disgusting!' Fagin said. 'But you cannot hide talent. Sometimes it leaps up at you like a viper from a mountain path.'

Twist watched as Fagin mimed a snake rising up and slithering across the desk, poised to strike.

'And so when Dodger says he's been bitten I sit up and listen.'

'Why did you have me followed?' Twist asked, watching as Fagin stared into his teacup as his paint-stained fingertip left a thin grey line around its rim.

'Because I don't like to see talent go to waste,' he said.

Twist looked at the clock on the wall. The hands had not moved for some time but this pantomime-like day had gone on long enough. He was tired and he knew that once the tea wore off he would crash. It was time to go and he stood, turning to the door to see that Dodge had anticipated him and was stood with his hands crossed in front of him.

'Listen, thanks for looking out for me today,' Twist began, 'and it's really flattering that you like my work but now I've really got to go,' he said, turning back to face Fagin.

The old man was smiling, his thin lips drawn back to reveal a set of broken yellow teeth. Twist caught his breath, asking himself why he had come here to this madhouse in the first place. But that was just hindsight talking. He could have broken away from Dodge on the far side of the bridge but he would not have escaped without him.

And then there was his natural curiosity with this peculiar art collector who employed roughnecks who climbed walls and jumped between buildings, and who forged signatures and served tea spiked with God knows what.

Twist could hear the blood pumping in his ears, as the pressure built inside him. He stared at Dodge who unlocked his hands and shifted his stance like he was getting ready to tackle him if he made a move for the door.

'Don't get carried away now, mate,' Dodge said.

Don't get carried away … *mate*?

Twist dug his fingernails into the palms of his hands and walked towards the door.

'First off, I'm not your mate.' he said, 'and second,' he went on, turning back to Fagin, 'I'm not an artist so don't even pretend it's my work you're interested in.'

Twist watched Dodge take a step back but he knew he wasn't going to fight his way out. There appeared to be only one way out and that involved crossing a ballroom full of gymnastic sociopaths resting up like chimps after a raid.

'You know the problem with graffiti?' Fagin began again, breaking the silence. 'You can't move it around. What's the point of art if you can't shift it?'

Twist stopped walking and turned back to Fagin.

'That is the point,' he said, 'it belongs to everyone.'

Twist watched Fagin shrug then reach into his drawer and pull out a thick wad of fifty pound notes, peeling off ten of them and offering them to him.

'Call it an advance,' Fagin said.

'An advance for what?' Twist replied as Dodge stepped past him, leapfrogged an antique rocking horse and swiped the wad from Fagin's hand.

Twist watched Dodge's face as he counted the money, then looked back to Fagin who was counting the same amount again, his mouth twitching as he palmed each note, before laying them down on the desk where Twist could easily reach them. But Twist didn't budge.

'Think you're getting more, do you?' Fagin asked.

Twist shook his head and Fagin looked skyward, clasping his hands together as if asking for deliverance. Then Dodge coughed and Fagin looked past Twist and spoke to him.

'What am I gonna do with a kid like this?' he said, speaking now as if Twist wasn't there.

Dodge rolled up his notes and stuffed them in his pocket before answering his boss.

'He's fast. Left the Feds for dust. I thought maybe we could train him up. Seeing as how we have a vacancy.'

'I'm not a thief,' said Twist.

'You said you're on the streets! What, you never stole a sarnie from Tesco's?' Dodge countered.

'Don't need to. They chuck out enough, if you know where to look,' Twist said, watching Fagin wince.

'Skip-diver,' said Dodge, as if he had just confirmed an earlier hypothesis about Twist's true standing in life.

But Fagin waved down his insult.

'We've all got to start somewhere,' he said, 'so tell me, Twist. You need a place to stay?'

'No thanks, I'm cool,' said Twist, thinking to himself that he was going to be way more than cool if he slept rough tonight.

'I think you've been misinformed, Dodger,' Fagin started again, changing tack. 'You see, your friend has other plans. Maybe a place at art school next autumn? I mean, even if we offered him five hundred a week … to come and train with us, it'd still be an insult to a gentleman of his prospects.'

Twist looked back and saw that Fagin was stroking his beard, staring at the boy, eyes alert but hands occupied like a man holding a conversation while petting a wet dog in front of a fire. The old man and Dodge were an unusual pair and he could not imagine how they had ever met.

Had a scene like the one that was playing out now occurred between these two in the past? Had the boy called Dodge wanted something as badly as he, the tagger formerly known as Twist, now wanted to learn? To escape the prison his life had become, to develop the only real talent he had? And had the peculiar old man looked inside Dodge's head and spoken aloud his innermost desire on their first meeting? And if he had and Dodge had accepted the offer that must have followed, had that wish been granted?

Twist thought not.

'No, er, actually … I'm off. Thanks for the tea,' he said, putting the cup down on a stack of hardback books and walking past Dodge towards the door.

'I'm cooking tonight, Dodge. You want spaghetti again, or I could do that goulash I did last week …?'

'Yeah, make it spicy,' Dodge replied.

Twist's hand gripped the door handle but he found himself struggling to turn it. He hadn't eaten in thirty-six hours, during which time he had outrun a Nigerian crime syndicate, a small army of cops and a police helicopter.

'So tell me … Master Twist,' Fagin said, addressing Twist's back with an almost perfect facsimile of genuine concern, 'what exactly is it in this life that you want?'

18

She let out the throttle on the bike and tried not to look at Newham. Riding kept her focused. There was no time for regret when she was riding fast like this, the lines and the cat's eyes a blur as they rushed up to meet her, putting the past behind her while the future lay waiting, somewhere in the darkness ahead.

When the satnav blinked she pulled into the slip road and took a look at the entrance to the new boy's estate. It would have been so much easier if this 'genius', as Fagin had described him, had decided to stay last night as well, but try as they might, he'd refused their clean sheets and mattress springs and returned instead to his bolthole in the condemned estate he called home. Saving his arse from electrocution clearly wasn't going to be enough, she thought. FBoss was going to make her go the whole nine yards and reel him in just like she had Harry before him. So she wasn't feeling proud of herself as she turned into the slip road that led into the rubble and broken buildings that were much as FBoss had described them.

'Picture the Siege of Grozny …'

She'd had to Google the Chechen capital of Grozny, the place the UN had called 'the most destroyed city on Earth'. It was strange finding such devastation here in London. At least the ruined tower blocks wouldn't be booby-trapped, she thought, as she saw the entrance guarded as Fagin had said it would be, by a fat man in a traffic warden's uniform.

She pulled the bike to a stop in front of the gate and watched the man look up at her. He had a face like a Rottweiler, folds of black flesh and dark rings around his eyes that turned to take in the girl on a motorcycle who had just materialised in front of him.

'Most girls walk in,' he said, peering at her face as she lifted the visor of her helmet.

'I'm not most girls,' she replied, forcing a smile as he walked past her and put his hand on the handlebars of the motorcycle, his bulbous eyes searching for a way inside her one-piece red leather race suit.

'Whatever turns them on,' he said, lifting his hand palm open to receive her crumpled twenty pound note.

The estate was even worse than she had imagined. The towers closest to the gate looked like a giant fist had punched them flat. The steel girders that had once held them together had twisted inwards and the concrete walls had collapsed, carpeting the areas around them with a fine white dust.

She cut off the tarmac and into the overgrown grass of the parkland to the north of the estate, counting the towers as she went until she reached the fifth. Pulling the bike to the left she killed the engine and let it glide silently down towards the rendezvous.

Concealing the bike behind a giant steel rubbish bin she walked round to the eastern wall where she quickly found the mark that Dodge had made to the left of the door. It was a red cross. As if the building had been visited by the plague and she imagined its inhabitants boarded up alive inside.

She moved to the window on the right of the door and prised back the board that covered it. Its screws were loose, just as FBoss had said they would be, and she quickly found herself on the stairs, taking them two at a time, feeling the burn in her thighs and wondering why they were going to so much trouble for a graffiti artist. He was scrawny and he couldn't run. They would have to train him – correction, she would have to train him – if, and it was a big if, they could first persuade or coerce him into joining them at all. Last night he'd said nothing when Dodge had told him the old man had plans for him. Plans that would not only give him a free pass on borstal, but also set him up with an easel and oils for life. But for all Dodge's words this strange boy had offered none. He'd just shaken his head and walked out. And half of her, in spite of her own situation, hoped he'd keep shaking it now.

She flicked on the light on her phone and lit up the landing. There were three closed doors and just one of them was slightly ajar. She walked towards it and pushed it open. There was a rope hanging there which went up through a broken skylight in the ceiling. She took hold of it, gripped her lower legs and shoes around it and began to climb up onto the roof.

Dodge and FBoss were crouched low on the far side, FBoss peering through a pair of binoculars. She dropped to a crouch and moved silently round behind them.

'How am I supposed to shift it?' she heard FBoss ask, making eye contact with Dodge who was shaking his head.

'You're not seeing the whole picture boss. It's like the estate agents say. Location, location, location.'

'Do you think you can get up there?' FBoss said, taking her by surprise.

She watched him lower the binoculars and turn to smile at her.

'Come,' he said. 'Come and take a look at this boy. Isn't he magnificent?'

He offered his hand and she took it, just as she had the first day they had met when he had come to visit her in the home.

'Why don't we ask him for dinner,' he said, '… or whatever it is you kids do together these days?'

19

He stood with his headphones on, lost in his own private world. It was music that Martin said would help him get 'in the zone', wherever that was.

He'd risen with the sun at close to nine and tipped half a jar of Nescafe into a hot mug of water he'd boiled on his meths stove. It was like a refrigerator in the steel engine room and he couldn't help thinking about the previous night he'd spent, comfortably numb from the tea, beneath a sixteen-tog duvet in the old hotel.

He shoved half a dozen Nurofen in his mouth and bit into a stale sandwich he'd salvaged from the back of Pret A Manger. The back of the paper bag said that French women ate whatever they wanted but stayed slim by eating only half of the food on their plates. It didn't say what they did with the other half but it had got Twist wondering if he wouldn't be better off in a café in Arles, sipping a pastis opposite a beautiful, slim French girl who kept giving her half his food.

He pushed up with his legs, gripping the rope, hand over hand, until he was back up on the roof of the block. Almost forty-eight hours had passed since he'd been tased and he had no desire to repeat the experience. He knew it wasn't safe here any more but he wanted to finish 'The Matador' so he could photograph it and use it as his calling card.

The sun was at its apex now, somewhere above a layer of fine white clouds which had no discernible edges and did not appear to be moving. It had to be about two or three degrees above zero. The lack of wind was some kind of bonus, he thought, as he unzipped his fly and leaned back, admiring the arc of his piss as gravity took it.

'I'm glad I climbed up the other side,' a voice spoke behind him.

He looked around and saw the Wrestler standing behind him wearing the same mask he'd worn the day before. It was crimson red with gold diagonal lines around the eyes but the wrestler had replaced the full red silk body stocking of yesterday with technical climbing gear, black cargo pants and a figure-hugging black ripstop Gore-tex jacket.

It was a sinister get-up. The kind of thing that a motorcycle hit man might wear in Cartagena, but what disturbed Twist more was the timbre of the Wrestler's voice. He sounded like a girl.

'Sorry, no toilets up here,' he said, turning, careful not to expose himself.

'Home sweet home,' the Wrestler said, taking in the litter and junk around him.

'I like the picture,' he went on. 'Not so keen on your pad though.'

Twist shook himself dry, pulled up his zip then turned to face the freak behind him.

'Thank you,' he said. 'You saved my arse.'

He watched as the Wrestler pulled off the red mask and felt the blood boil in his cheeks. She had green eyes and auburn hair tied in a knot at the back and she was about twenty years old. He held up his hands, desperately trying to unscramble his thoughts.

'You got anything to eat?' she asked.

'Don't get many visitors,' he replied. 'I've got some cream crackers … and cooking chocolate.'

'Hmm. Carbs and chocolate – the athlete's diet.'

'Beggars can't be choosers,' Twist said, walking back towards the engine room and the cardboard box that doubled as a fridge-freezer.

'I'm sorry if I scared you,' she said, shaking the mask at her side. 'The cameras, you see.'

'I thought you were a guy.'

'You say the sweetest things,' the girl said, smiling as he handed her a cream cracker with a lump of chocolate-flavoured fat on top of it.

'I meant the way you move …' he said.

'What, so girls can't be fast?' she replied, clearly offended. 'Fuck off!'

Twist didn't have enough experience of girls who ran down walls dressed as Mexican wrestlers to draw any hard and fast conclusions. So he bit his lip, then just went for it.

'This is always what happens,' he said.

'What?' she replied, watching him as he disappeared into the engine room.

'*What* always happens?' she said again, watching him as he emerged clutching his meths stove.

'I see a girl I like and shit just starts pouring out of my mouth,' he said, busying himself with the blue fuel, spilling most of it on his hands.

'Better stick to the drawing then,' she said smiling, 'you're good at that.'

Twist pulled a packet of safety matches from his pocket. He opened the box and found it was empty.

'Here,' she said, offering him a lighter then laughing as a blue flame shot up his arm and he danced in a circle slapping his hand against his jeans trying to put it out.

'So what do you want?' she asked when he'd successfully lit the burner.

'Me, paint, a wall,' he said. 'The rest of the world down there. Suits me.'

'You can't stay up here forever, you know,' she said, staring at him as he examined the small hole he'd burnt in his new tracksuit top.

'I don't see why not,' he countered. 'When I was younger I used to climb trees. They moved me around a lot when I was a kid. Foster parents, care homes, social workers with padlocks on their handbags talking about me behind closed doors. The only way I ever got any head space was climbing things that were really, really tall where nobody could reach me.'

'Except me,' the girl said.

'Yes,' Twist was forced to admit, handing her the less dirty mug, 'except you.'

'Thank you …' she said, looking at him from the corner of her eye, sly or coy, he couldn't tell which.

'Actually, I came to ask you out,' she said.

'What?' Twist spat.

'To a party,' she said. 'You know, food, drink, dancing ... a PAR ... TEE?'

Twist recovered himself and fished something unspeakable out of his mug.

'Where?' he asked.

'At Fagin's.'

'The creepy Russian dude in the hotel?'

'Romanian,' she corrected him.

'Right,' Twist said, unconvinced, watching her nervously as she stepped closer to him, looking into his eyes.

'Look,' she said, 'I know he's eccentric but he's got that huge big place all to himself and forgive me for saying this but I really don't think you should stick around here any longer than you have to when there's lots of room there to do your own thing. No social workers – and believe me when I say: been there, done that too. He won't tell you how to live your life. He's cool. A good cook too ... so will you be my date?'

She paused for breath, her eyes glancing down at the floor.

'... I mean, unless you've got something better to do.'

20

Twist pushed his plate away from himself and gripped the sides of his stomach which was fit to burst. He couldn't recall last being in such entertaining company and when he looked up he said a small prayer to whoever it was who might be watching over him.

Three boys, excluding Twist, one girl and at the head of the table the peculiar-looking Romanian called Fagin watching them eat with a silver ladle in one hand and a bottle of what looked like home-made vodka in the other.

'I told you he was a good cook, didn't I?' said Dodge.

Twist looked up and saw that Dodge was dabbing goulash from the corners of his mouth with the linen napkin he had tucked under his chin. It didn't surprise Twist that he had finished first. He was a little bit faster than the others.

'The French drink wine, the English drink tea and we Romanians drink a lot,' began Fagin, standing up and working his way around the table, dispensing the spirit from his bottle into each of the diners' green teacups.

Twist grew nervous, not wanting to appear ungrateful after the food and the hospitality but nervous about drinking the liquid, recalling the strange effect Fagin's tea had had on him.

'I don't drink,' he said, placing the palm of his hand over his teacup when his turn came, feeling all faces at the table turn to look at him as if he had gone out of his mind.

'Of course, there are times when we must stay sober,' Fagin countered, 'just as there are times when we must stay drunk, and there are other times too that we owe a toast for the gifts the Gods have given us and to welcome a new comrade into our humble assembly.'

Twist could feel Fagin hovering behind his right shoulder, his nose just visible along with his teacup which he raised to meet the others' cups in turn.

Twist drew back his palm and watched the clear liquid flow into his cup.

'In Moscow they drink vodka, in Bucharest we drink *tuică*,' Fagin declared as Twist raised the cup to his lips and drank what tasted like rotten plums burning in a pot of flaming turpentine.

'*Noroc!*' Fagin roared when his turn came, the toast circling the table burning each throat in turn.

'Come, come!' Fagin shouted, slamming his teacup down on the table top. 'This is no party. Now we must dance.'

Twist could not recall most of what followed. The shot had hit so hard and fast that it was hard to tell when the music had begun. Like the *tuică* it was like nothing he had experienced before. A wailing, enchanting gypsy song driven forwards by a deep, driving house rhythm that had everyone on their feet, throwing impossible shapes, backflips and somersaults all somehow in step with the Lord of Misrule, Fagin himself, who strangled an old violin while dancing intricate jigs on the tips of his toes.

Flashes came back to him now as he sat up in bed. Images of the girl, the one they called Red, who danced them all to submission as she gyrated and spun, challenging the boys to keep pace, making fools of them, her elegant moves in stark contrast to their ape-like manoeuvres.

Twist's head hurt as he peered over the top of the duvet at the other boys sleeping in the room off the ballroom where they had danced the night before. As he pushed himself up in bed he felt something hard dig into his ribs. Reaching down he found an art book beside him with the corner of one page turned inwards.

It came back to him now. Not in snatches but in a complete sequence. How Fagin, taking a break from the violin, had caught him watching Red and beckoned him into the quiet of his office where they had sat, side by side with their backs to the wall.

'When I was your age, I wanted to be an artist, just like you,' Fagin had begun, 'but more than that, I wanted to eat. You like the goulash. You want another helping?'

'I already had four.'

'A big full stomach, I hope you're not planning on doing any climbing tonight?'

'Can I crash here?'

'Of course you can. We're like a family for people who never had one.'

'Is Red …'

'You mean Nancy? Yes, she is a particularly talented member of the family.'

'Nancy?'

'Yes, it's a beautiful name. But such a proud girl. She needs someone to train with, someone who is her equal. Now the boys ... they're good at what they do but they lack ... imagination.'

'I suppose I could stick around a bit. If she agreed to train me ...'

'I think she will agree but first you must offer her something.'

'Like I'm loaded.'

'I don't mean money. She needs an education, Twist ... I can't keep calling you that. It sounds like I'm in a casino. You must have a Christian name. If I say I am Cornelius ... who are you?'

'Oliver.'

'I saw you checking out my little art collection earlier. You've got an eye for painting, Oliver. You can teach her about art.'

'Oh yeah?'

'I see you like Bacon.'

'Bacon?'

'Francis. Dodge showed me your *chef d'oeuvre* on the back wall of the gallery ... Bacon's Pope.'

Twist recalled now his embarrassment, not even knowing the name of the famous painting he had shamelessly photographed and sprayed up onto the rear wall of the Tate Britain until Fagin had opened the book on his lap and leafed through it, finding the original and offering it to him, beginning with a quote and continuing without a hint of condescension in his voice.

In the midway of this our mortal life,
I found me in a dismal wood, astray.

'When the poet Dante found himself stalked by a wolf after becoming lost in a dark wood at the foot of a great mountain, he was beckoned into a cave by the spirit of the Roman poet Virgil and led across the river Styx down into a place where the sun never shone ...'

'Into hell?' Twist asked, watching as Fagin made horns of his index fingers.

'... Which has nine layers which they descended, seeing many horrible sights until they reached the sixth level where they found him ...'

Twist recalled Fagin's paint-stained finger pointing at the picture of the Pope that he had copied from the photograph he had taken inside the gallery.

'... Your Pontiff. Pope Nicholas III who was guilty of simony, which is the sale of a place in heaven to those foolish enough to believe the stairway can be bought and who was therefore punished by being suspended head downwards in a well of fire.'

Twist looked again at the picture in the book. He wished now he hadn't told Fagin that he never read the captions in the gallery and mostly only went there to get out of the cold and the rain. And how Fagin's face had changed then, as if he'd opened a door to a place in his past which he preferred to keep locked.

'I didn't always live like this, Oliver,' he'd begun, slowly at first, his eyes looking down at the space between his knees. 'I grew up in Romania. You heard about the orphanages they got there? *Sheesh* ...'

Twist had watched as the shadow of the past had fallen on Fagin as he'd begun his tale, which like Dante's own had started in a dark wood running from the secret police as his parents, uncles and their families had been bundled onto cattle trucks and driven from their ancestral village in the Fagaras mountains on the eve of his fifteenth birthday.

Only moving at night when the moon was hidden behind the clouds, Fagin refusing to look back, never knowing what had happened to them and cursing the fatalism that had left them rooted to the spot, refusing to believe the dark rumours, until it was too late and the writing was on the wall.

Twist had remained riveted. It was a story of escape, a coming-of-age story brimfull with adventures, travelling through ravines teeming with bears on the furthest reaches of the Carpathian Alps, learning to be self-sufficient, studying the stealth and guile of the snow fox, avoiding the towns where every fourth citizen was Securitate, a Janus-faced spy for the dreaded secret police.

And how, wintering in the mountains, sleeping in snow holes and mountain huts with other refugees, he'd pieced together the truth about his family and heard the first stories of the orphanages where, if they caught him, he would be taken, his head shaved and a number burnt into his scalp.

And so Twist had listened, rapt, Fagin pausing only to dab a tear from his eye and pour *tuică* into his teacup as he recounted his last night with his grandparents who both refused to leave their home, even after their daughter, his mother, and his father had been taken.

And his attention to detail, even after thirty years, had surprised Twist and brought the story to life so that he felt as if he'd been back there with him, feeling the frost crunch beneath his feet on the path of his grandparents' home as he'd tried to tiptoe out without waking them, only to feel the pressure of his Grandfather Bodbeg's hand on his shoulder when he'd stepped into the silence of the trees and turned to take one last look at his family's home.

And to his surprise, Twist found Fagin could still recall old Bodbeg's parting words as he'd pressed an old service revolver and a bottle of *tuică* into the young man's hands.

As you go forth in life, there will be a great chasm — jump, it won't be as far as it looks.

21

'Oi! How about showing us what you can do? There's a wall on the roof. Here ...'

The challenge had come at breakfast. Now it was half past eleven and he was still staring at the wall, a duffel bag full of cans at his feet and a voice in his ear telling him he was a fake. The only thing he had managed to get up was a smiley face in gold and it sat there now, a footnote to his lack of talent.

Not much then after all the big talk with Cornelius 'FBoss' Fagin. Talk that had gone on into the early hours, sitting with their backs to the wall sipping *tuică* as FBoss held forth on beauty, art and the corruption of the art world which meant that the few *special* people with the *aesthetic* faculties to genuinely appreciate it had deliberately been shut out by the *MAN*.

At times Twist had watched him spring up animated from the floor as if the *tuică* had rolled back the years, forgetting that he was no longer a fifteen-year-old acrobat travelling incognito with a Chinese circus in Yugoslavia.

'People like you and me, Oliver, we're special,' he'd kept repeating as he'd navigated his mess of catalogues, pictures and antiques to illustrate whatever point he was making, all the time returning to what he described as 'the gift' and the unique qualities of those who possessed it; on the one hand sensitive to the beauty of the world and on the other tough enough not only to survive but to take what they deserved from it.

With the *tuică* burning his throat and with tears of laughter in his eyes, Twist had listened to FBoss's stories. How he escaped the Eastern Bloc disguised as a performing bear in a travelling circus, and all the hard moral choices that had imposed on him, not just as a showman but as an artist.

Of the hunger that had stalked him like a wolf in those days, a hunger which was not a crime and which had only abated after a chance encounter with a Roma called Armond Griot, who he referred to only as 'The Master', and who could whisper to horses and women and who not only possessed 'the gift' but had the ability to see it in others.

Who had spotted Fagin, then aged sixteen, as he'd walked a tightrope stretched between the church steeple and the clock tower of a town hall in a village just north of Seville, and invited him to his birthday celebration in a lemon grove where Fagin had sworn to join Griot and his band of criminal deviants for a year after an eleven-hour drinking bout that had left one man blind.

Looking bleary-eyed at the wall now, Twist found it hard to believe in any kind of 'gift' at all. He wasn't special and in the cold light of day he wasn't convinced by Fagin's stories of 'The Master', and his inheritance of his talent for spotting 'the gift' in others.

Stealing back beauty, reclaiming the works of genius from the private collections of the global elite, and Fagin's Robin Hood of the art world shtick had been all very plausible at four in the morning but now with his head throbbing and a dose of the runs it all seemed a long way from Newham.

'Bit of a hippy, are you?'

Her voice startled him. It was the girl again, sat directly above him on the top of the wall.

'And I thought you were going to do me some pretty little bunny rabbits?' she went on, goading him.

Twist could tell she was being sarcastic but he raised the black can anyway. It was a relief finally having someone to tell him what to do. He crouched and in four coordinated movements a jumping rabbit appeared on the wall.

'Maybe a cute little kitten?'

Twist flashed the can again and a leopard appeared, stalking the rabbit. He heard her laugh.

'And a helicopter gunship blowing them both to kingdom come ...'

Twist turned and saw that Dodge had snuck up behind them. He watched as the smile fell from Red's lips as he approached and he turned, busying himself with the rotor blades of an Apache attack helicopter.

'Come on, Twist,' Red said, 'we've got work to do.'

She led him round to the far side of the roof past the giant tin ventilation ducts that looked like the chimneys of an old cruise ship. With no surrounding buildings the roof was invisible to anyone at ground level, which was just as well considering what they did up there.

Pieces of scaffolding had been bolted together to make a series of bars, about four feet apart, ascending to some ten feet off the ground. Traffic bollards filled with cement were laid out in an S shape and to one side there was a makeshift gym, dumb-bells made of paint cans filled with cement and scary-looking ratchets and pulleys strewn at the foot of a bouldering wall with a plywood overhang.

The least scary thing was a two-foot-high wall and Twist had to laugh when Red motioned for him to get up onto it. But Red wasn't laughing and Twist sensed a sudden shift in the mood, the drunken revelry of the night before replaced with a professionalism and a focus that boded badly for the day ahead.

'Head tucked, roll from the shoulder,' she said.

Twist looked down at Red.

'I feel stupid,' he complained.

'You look stupid,' Dodge replied, grinning gargoyle-like from the top of a ventilator duct, breaking into laughter when Red punched Twist hard in the chest, sending him crashing off the wall to the ground.

'You can't land right from two feet, you can't land from twenty,' she said, watching him pull himself up off the concrete. 'If you're not going to take this seriously, I've got better things to do,' she added. Twist followed her with his eyes as she walked away, dropping into a roll as she passed, then Dodge showed them all how it was done.

'As much as I'd love to stay and watch you fuck up, me and Batesy got real shit to do. Recon duty. You just watch your step now, Twist,' Dodge said, leaping down off the duct and landing on his feet like an alley cat.

So Twist got back up onto the two-foot wall and launched himself head first at the floor, dropping his shoulder and rolling into a neat tuck turn.

'I'll do whatever you want me to...' he said, looking at Red and meaning every word of it.

*

The two-foot jump and roll rose to four, six, eight and finally ten feet, bruising Twist's shoulder blades and right hip. Next came the poles that were four feet apart, just too far to step from one to the next, forcing him to jump but maintain a standing position, effectively running up them one to the next, Twist freaking out that he was going to slip, miss his footing and slam his balls up into his midriff.

And the names were harder to remember than the moves. The tic-tac, cat something and the under bar were the only ones that stuck, which turned out to be a problem because before too long Red was shouting them at him as he ran in circles around her like a dog on a chain.

And watching her move was perfect hell, watching her perform complex moves without thinking as he over-thought them and slipped up and fell at her feet trying to remember if and when he'd actually signed up for this abuse. Being crap was one thing. Being crap in front of a girl you were into who had been somehow coerced into making you less crap was another.

He looked up from the floor as she sprinted along a half-inch plank, dived off the end, cleared twelve feet, grabbed a bar using her momentum to swing her legs under it, let go with her hands, hooked her legs over a second, higher bar, spun round it backwards then launched herself up to catch the corners of a wall some fifteen feet up.

'Do it again. Again. Idiot. Once more. Again ...'

The abuse was relentless until he couldn't meet her eye and the pain made it difficult to respond in words of more than one syllable, lying winded on his back hoping maybe she'd surprise him and tell him ...

'No, you've got it wrong again, but I do really like retarded mute guys who can't backflip.'

22

Fagin had woken flat on his back a full forty seconds before his alarm had gone off at a quarter to six. After gargling and swallowing what was left of the *tuică* in the teacup on his bedside table, he'd stepped into his lambswool slippers, pulled on his purple dressing gown and shuffled, more dead than alive, into the storeroom where a bank of computer monitors sat blinking and whirring in the darkness.

It was a cruel twist of fate that his surveillance suite had chosen to malfunction at the exact moment that opportunity had once again come knocking. This time it was via Sikes, who swore he'd heard it from the horse's mouth, the body-guard of a Russian crime kingpin who collected art and was after a set of six original Hogarths, valued at sixty mil and thought to have been destroyed in a fire two hundred and fifty years ago, which had just resurfaced and fallen into the hands of a notoriously crooked Mayfair dealer who was at this very moment preparing them for auction.

He shuddered to think how much he'd spent on this CCTV monitoring equipment and how ill-favourably it had performed versus the uSpy, an iPhone app which at just sixty-nine pence had, for a short, glorious two-week period, given Batesy unfettered access to over fifty per cent of Mayfair's privately owned CCTV cameras.

But what worried him even more than their loss of video surveillance was the lack of any real intelligence on the true identity of the wealthy Russian collector who had commissioned them. It was all very well Sikes claiming this to be a cut and dried, cash in hand contract but Fagin had never embarked upon a job without knowing exactly who he was working for.

He sat down and stared at his reflection in the blank glass of the dead monitor and asked himself what good, apart from the six million dollar fee, could possibly come from agreeing to steal six high-profile pictures for a Russian crime lord.

He had learnt some information about Arkady Rodchenko from his friend Grigoi but not enough and it bothered him, not least because a man willing to attempt a stunt like this was more likely to whack them as pay them when it came to delivering the goods.

And Sikes wasn't helping. Fagin's questions about the Russians were met with stony silence. Ten minutes with Rodchenko and Fagin was sure he'd be able to get a read on the situation. Sniffing out money and sensing danger were his special skills and employing them now could mean the difference between walking away with a suitcase full of cash or resurfacing with the Thames tide, without teeth or fingertips.

So Fagin couldn't work Sikes's attitude out at all but he did know one thing. The tough kid he'd picked up ten years ago, whose debts he'd cleared and who he'd fed, housed and schooled in all the subtle tricks of his trade, had changed. He had fallen after being chased from the roof of a jewellery store in Bow. He'd slipped and plummeted two floors to the street, turning himself in the air like a diver off the high board so that he'd landed feet first, the impact shattering his leg and forcing shards of splintered bone up and into his knee.

It had crippled him and left him bitter and resentful. And whereas Fagin had hoped he would change for the better and coach the younger boys instead, he'd fallen back on his brute strength to intimidate and coerce them. And that, as far as Fagin was concerned, was fine for as long as he played ball. But when he started drawing down scores on his own and disappearing for days on end with his new 'associates', he would have to see that sooner or later he was going to take another tumble.

So with a bogeyman for a client and a recalcitrant psychopath on his payroll, Fagin felt his only option was to advance with the reconnaissance and plan the job. He would use the announcement of the discovery of the paintings and the imminent date of their public auction to light a fire under the agent, secure the ID of the client and, if he was lucky, secure an advance that would cover the costs of his disappearance if the client turned out to be the devil himself.

And although intelligence-gathering could become prurient and an unhealthy obsession, in this instance it was invaluable because without it you were working in the dark and as his mentor Armond Griot had consistently pointed out:

If it feels wrong, it IS wrong.

And it was never too late to walk away. If you didn't trust your instinct, sooner or later you were going to walk into a police sting or surface, beaten and bloated, by the Isle of Dogs where the bodies of fools who should have looked before they leapt get washed up.

He clicked the mouse and shuffled through the grainy images that Batesy had been able to mine via uSpy during the two-week window before the firewall had picked up unwelcome attention from a security firm in the area and they'd been forced to shut it down. From this footage alone a dynamic profile had already begun to materialise. Not perfect yet but enough to have established Losberne's eating habits, lunch partners, sexual proclivities and the timing and variations of his daily walk to and from work.

And with this information to hand, Fagin could begin to plan, using a strategic planning tool he'd been gifted by an old business associate, a retired British Army colonel whose 'souvenirs' Fagin had helped place when his tour in Iraq had ended in 2003. Drug-crazed Liberian rebels annihilated, Taliban defeated on home turf and a small island off the coast of Argentina reclaimed, the tool had impressed Fagin with its simplicity.

'First you get clear on what it is you want,' the colonel had told him, 'then you write down three supporting effects that have to be in place to bring the job off and then you get creative and list all the things you can do to make sure all three of those effects stack up in the right place at the right time.'

Fagin had planned jobs successfully on his own before and he had never been much of a fan of the military but the colonel was living proof that the tool he called 'The Estimate' worked if you fed it high-quality data and were prepared to walk away if you didn't have the resources needed to stack up the three supporting effects.

Fagin stepped into his planning room and looked at their objective; steal a set of six paintings. First a set of three that had been missing since the year dot, then the remaining set of three from a public auction. He scratched his beard and ran his finger down a line of Post-it notes on the wall, each of which had a title.

1. Create a diversion.

2. Take possession of the paintings without detection.

3. Get paid on delivery without getting whacked.

He drained the dregs of his coffee and rubbed his red eyes. Sleep, his fickle mistress, had deserted him a couple of weeks ago after Sikes had brought him the new gig and as he shuffled up to the wall with a fresh idea on a Post-it note, he wondered if she would ever come back. Probably, he thought, when he had his share of $60 million tucked safely away under his mattress.

He walked back into the monitor room and clicked the mouse to the right then double-clicked on the letter H, bringing up a folder with ten icons inside it. He hit R and clicked the camera on the roof into full screen mode so that he could see how the new boy called Twist was getting on.

According to Red he'd passed the first test with flying colours. He was fast, smart and keen to impress. Her one reservation was his attitude.

'He's a funny one,' Red had said. 'He's done time in Beltham but he's a sensitive soul. You see an old lady crossing the road, he's going to carry her and her dog over to the other side. I'm not sure he's stolen a two-penny sweet let alone sixty-million-dollar works of art.'

So the boy had a moral compass. Surprising, after a spell in Beltham, which was considered by many old pros as a kind of criminal finishing school. But principles, like drinks, could be fixed and the more Red told Fagin the more he knew which buttons to push. Twist wasn't interested in money but he was interested in going to art school and, from what Fagin could see of the boy now, watching wide-eyed as his instructress pop-vaulted the double bars on the roof, he was interested in Red too.

'He looks like he's been run over.'

Sikes's voice took Fagin by surprise but he knew he must not show it.

'He's done well,' he replied, clicking the monitor off with the remote control in his hand as he heard Sikes's footsteps drawing closer.

'Can we trust him?' Sikes asked.

'There is only one way to find out,' he said.

There was a knock on the door.

'Come in,' Fagin shouted, starting up from the monitor to greet Twist with his lopsided grin and firm handshake.

'Now, Twist,' he began, his face earnest as Bill sidled out of the room, 'I know you have your concerns about the work we do so I just wanted to set the record straight.'

23

Twist could see Fagin's reflection in the dead monitor. Their conversation had begun ten hours ago, here in the monitor room, with a brief lecture of the vital work his gang did as 'repossession men' for large insurance companies.

Twist had heard of specialists who 'repossessed' cars whose lease plan buyers had failed to keep up their payments, and Fagin had used this analogy to explain the service he provided for the insurance companies who contracted them.

If art was listed as stolen on the Art Loss Register, insurance companies paid out vast sums to the victims, which effectively meant that were the art to be recovered, it would now belong to the insurance company and not to the previous owner.

As a result they spent equally large sums of money trying to recover the art and recoup their losses. To do this they employed private detectives, often former Interpol or Scotland Yard art squad specialists, to track down the art.

Due to the involvement of organised crime in many art thefts, most private detectives were unwilling to take on the risks of breaking and entering criminal strongholds to 'repossess' the art. Which was why the major insurance companies contacted Fagin and his outfit to do the dirty work for them.

Dirty because, as was the case in the 'Losberne Repossession', missing art that may have been stolen by career criminals often resurfaces in the hands of crooked dealers who in turn sell to high net worth individuals who prefer not to probe too deeply into the provenance of the work hanging on their walls.

And this, Fagin had concluded, brandishing his contracts from the insurance firms all underwritten by Lloyds of London, was where the confusion about his work always began.

For far from being like the thieves who had stolen the work in the first place, they were in fact far more like bail-iffs, unpopular, no doubt, but in fact performing a valuable service, not just to their employer but to the art world at large by recovering great art works that would otherwise be lost to the British public.

And so, Fagin had finally come around to asking the question that Twist had guessed he'd been building up to all along.

'So now you know what we do,' he'd begun, slowly, looking straight at Twist, 'do you think that this is the kind of work that you could be interested in trying out for?'

And so Twist had agreed to a 'trial run' which was how he'd come to be standing here the next day, watching Fagin playing the puppeteer, each click of the mouse propelling 'the mark', portly Dr Crispin Losberne, dealer in fine art, on his morning walk from his town house in a private mews off Belgrave Square to his gallery on Savile Row, Mayfair.

*

Twist scanned the monitor room, crossed it and sat in an empty chair directly in front of where Fagin was standing scratching his crotch impatiently, like a derelict university professor waiting for latecomers to arrive.

A boy who had been introduced as Cribb was fiddling with a remote control by what looked to be a digital receiver unit, while across the room Red examined her nails as Fagin's briefing began, both Dodge and Batesy notable by their absence.

'You cannot con an honest man,' he said, framing the moral of the story then pointing a toy golf club at Cribb, who hit play on the remote, before turning to point at the monitor which now whirred into life behind him.

'Six foot three inches tall and just one point seven miles in forty-five minutes,' Fagin said.

'He's moving slowly,' Twist commented, stating the obvious.

'Or stopping off en route,' Fagin replied. 'Cribb, if you wouldn't mind?'

Twist had not had much to do with Cribb so far but Red had filled in his backstory and Twist had been surprised to hear it closely resembled his own. A car thief with over forty-two violations for joy riding against his name, Cribb had done a bunk following an apprenticeship scheme with a mechanic in Swindon who'd specialised in German cars. Making his way up to London he'd fallen back on his skills and fallen in with a breaker in Tottenham who pulled them apart and made a killing in spare parts sales.

Which is how Dodge had first stumbled across Cribb, tripping over his beanpole legs that had been sticking out from beneath a Mercedes S Class off Bow High Street. Picking himself up, Dodge had helpfully informed the body under the car that if he didn't want trouble he should stop what he was doing and make tracks, as CID were hard on his heels. Cool as a cucumber Cribb had crawled out from under the bonnet, walked round to the back of the car and jacked open the boot, ushering Dodge inside where he'd lain, hidden, until the Feds had disappeared leaving only a trail of expletives in their wake.

Fagin nodded to Cribb, who clicked the remote again to reveal a photograph of a much younger, fitter Losberne sitting in a rowing boat on the River Thames.

'History of Art at Ruskin, Oxford, followed by Fine Art at St Martin's, where he slummed it in his aunt's empty flat off the King's Road before getting kicked out for cheating in his finals and moving to a farmhouse just outside Puglia where he lived until Black Monday bankrupted his old man in 1987.'

'Black Monday?' Twist asked, wondering why it was necessary to go into Losberne's complete life history in such detail.

'Programme trading,' Fagin explained, 'overvaluation, illiquidity and the madness of crowds were all cited as causes of the perfect financial storm that meant that young Crispin, perfectly useless aged thirty, had to go out and do the unthinkable … and *work* for a living.'

Fagin stood up at this point and turned to face his audience, forcing Twist, Red and the boy called Cribb to back up and give him more room to perform.

'So, rather than go without, Losberne set himself up as a "knocker". His timing was immaculate. When one in eight of Wiltshire's population was middle to upper middle class, elderly and living alone, he used his family name and working knowledge of fine art to get inside their homes and identify targets for an organiser who ran several burglars and supplied several local dealers.'

Twist watched as Fagin clicked on the mouse and a dog-eared photograph of a man in a Navy pea coat appeared alongside Losberne in the car park of a pub called The Assizes.

'Just popping in to see how you were doing, Mrs Peabody. I must say that's a delightful Regency grandfather clock ...'

Twist could see that Fagin had left no stone unturned as he went on, cycling down the crooked path that Losberne's life had followed.

'Losberne began to dabble as a dealer in the early nineties, circumnavigating the local auctions which were now too high risk. There was no single stolen art register at that time and Losberne kept himself off the Yard's radar ... Cribb!'

Twist watched as Fagin cuffed Cribb round the ear with a backhanded swipe, and a series of images flashed up on the screens as he raced to catch up.

'But his big coup came in 1994 when a tip-off from a fence who declared himself to be "out of my depth" led him to the semi-detached, pebble-dashed council house in Slough of the thief who worked into the fence. Who led him up to the attic where he found an original Braque, believed to have been taken by Franco himself after dynamiting the Mayor of Guernica's vault twenty minutes after the Luftwaffe flattened the Spanish town's municipal HQ in 1937.'

'Fortuitously his find coincided with a MOMA, New York exhibition entitled "Stealing Beauty" and he wasted no time in worming his way to become the go-to guy for the private seller keen to authenticate and quietly sell on any high-profile work of dubious provenance. He became the Swiss banker of the art world. Drug dealers who had taken art as collateral on a debt, unscrupulous property developers seeking cut-price kudos, oligarchs, dictators and anyone filthy and rich enough to want a masterpiece, all found his double-blind, triple-encrypted online auctions the perfect way to sell and secure priceless works by artists that even their vulgar friends would recognise.'

Twist stared at the screens open-mouthed as art and sketches by major artists flashed before his eyes. Van Goghs, Rembrandts, Picassos, Constables, Bacons and Goyas all appeared on the monitors in front of them. Fagin did not bat an eyelid.

'A paper millionaire by thirty-five, Losberne bought his Mayfair gallery aged forty and his Tribeca space a year later. Based in London in the summer he spends his winters in LA in his Malibu beach shack sourcing missing work for the Gettys.'

'All very interesting, Fagin.'

Twist turned and saw a man stood in the doorway, smiling. He was in his late twenties and built like a boxer and he had a livid red scar running from his scalp to his right cheek.

'Good of you to join us, Bill,' Fagin replied, smiling as he took the remote from Cribb and switched the input to a hard drive containing CCTV camera footage.

'Each morning for the past two weeks the good doctor, as he has titled himself, has been blissfully unaware of his shadow, an *Evening Standard* vendor in a purple fleece and a baseball cap with "D" embroidered on the front.'

Twist focused on the middle screen as a figure matching the description Fagin had just given walked into shot keeping pace behind Losberne.

'Now you see him ...' Fagin said, pointing at the man in the purple fleece who stopped in the middle of the screen, turned his head up to the camera and waved. 'Now you don't.'

Twist heard Red laugh on the far side of the room as Dodge disappeared from the centre of the screen and the clock jumped back ten seconds to a fresh sequence in which Losberne crossed the same street at the same time the next day without being tailed.

'Now, Twist, if you were wondering why I keep Batesy on ...' Fagin said, 'watch this.'

Twist stared as the monitor switched out of CCTV view and into first-person camera mode. The lens was fixed at eye height and gave a clear view of Losberne's back as he ambled relaxed through Mayfair, stopping to buy his coffee in a Carluccio's on the corner, smiling at the dark-haired girl behind the counter, waving away the change she offered him on a small silver tray.

Twist studied him as he walked on. Sipping from his coffee as the camera zoomed in on a sign held up by a homeless man who was shivering beneath a tartan blanket under a fire escape at the corner of Burlington Gardens.

Twist heard Red laugh as she read the sign in the tramp's hand and was the first to clock Batesy winking up at the camera.

Family kidnapped by ninjas. Need 2 quid for karate lessons.

Fagin clicked twice with the mouse and the camera angle changed to a CCTV camera overlooking a covered arcade. There was a shop selling vintage prints of old sailing boats that Losberne glanced at as he walked, face forwards into shot.

'The arcade, you klutz ... get out of the arcade!' Fagin barked, clicking back onto Dodge-cam as he sped up, jogging to cross New Bond Street before the lights turned green, catching Losberne just as he turned into Savile Row and his gallery, one street down on the corner.

'Keep tight,' Fagin spat into the microphone on his desk and nodded as Dodge raised the thumb of his right hand as he upped the pace to something approaching a slow jog, as white columns appeared ten deep each side of the gallery door's thick glass, through which blue lights danced on and off inside, offering brief glimpses of the art Losberne had chosen to display.

'All front,' Fagin said. 'The real gems never see the light of day ... like the three painted ladies our source tells us he's keeping in his storeroom ... hello ... what's this ...?'

They watched as Dodge's hand appeared at the right of the screen, pulling a hood down over his head, partially obscuring their peripheral vision until he pulled what had to be spectacles from his face to hold them at waist height, picking up a natural blonde in her early twenties who stared blankly at Losberne as he fumbled with the front door's several keys.

Then Dodge was moving again, fast towards the corner, pitching forwards, appearing to fall flat on his face but still managing to keep the specs in his hand as he went down. He caught the look of concern on the girl's face as she knelt down to help him to his feet and then came in and out of shot as the camera jerked towards her, forcing her to retreat, his hand visible on her left shoulder then panning perfectly over Losberne's left shoulder to zoom in on his fat fingers as they punched the code to the gallery's front door on a small metal keyboard.

Twist stared at the screen in disbelief as Losberne turned angrily on Dodge who continued to film what looked like a portcullis rising up from the ground and Losberne turning his back on Dodge to push the gallery door open and disappear inside.

Twist looked across at Red and Cribb and the man who still hadn't introduced himself, then back at Fagin who was smiling, stroking his beard as his right hand worked the mouse, rewinding the footage then hitting pause, all eyes on the screen as he clicked play then pause, revealing one frame at a time.

'1 ... 6 ... 9 ... 1 ...'

'Bingo!' Fagin said, turning his gaze on the hard man in the doorway as if to say:

I told you, I told you they could do it.

24

'Sorry, Mr Fagin,' Twist began, cutting in mid-sentence as Fagin continued to vent his spleen against Losberne, 'but I've really got to go.'

'I'll be right back,' he added, stepping into the corridor in time to catch Red, who had slipped out almost unnoticed, as she turned to open the door to her bedroom. Hers was two doors down from the room that he'd been sharing with Cribb since he'd agreed to his work trial.

'What are you up to later?' he asked, leaving the question hanging as she reached into the pockets of her track top, her hand movements quick and deliberate, as if she was in a hurry to find her key, unlock her door and disappear inside.

Twist waited, watching her face as the door to the surveillance room opened and closed and she turned, forcing a smile, her eyes looking right through him at whoever now stood in the corridor behind him.

'You out tonight?' he asked again.

'You'd better watch it,' she replied.

'Watch what?'

She stared at him, raising her eyebrows, trying to tell him something without actually having to spell it out. And then it clicked. He got the message. *He's behind you!*

And when he turned he saw that the man Fagin had addressed as Bill was standing directly behind him, smiling at him, not friendly but mocking him in some way. Twist saw the scar again in the spotlight and thought twice about asking him what he was looking at.

'Twist's been eating too many hot dogs,' Red said.

Twist lowered his head and looked at the floor. Red's comment made no sense. It was a cover for her earlier warning but, more than that, it was a get-out. A way for him to stand down, accept his place in the pecking order and avoid a confrontation with the alpha dog who had appeared silently behind him.

He watched as she pushed the door open and stepped into her room then felt the draught on his face as the man called Bill walked past him, leading with his right leg because his left leg was set rigid in a brace, until he was standing facing Red who was holding the door open for him.

And when the man turned and looked back at him, Twist felt the scorn in his look as he reached down to tap the metallic frame on his left leg.

'You know how I got this?' he said.

Twist looked down at the leg then back up at his face.

'I slipped up,' Bill said, 'watch you don't do the same.'

25

Pulling the bike across the road, Twist watched Losberne use the crossing just as he'd seen the portly dealer do on Dodge's spectacles cam the day before. Listening through the crackle of static in his headset for Fagin's voice, he ducked beneath a plyboard tunnel built to shelter passers-by from the builders working on the scaffolding above, out of the glare of the morning sun which had just topped the grey slate tiles of Mayfair's rooftops.

He was under no illusions about where he was at or what he was doing. He was a young offender who had broken parole and fallen in with a gang of professional art thieves who'd sent him pedalling out into an arctic headwind to track Losberne disguised as a lycra-clad cycle courier, as the mark stepped out from Carluccio's sipping a steaming hot latte, trussed up against the biting wind in a full-length navy blue cashmere overcoat.

Hastily pulling the tracksuit from his rucksack he picked up Losberne and his latte as he strolled on his way to his gallery.

'Hot coffee,' Twist spoke into the mouthpiece.

'Roger that,' Red replied, stepping out from the café in a pair of DM's, adjusting the horn-rimmed spectacles on her face and zipping up the biker jacket against the biting wind.

Twist watched as she half ran, half walked, drawing level with him on the pavement on the far side of the road. 'Sexually liberated St Martins' had been Fagin's advice to Red when she'd been picking her outfit.

Twist followed her to the corner then watched her turn and scan the street ahead. Jet-black eyeliner and thick-rimmed spectacles framed her emerald-green eyes which stared diagonally across the adjacent street corner. Dodge was there in a blue puffar jacket, jeans and a pair of Nike basketball boots. He beckoned them with a flick of two fingers against his thigh and, as they drew level, Twist saw Batesy crouched beside him, his hands hidden, rifling inside an old attaché case.

'Right pocket,' Twist said to Dodge as he passed him without looking back, knowing that Red and Dodge would already be on the move, walking then running when they were out of sight so that they could get into the covered arcade, the CCTV black spot, before Losberne.

It surprised Twist how all three of them appeared to be improvising, taking liberties with Fagin's script which they had rehearsed into the early hours of the morning, and he wondered if this was how they always did things and if it was only because he was new to the game that he was sticking doggedly to the role he'd been asked to play.

But Fagin had been very clear. Twist wasn't the leading man. He was there to learn, to tag along and sure, play his part when the time came, but most of all to watch the others, not act too soon, and on no account try and be a hero if something went awry.

So Twist pulled up the hood of his track top and cycled fast around the corner to the far end of the arcade where he clocked Dodge, standing, staring into a estate agent's window, both hands cupped over his eyes as Red whispered something into his ear as Losberne passed behind them.

And although he'd been specifically instructed not to gawp, Twist could do nothing else, as Dodge stepped back, exclaiming wildly, and hit Losberne's right hand, sending a geyser of hot coffee shooting up into the air above him to land bang on target down the front of his thousand-pound cashmere coat.

'For God's sake!' Losberne shrieked, stepping back, hand on chest like he'd just been shot, his voice audible on the far side of the road. This was the cue for Twist, who started out towards them as Red began dabbing at his coat with a clean handkerchief, Losberne's rage fading to a whimper of protest as Red looked up at him and smiled.

Twist watched wide-eyed in admiration as Dodge moved in close, aiming at Losberne's right pocket with a few targeted jabs, giving a quick nod as Losberne pushed past him and Red; the good doctor was hot, bothered and completely oblivious to Dodge's fingers in his pocket as the young thief stepped out into the flood of commuters filing through the arcade and hit Twist square in the chest with Losberne's iPhone.

Twist looked back just once as Red's performance began again and then he was free of the crowd and running for the plywood tunnel he'd come from, and Batesy, who was waiting on the first-floor scaffolding still rifling inside the leather attaché case.

*

Jack! Get a bottle of water. Just do it!' Red barked at Dodge.

'No, really,' Losberne stammered, showing every sign that he was beginning to enjoy the young nubile patting at his chest with her frilly handkerchief insisting that it was 'the least she could do.'

Oblivious to the fact that behind the green eyes she was counting every second, calculating how long it would take Twist to reach Batesy and his new scanner that he claimed could hack a password and clone iOS 7 in under sixty seconds.

'We were just on the way to the Royal Academy. To see the Gainsborough exhibition,' she rambled on, breathless, dizzy but watching a flicker of something like interest appear in Losberne's eyes.

'Oh have you been?' she asked, watching the smug satisfaction spread across his face as he leant forwards and said:

'As a matter of fact I curated it …'

Twist was running full tilt but he was still thinking. That he had never had an iPhone or a PlayStation 3, which had made him stand out in Beltham as maybe the only boy who hadn't spent every waking hour of every day sat in front of a console waggling his joystick or scrolling mindlessly through Facebook trying to convince girls that he wasn't a complete loser.

But then he reached the end of the tunnel and the thinking stopped as he pushed up off the base of the wall the way Red showed him, caught the planks of the scaffolding and pulled himself up until he was level with the first floor of the empty building looking along the covered gallery at Batesy.

'You got it?'

Twist nodded and pulled the phone from his pocket and was just about to slide it along the planks when Batesy raised his hand, indicating he should chill and bring it to him in person because they had a ninety-second window to get it back to Losberne. So why hurry?

Twist watched him work, connecting the iPhone to a brick of a laptop, two fingers tapping away, humming something to himself as Twist played Red's script in his head and pictured her telling Losberne that Dodge wasn't her boyfriend.

Then he heard the slap of Batesy's hand hitting a wooden plank and the sound of him swearing.

'Shit! Shit! Shit! It's not working!'

Red had him now. She'd delayed Losberne for over three minutes with her inane chat about street art and watched with satisfaction as his hand searched inside his calfskin wallet for his business card which he handed to her with a smile, the finger and thumb of his right hand making the 'call me' sign then reaching out to hail a black cab as it turned the corner.

'So I should call you?' she asked, feigning surprise that so great a man should be interested in her, as he got into the cab.

'The cab went that way!' Red screeched, pointing Twist to the corner of New Bond Street.

'Rush-hour traffic,' Dodge shouted after him as he took off in pursuit, 'he can't've got very far.'

Pedestrians, cyclists and cars cluttered the street, breaking his pace down to a shuffle with every fifth step a half jump to get the height needed to locate the sixteen black cabs caught in rush-hour traffic. He zigzagged between them, ducking to peer inside and discount the Filipino with the recalcitrant toddler, two boys with a pug, and assorted suits clutching their coffees and handheld devices of their own.

Until he saw the lights beginning to change and he knew he was never going to find Losberne by staring at the backs of people's heads. He had to get in front and clock them as they drove past, so he turned, dived past a courier coming fast down the middle of the road and started sprinting down the middle of the road to the traffic lights.

He made eye contact with the driver of an oncoming lorry which braked, forcing the Vespa behind him to skid, swerve and come slewing up at him, forcing Twist to leapfrog a traffic bollard, then roll across the bonnet of a stationary Saab and hit the pavement on the far side, somehow on his feet. In one fluid movement he continued running again, hoping the cab that was indicating left was Losberne and that he was telling it to pull in – he'd walk as opposed to he'd lost his iPhone and he was going to call the police.

Twist watched as the traffic began to move through the lights and the cab pulled left then accelerated, his heart sinking before seeing it pull in at the kerb and the rear passenger door open and Losberne step out.

And as he slowed, watching as Losberne patted himself down, searching for a phone that wasn't there, Twist heard Fagin's voice in his ears, telling him not to try to be a hero if the shit hit the fan … He shoved the mobile into the elastic waistband of his track pants, reached for the handle on the roadside door of the cab, opened it and jumped inside.

'Get out of my taxi!'

Twist looked up. He could see that Losberne was furious so he pulled a leaf from Red's book and grinned right back at him.

'Sorry, mate. I thought it was free!' he said, bowing out, pulling on his waistband and shaking the iPhone, feeling it slide down the inside of his left leg and watching the expression on Losberne's face change from a scowl to a smile when he pointed down to it through the open door and asked:

'Is that your iPhone, mate?'

26

Twist watched as Dodge made short work of the wiring, cradling the magnum of champagne in his crotch, pushing gently, turning the bottle in a wide arc, weighing up each target in turn as they presented themselves to him.

'I'm telling you … If it wasn't for Twist here …'

The gang had returned to home base half an hour ago to jubilation from Fagin who had cracked open his private stash of *tuică* to protests from Dodge who'd walked out and returned five minutes later with a magnum of chilled champagne and two kilos of smoked salmon in a JJB Sports duffel bag.

The five of them sat facing one another in a large horseshoe on the polished wood floor of the ballroom – Dodge, Batesy, Red, Cribb and Twist – each slumped on a giant beanbag running the champagne between them on a skateboard while Fagin moved amongst them, all smiles, clutching his bottle of poison.

'We'd have been up shit creek without a paddle without him … you should have seen him move, FBoss,' Dodge went on, turning the bottle on Batesy, whose failure had forced Twist to make his mad run.

Fagin made a big play of the effort involved in dragging one of his knackered armchairs over to the group. 'Don't get up! No! Oh so kind of you but no!' he muttered. They all laughed, but nobody lifted a finger to help him.

Twist watched as Fagin slumped down on the armchair, leaning forward and taking a big swig of *tuică* from the bottle before giving out a sigh and sinking back into the collapsed springs of the seat, his eyes narrowing into slits so that it was impossible to tell if he was scheming or falling asleep.

There was whispering and Twist turned to see Dodge reposition the bottle, compensating for gravity, as he gently squeezed the cork which shot fifteen feet across the room and hit Fagin between the eyes.

'*Du te'n pizda ma tii!*' Fagin shrieked, leaping up out of the chair, taking swipes at Dodge with the *tuică* bottle as he rolled backwards using the beanbag to fend off the blows.

Probably just like old times, Twist thought, looking across at Red as her laughter rang out above the shrieks and the screams and he wondered, not for the first time, why there was one beanbag empty and nobody ever talked about the kid whose job he'd taken, the one called Harry.

'Got a good appetite, I see,' Fagin said, sitting back down in the armchair, his shirt wet with *tuică*.

Twist turned away from Red to Fagin, who smiled and held up the empty bottle of *tuică* for Cribb to get up and replace.

'Well done continued boyee,' Fagin said, leaning forward nodding at Twist as the double doors to the ballroom opened and Bill Sikes stepped in to join the party.

'That was the easy bit,' Sikes said.

It was hard to tell how long he had been listening or watching Twist ogling his girlfriend.

'But I've never seen anyone move like that. Not even Harry,' Dodge said, staring at Sikes.

Twist tried not to meet Sikes's eyes as he walked across the room chewing a chicken leg and sat down in the empty beanbag facing Twist.

'Bill's right,' Fagin joined, siding with Sikes but reasserting his authority, 'you did well today, Twist, but today was just the hors d'oeuvre. Batesy, you are a talented boy but you must be focused from here on in. Any peep out of Losberne – I need to hear it. Dodge, you *are* washing up.'

Dodge's protest was ignored by Fagin who turned towards Red.

'And Nancy, my girl, I want you to get Twist ready. He's fast but he knows nothing about B&E.'

'Tonight?' she replied, filling a teacup with champagne.

'It's about time you and me had a night out, Nance ...' Sikes began, but stopped mid-sentence as Fagin pointed the champagne bottle at Twist.

'Tonight,' Fagin continued, pointing the bottle at Red, 'you will take Twist out and show him the ropes. You're always whining about how Dodge gets the plum jobs but this time you're going in and Twist is going to back you up.'

Twist risked a glance at Red but she didn't return it. She was walking towards Sikes, smiling, passing him the champagne bottle then leaning down to whisper something in his ear. Twist watched Sikes. His face was blank, staring at the floor in front of him, but then his eyes snapped up and met Twist's own as Red leaned in and pecked him on the cheek.

'I won't be late,' she said and Twist squirmed as Sikes reached up, grabbed her wrist and pulled her in for a kiss.

Twist pushed himself up out of his beanbag and smiled at Dodge who as usual had missed nothing on his way to the kitchen to wash the dishes. He followed Dodge, stopping at the door to look back as Sikes broke off the kiss and stared straight back at him.

'I'll wait up,' Bill said.

27

It didn't make sense being back at the Tate. It was illogical to return to the scene of one crime just to escape another more recently committed, but his behaviour around Red was beginning to appear increasingly irrational.

'B&E' was pretty much like the stuff they'd been doing on the high wall of the roof, only this time the drainpipes and window ledges had been a means to an end, not an end in themselves.

It hadn't bothered Twist as much as he'd thought it would. Perhaps it was the way that Fagin had framed their mission. Telling Red and him that they were on a training exercise and the palm-sized scanner – used to pick up signals emitted by keyless entry fobs – was just the evidence Twist needed to show that he'd made the grade, a small but vital part in Fagin's bigger plan.

The idea to steal the device had been Cribb's. He'd used them before, during his days as a car thief, and knew that you needed a licence to buy one. If they could get Red inside

Losberne's gallery with it they might also be able to get her into the safe room at the rear of the gallery.

Red had jumped first from a twenty-foot-high brick wall over razor wire to land on the near edge of the warehouse's tin roof. Twist had followed her lead, falling flat on his face to avoid the risk of tumbling and becoming ensnared in the razors below.

Once inside, Red had put on night vision goggles while Twist watched for movement from the security guard's shed through a toilet window. There had been none. Asleep or otherwise engaged it had hardly mattered. They'd given themselves a time limit of ten minutes to find the device but Red's smile had lit up the gloom within five, Twist squinting in the darkness to see the tiny black box attached by a wire to an equally compact keypad. He'd reached out to give her a celebratory hug, feeling her hands and fingers grip his back and then let go, her body twisting to the side to break his embrace.

'You're not in yet,' he'd heard her whisper as she turned, placing her fingertips to her lips to listen for any sound in the warehouse that might indicate they were not alone. And then it had hit Twist like a tiny taser shock.

He had a spiralling sense of panic and then he was stepping past Red at the doorway and beckoning her down the steps to the ground floor of the warehouse from where she'd come, breaking into a run when he'd reached it because they had grossly underestimated Fagin and the test that he had set them.

There had been neither sight nor sound of the security guard because there had been none. And rather than this realization triggering alarm bells, like it should, it had lulled them into a false sense of security. The pair of them standing, celebrating their success in the middle of a high-tech firm specialising in next generation surveillance and security, somehow secure in their belief that they were safe just because they had seen no signs of human life or heard the blare of an alarm.

It had taken them ten minutes to attempt to correct their mistake. Ten minutes to run, walk and backtrack just over a mile in total, as the sound of sirens had grown loud and shrill from the direction of Millbank. Once they'd reached the river they'd taken off their tops and their beanies and dropped them over the edge and Twist had looked back once to see the curling turbulence suck them under before pacing out to catch Red, just another pair of night runners eating up the miles in training for the marathon in April.

And it had been during that run that Twist had realised where they were heading, that without even knowing it, they'd taken an almost direct course to the Tate Britain, to the scene from his past life, before he'd met her, where his Simoniac Pope was still displayed. And it had occurred to him then that she had to see it and that if she didn't she might never be able to *get him* like he so badly wanted to be got.

And so he'd suggested they take the detour. Get off the main drag away from the obvious approach route of the police on their way to the warehouse. And as he'd explored the set of her lips and the slight flare of her nostrils for a micro signal that might reveal that she was thinking what he was thinking, a cop car sped past then slowed momentarily, perhaps for a double take, the blue lights illuminating the buildings along Millbank and the riverside in turn.

And that had been enough to convince her to let him lead
her here. To his picture, on the rear wall of the gallery, of a
tormented pope, sitting in the shadows, sandwiched between
the ivy, away from the sterile glare of the gallery lights inside.

Now, standing beneath his most daring piece of work, Twist
explained how he'd at last been recognised and forced to
escape the gallery and a team of security guards. He watched
the expression on her face as the sweat chilled on his skin.
She stood there looking up at it. Not saying anything for a
moment but then turning to look at him, in disbelief.

The gallery was open late for a special exhibition. At the
entrance Twist recognised the same security guard as before.
He was slumped on a plastic chair just inside the front door
next to a security gate, thumbing through the sports pages
of yesterday's *Mail*.

Twist watched as Red stepped forwards and smiled sweetly
at him, watching as he struggled to sit up out of his slouch,
pushing down on the plastic arm rests then placing his hands
in front of his chest like a dog begging for a bone.

Twist followed Red up into the galleries. She turned and
smiled at him from the first landing of the stairs, daring him
to climb higher, sensing his reluctance to get drawn further
into the maze of art where the guides might recognise him
and be less slow this time in sealing him inside the great
partition doors that closed the end of each gallery.

'Come on,' she said. 'I want you to show me how you
escaped.'

Beginning beneath the bench, he started to re-enact each
scene of the chase, forgetting the danger in her smile and
her laughter as the drama unfolded. At the top of the stairs

he launched himself, Errol Flynn style, onto the banister, sliding down sideways on his belly before springing off and half running half walking, turning to beckon her with quick, half-concealed movements of his hand towards the Ladies. He went back into the same cubicle, getting stuck, once again, head dangling as she pushed him, laughing hysterically until he was clear and dangling from the ivy looking up as she emerged, effortlessly, from the window to join him.

It was insanity. To return here and take this risk but even the ogre who had tried to kick the door down in the cubicle and tear his head off his shoulders was nothing to him now as they climbed down the ivy and stopped at the bottom to look once again at the demonic figure he'd put up on the wall it grew upon.

It had been ring-fenced almost like a crime scene but incredibly it had been left intact.

'Who is the man?' asked Red, staring up at the wall.

'*The Simoniac Pope*,' Twist began. 'Simony was the sin of exploiting one's position in the church to make money and the eighth circle of hell is a chasm containing the popes guilty of this sin. According to the audio guide inside, their punishment is to be thrust upside down into a stone hole with the soles of their feet on fire.'

'That'll teach him, won't it?' Red said.

'You'd have thought so, wouldn't you?' Twist replied, clutching himself against the wind which had whipped up while they'd been inside.

'Come on,' Red said, 'it's cold. Let's go back inside.'

The guard couldn't understand how they'd left without him seeing them but he didn't stop them. The temporary exhibition was a retrospective on a miserable painter called Lowry who Twist had never heard of. He painted miserable people in grim industrial towns moping along in front of steel mills and factories.

'At least working for FBoss is fun,' Red said, staring at the last picture in the exhibition.

It was true, Twist thought. More fun than working in a factory or working sixteen-hour shifts for a necrophiliac undertaker called Sowerberry.

'Fagin will help you get what you want,' Red said, turning to look at him. 'If you tell me I can tell him.'

Twist wondered if Fagin had put her up to this. It seemed strange why he'd set it up for the two of them to hang out together.

'If you need to get overseas he can fix it. Maybe not America but Eastern Europe. Berlin or maybe Prague. He's got connections out that way. A fake ID, passport, anything ...' Red's voice trailed off as she walked out through the exit and into the twentieth-century gallery.

'"Three Studies for Figures at the Base of a Crucifixion",' Red said, reading from the description by the side of a disturbing painting by Francis Bacon.

'Come on,' Twist replied, taking her hand and pulling her gently but finding her anchored to the spot, fixated on the painting.

'What do you know about that picture?' Red asked him as he craned round to see the dwarfish guide who had first found him sleeping beneath the bench, whispering to a man-sized colleague who was sat bolt upright on a stool in the far corner of the gallery.

'Bacon said they were the furies. The vengeful spirits of the Greek myths ... but he threw in all kinds of other stuff.

Like ectoplasm which shows the materialisation of ghosts, and they say he stole something from Picasso.'

Twist ignored Bacon's grotesque white half-goose half-dog monsters and looked back into the far corner but the small guard had vanished. Jogging back up the gallery he checked left and right but there was no sign of him and when he turned there was no sign of Red either.

He turned three sixty and saw that there were two exits facing one another on opposite sides of the gallery. He chose the right one that led into the Romantics and found he had guessed correctly. She was standing in front of the original; William Blake's *Simoniac Pope*.

'We've got to go,' Twist said, turning to see the little guide reappear, reflected in the painting of a giant black dog to the right of the flaming Pope. He had an impish grin on his face and Twist knew the game was up.

Red turned and Twist nodded his head to the right and finally she understood.

'Come on,' he said, turning to his left and beginning to walk casually up the gallery, sensing the guide's eyes tracking him until they passed Millais's *Ophelia*.

'That's Ophelia,' Twist said, breaking into a slow jog. 'She went out with Hamlet, went mental and then drowned herself.'

'Reminds me of this girl I knew in the care home,' Red said, catching Twist up as he opened the fire exit door on the first floor. 'Used to lie in the bath tripping.'

28

Fagin stared at the racks of clothes that stretched round what had once been the hotel's cloakroom and asked himself what a billionaire Russian art aficionado would wear to an informal business meeting.

He ran his hand along the shoulders of the clothes, feeling the cotton, silk and fur brush against the tips of his fingers, releasing the odour trapped inside them and, with the heady mix of dry cleaning detergent, dust and stale body odour came a memory of Ivanka, the trapeze artist turned wardrobe manager who had beckoned him up into the costume trailer during a power cut in Brazov and made a man of him.

A fugitive at fifteen, all skin and bones, struggling on the mound of dirty laundry as she bit him repeatedly on his nose all through the long intermission as the clowns pedalled furiously, juggling burning torches on unicycles to quell the tide of terror that had risen up in the crowd in the big top as the geriatric lion had begun to roar inside his cage.

His hand reached a gap in the rail and touched a suit bag which he pulled out and held up, using it to shield himself from whichever of the boys had sneaked in and was working his way along the far side of the rack hoping to take the fifty pound note he kept in his pocket to keep their skills sharp.

'You know when I was your age ...' he said, snatching through the gap in the railing and catching Dodge by the hair, 'I used to enjoy dressing up.'

Dodge smiled in defeat.

'What are you up to, FBoss?' he asked, as Fagin released him.

'There's one role in this charade that only I can play,' Fagin said, unzipping the bag and pulling out the navy blue woollen suit.

'I mean with Red,' Dodge said. 'Buddying her up with Twist the whole time. You must have seen the look on the boy's face?'

Fagin let the suit bag drop to the floor as he slipped his fingers inside the front of the jacket, tracing the stitching that held the silk lining to the wool of the jacket's exterior and listening to Dodge whose instincts he had learned to trust.

'Oliver's not quite part of the family yet, Dodge. We still need a hold on him. Some boys want respect. Some boys just want a place in the pecking order. What does Oliver want?' he asked, pulling the jacket over his shoulders and checking his look in the full-length gilt mirror opposite him.

'Spray cans?'

'He wants what no one ever gave him, Dodge ...'

Dodge watched Fagin unfasten his belt, kick off his slippers and drop his threadbare corduroys to the floor. He was wearing a pair of off-white long johns and he looked up, aware that Dodge was still standing in front of him, unsatisfied by his answer.

'Is something else troubling you, Dodger?'

'Yes,' Dodge replied, 'as a matter of fact there is.'

On their way back from the gallery they reached a bridge. A plaque showed a picture of a Victorian man with a moustache who Twist recognised as the royal consort, Prince Albert, who'd had sixteen children with Queen Victoria. There was a shiny gold monument in Hyde Park that he knew about and he wondered how many other things, like this bridge, she'd had built to remember him by. It was hard to believe, looking at the picture of the stern-faced grandmother on the plaque next to the husband she'd outlived by over thirty years, that they'd ever had sex at all.

He turned to look at Red and wondered what she would do if he reached out and took hold of her hand. Probably nothing, he thought, turning instead to stare at the life-size replica of a triceratops on the far bank, wondering what it would look like painted neon pink, until Red broke the silence with a question.

'So, er, how did you get into art?' she said, catching his eye as he turned back to face her.

'They never liked the tagging at the homes or the schools I went to, but the way I got shifted around, by the time the teachers figured out who I was, they didn't know who to come after ...'

'I used to like PE,' she replied.

'Were you always so fit ... I mean, in such good shape, er, physically,' Twist blurted, shrinking as Red shot him a look and he found himself staring down at the path, coughing nervously. 'I mean ... good at athletics ... Rio Twenty Sixteen.'

He liked the sound of her laughter even when the joke was on him.

'You don't know much, do you?' she said. 'Everyone knows I'm gonna be a dancer.'

He watched as she turned slowly, lifting her arms above her head, folding her hands in neatly at the wrists and rising onto her tiptoes, taking tiny steps that grew bigger until she was reversing her entire body, facing him then facing away with each new step in a wide circle, tracing the air with her hands.

He watched her hair spread out behind, then she drew her hands to her chest before releasing them to spin her faster and faster around him, each step becoming a leap, turning like a twister tearing around the cobblestones, spinning towards the river, out of control and out of reach.

29

'You number one driver. Fast like James Hunt,' the oligarch said, leaning forwards, his ash-white face visible in the rear-view mirror of the S-Class Mercedes limo as it edged forwards in traffic that had backed up all the way from Piccadilly Circus to Green Park and the Ritz Hotel.

Cribb, the chauffeur, nodded, accepting the compliment with all the deference he could manage beneath his black peaked cap. His suit was straight out of central casting but at least it was sticking to him, which was more than could be said for his boss's moustache. It was glued so badly to the oligarch's top lip that he had to fix his mouth in a grimace just to keep it in place.

But at least he was in character, which was more than could be said for the toerags who had ignored his lesson in Constantin Stanislavski's 'Method', preferring instead to improvise in their own inimitable style.

'Right turn here,' he barked from the back seat, gripping the handrail as the fourteen-foot behemoth slewed to the right down a narrow side street then nudged out across Jermyn Street where he waved it in to park up outside a white-fronted Georgian building.

'If anyone comes you cruise round the block. Then call me,' Fagin said, circling his finger in front of Cribb's nose. Cribb duly doffed his chauffeur's cap, then closed the passenger door behind him as he swept across the pavement and up the front steps of the architect's office with his bodyguard, a well-dressed Dodge, scanning the street behind him for hostiles.

The building was high Regency, its geometrical precision a shadow of the classical symmetry of the buildings of classical Greece and Rome. The history was not lost on Fagin. He knew that these empires had been held up as models for the education of the ruling elite of the Georgian era as they were instructed to be the colonial administrators of the British Empire, the civilisation which they considered their birthright and which they never doubted would be a legacy that would last one thousand years.

They walked up the marble steps beneath the triangular fresco of the porch, its workmanship undiminished in the face of two hundred and fifty years of weather. He motioned his assistant forwards and Dodge, looking every inch the part in a shiny, fashionably tight-fitting silk Hugo Boss suit, stepped forwards and pressed the button above an etched stainless steel sign which read *Spender Ltd. Architects since 1838.*

'Keep your mitts to yourself,' Fagin hissed as they heard the electric circuitry of the door buzz and the lock click open.

'Alex Spender,' said the man who opened the door, 'architect since 1838 at your service.'

Fagin extended his hand, making sure the upper middle class Englishman clocked the huge gold Rolex on his wrist as Dodge gave him the once-over for concealed firearms and Batesy nodded from the illegally parked S Class in the street behind him.

The handshake was firm if not vigorous, Fagin reaching forwards with his left hand to secure the power grip, beloved of senior statesmen and power brokers, searching deep inside his eyes as if anticipating some kind of foul play.

Then he smiled, nodding to himself as if his expectations had not only been correct but had, in some surprising way been surpassed. Looking suitably perplexed, Alex Spender, owner and managing partner of the firm, turned and led them across the threshold of the building where his family had worked for almost two hundred years.

'We speak on telephone, about conversion you do at number ninety-two,' Fagin said, his accent as thick as crude oil in a Siberian pipeline.

Spender ushered them into a large office at the back, a space which was entirely his own. A single glass table reflected the light that spilled into the room from a glass ceiling some thirty feet above their heads. The sound of tiny wings beating in the air above drew their gaze upwards towards a tiny bird which was dipping its long beak into a beautiful flower which appeared to be growing in thin air.

'An East African hummingbird pollinating a ghost orchid. *Arachneea Sprilunias*. An agrophocic plant. It draws all its moisture from the environment.'

Spender waited until they were seated before taking his own place behind his desk in a black leather Corbusier chair.

'The Losberne Gallery?' he asked.

'*Da*,' Fagin nodded, 'I buy building opposite. Want make modern. Like ninety-two. You show me plans, *da*?'

Spender leaned forward, his forearms flat on the glass desktop and smiled at Fagin, who noticed that the Englishman was more focused now that he was looking a three million pound account in the eye. Fagin could also tell from Spender's slight hesitation that it was not his usual practice to share the layout of client's premises with anyone but that there was something about an oligarch that was forcing him to seriously consider dispensing with protocol.

'Of course I can show you our plans for Dr Losberne ...' he coughed, standing up and walking to a recessed black cabinet to his right, unlocking its glass door and pulling out an aluminium tube from a shelf labelled 'L'.

Fagin watched him walk towards the clear glass table and unfurl a four foot by four foot set of plans, pausing only when Fagin's mobile phone began to hum.

Turning his back on Spender, Fagin crouched low at the table, pulling his phone from his pocket and shielding it secretively from Spender who showed no sign of trying to listen in at all.

'*Da?*' he began.

'Eleven-o-five, on the dot. Just like you said!' he heard Batesy shriek from the car outside.

Dodge watched Spender look over at Fagin as he pulled the mobile phone away from his ear then calmly replaced it and shouted a thick stream of expletives in Russian into it before turning to glare at the architect, shielding the earpiece of the phone with his free hand.

'Is private!' he growled.

'It's all right,' Spender demurred, 'I don't understand Russian.'

'You want my business?' Fagin asked bluntly, watching as Spender finally got the message and offered up a little bow – *whatever sir wants* – before slipping into the next room with the flats of his hands pressed tightly against his ears.

The moment he was gone Fagin stood up and scuttled to the door, getting firm purchase on the handle with both hands as Dodge stepped up onto the glass table, pulling out a high definition pocket camera, the flash illuminating the room and startling the hummingbird which Fagin watched climb steeply and hit the glass ceiling with an almost inaudible bump.

30

The plans were on the wall but Fagin looked strained. There were dark rings around his eyes and while he was never short of ideas he was having trouble placing them in a sequence that made sense. The job itself was not easy but the client posed his own risks and the fact that it had been Sikes and not Fagin who had brought him in made Fagin doubly nervous. But it was Sikes that worried him above all else.

Sikes, who had known him almost half of his life. Sikes, who had been both raised and schooled by him. Sikes who had always, no matter how much care and charity Fagin had given him, lived in his mind with a question hanging over him. A question only a psychologist could answer.

And if Dodge was right, if a potential *human resource* problem was emerging with the new boy then it was by no means inconceivable that one of Sikes's symptoms, his predilection for violence, might reassert itself, which would derail the entire operation and expose them to a heat that no amount of firefighting would extinguish.

Fagin looked down at the fat gold Rolex on his wrist. It was half past six and Twist and Red had still not appeared, a full thirty minutes after the briefing had been scheduled to start. Crossing himself, he turned back to the members of the gang who were present while offering a silent prayer that Dodge's superior instincts for trouble were, for once, wildly off the mark.

'No windows. Reinforced wall here,' he began, pointing at the rear wall of the open-plan gallery space on the ground floor and a smaller room beside it.

'We'll have a job getting in there,' Sikes replied.

Fagin looked across at the brute. He was sat next to Dodge on one of the fold-down chairs.

'You don't have to worry about that, Bill,' he countered. 'We don't go in. They bring them out.' Fagin said watching Dodge shuffle uneasily as they entered unknown territory.

'Bring what out?' Dodge asked.

Fagin glanced up. Batesy was checking his iPhone.

'In your own time, Master Batesy,' Fagin hissed, watching as the young man fumbled and dropped it, leaving it on the floor, returning to the remote and clicking onto the next slide, which was a page from a Sotheby's catalogue.

It showed a single painting, one of three existing originals from a 'complete set of six' that was due to go on sale in their next auction. There was a title for the auction at the top of the page that might have been Sotheby's marketing team's finest hour. It read:

The Greatest Sale of Eighteenth-Century Art Since The Eighteenth Century.

Fagin was not often lost for words but he found them difficult to retrieve now. He paused for thought, looked up at Dodge's face and saw the boy watching him expectantly before looking down at the ground once again.

'So, my dears,' he began, 'our client, for whom we are going to all this trouble, is not an unreasonable man. I have not introduced him by name until now to preserve his professional … integrity, but it is important for you to know the essential facts about him as they pertain to the success of this job. He is a Russian from a Siberian city called Krasnoyarsk, a businessman of considerable means who is also, as you may well already have seen by his selection of said Hogarths, a person of considerable taste. Such a man can be persuaded. He has just paid the visit he had promised he would make to the owner of the existing three Hogarths and has, Bill has reliably informed me, *persuaded* him to sell via Sotheby's which means …'

Fagin looked up at this point and saw Sikes's dark eyes attempting to read him from across the room. He recalled their agreement not to mention Rodchenko's actual name to the boys. Instead he coughed, looked back at the floor and sucked half his entire beard into his mouth, before looking up again to meet Dodge's questioning eyes.

'So … where does that leave us?' he went on. 'Well … it means that we've got about a week to retrieve the missing three from Losberne before our Russian friend, Mr Arkady Rodchenko, comes and severs our vital functions with a pair of rusty pliers.'

There was silence in the room as he picked up the miniature golf club from the desk and pointed at the picture of Moll Hackabout, the heroine of Hogarth's cautionary tale in the first of her appearances, just off the mail coach, standing next to a toad-like woman in a black shawl.

'Enter stage left our heroine, one Moll Hackabout, seventeen years old and served up fresh from the provinces into the hands of old Mother Needham, one of the Seven Dials' most notorious brothel keepers,' Fagin began again, glancing nervously at Sikes who showed no reaction at all.

'This is the first episode in her infamous decline, rendered by none other than William Hogarth, the pre-eminent satirist of his age, that being the reign of George I, and titled *The Harlot's Progress* – a series of six original plates ...'

'Says Sotheby's,' Dodge butted in. 'So why are we casing Losberne?'

'A series of six, I said. Three are up for auction at Sotheby's, as you can see from the catalogue, at the rear end of next week. The other three have been missing since 1755. The story is they were destroyed in a fire. But some people say that the fire was merely a diversion to cover the theft of the paintings. That all the time they have been off the radar ... until now, that is ...'

Fagin looked at Sikes, wondering what the real story was behind the tip-off, guessing that Rodchenko's thugs had most likely tapped up the insurance agent or underwriter who Losberne would have called in to protect his Hogarths before they reached auction.

'So you're saying Losberne has got the three missing paintings?' Dodge asked.

'So my man tells me,' Sikes replied, eyes forward on the prize.

'I don't mean to be thick,' Dodge said, 'but to clarify, we're stealing these to order?'

Fagin stroked his beard, nodded, then craned his ear towards the door. The others heard it then. It was the sound of the hatch to the stairwell being unlocked. Fagin nodded at Batesy who left the projector and stepped out to greet the latecomers who filed into the room seconds later, smiling and relaxed in one another's company.

Fagin watched them come in. No apology from either of them and no sign of guilt on their faces, which, he reflected, could only be a good thing.

'Did you get the scanner?' Cribb asked.

Red reached into her jacket pocket and pulled out the palm-pilot-shaped device she and Twist had taken from the warehouse.

'And … I saw a Bacon, a Blake and a new artist called Twist …' she said.

'They're all a bunch of Cuntstables,' Batesy interjected, receiving a slap from Fagin as he filed past him back to his place at the projector.

'Show some respect,' Fagin said, watching Sikes who followed Red, eyes blank as she walked in front of him and pulled a fold-down chair from the stack to sit down on it next to him.

'I'm not sure you've been *formally* introduced to our latest recruit, Bill. I give you Oliver Twist. Street artist. Traceur and soon to be …' he paused for effect, 'Robin Hood of the art world.'

'Heard a lot about you,' Sikes said, smiling at Twist this time.

'All good, I hope,' Twist replied.

'So far,' Sikes said, offering him a friendly wink as he stood pushing up off the back of the chair with one hand to balance on his bad leg while offering his free hand for Twist to shake, holding it there, wondering why Twist had stopped short of taking it.

'Hello, boy,' Sikes said, feeling the pressure against his good leg and hearing the growl that accompanied it.

Twist's hand lowered as he went to pat the bulldog on the head.

'Don't touch him!' Sikes said.

Twist looked up at Sikes, surprised by the urgency in his voice.

'You're going to need your hands later,' he said.

31

She looked round at the others crouched in the back of the white Bedford van. Twist and Batesy were sat opposite one another on the metal arch frames of the rear wheels and Bill sat watching her as she straightened the straps of her dress.

She looked across at Batesy who was watching the entrance to Losberne's gallery on the screen of his iPad.

'Don't worry,' he said, 'I've been checking his messages. He's got nothing on this evening. Now ... go. He's coming out now.'

She shot him her brightest smile, looked once at Sikes then turned and waited as Twist reached for the door handle opening their secure, self-contained world to the cold and dark one outside.

As the door slammed shut behind her she saw that *Plumbing Services* had been painted on its side. She crossed the street to the gallery side and walked straight up to the front door just as Losberne was turning, regular as clockwork, to lock it.

'Is this a bad time?' she asked, watching his eyes light up.

*

Ten minutes later Losberne was leaning over his fridge in his small private office next to the room Fagin claimed held the Hogarths. It was not a large office and in the corner she noticed a spiral staircase.

'I have a bedroom up there with a shower,' he said, turning to face her as he poured her a glass of champagne. 'One never knows when one will get busy.'

Red took the flute and smiled politely back at him as he sat down on the patent leather red two-seater sofa next to her.

'You were saying, it'd be answering the phone, a bit of filing …?' she asked.

'Nothing a girl like you can't handle,' Losberne replied, placing his hand on her knee and keeping it there as she turned hastily to rummage in her bag, pushing it sideways across her lap as she switched on the key fob scanner inside.

'I did want to show you some of my art,' she countered, pushing the iPad at him with her right hand as she probed the bunch of keys in his pocket with the scanner inside the bag with her left.

'I've got it all on here,' she said, turning it a full half circle, scanning the room just as Batesy had instructed her but all the time worrying, wondering, how far Bill would let Losberne go before he reacted.

'This one's based on —'

'*The Simoniac Pope*, of course. Very interesting … you've really got the line …' Losberne said sitting up now, really paying attention.

Red scrolled across to the next page. She hoped Twist was listening too. He was terribly earnest but there was something about him that she liked. If he was going to be an artist when this was over then what was stopping her becoming a dancer?

'I'm afraid this isn't my area, but I have to say these look rather intriguing ...' Losberne went on, pulling the iPad closer to his face, zooming in to examine the details.

'Fuck me!' Red said, watching Losberne register the change in her accent.

'Sorry. That's my "graffiti" voice,' she beamed. 'It's the only way to get taken seriously on the street.'

'I see. More champagne?'

'It's going right through me. Must pay a quick visit to the little girls' room,' she said, standing quickly and walking back towards the entrance to his office and the gallery toilet outside.

It was dark in the gallery but there was an unmistakable glow coming from the glass encased server which stood locked behind Losberne's PA's desk.

Red approached it and ducked down behind the desk as she heard Losberne come out of his office and stand in the doorway scanning the room for her. She took a generic remote-entry key fob from her hand and hooked it up to the wire that linked it to the scanner and its tiny built-in hard drive. There was a whirring sound as the data downloaded onto the fob. She worked quickly, detaching the USB cable and placing the fob up against the reader on the face of the server stack.

Nothing happened. She reversed the fob hoping that the other side would transmit but it didn't. She held her breath, listening to the sound of footsteps leaving Losberne's office. Crossing the gallery space she texted blind into her mobile phone.

'I'll do it,' Twist said, watching a mixture of surprise and relief play on Dodge and Batesy's faces.

'Whatever you do, don't drop it,' Dodge said, passing it to him and watching as he slid the key fob into the coin pocket of his jeans as Batesy muttered something about cheap Chinese shit.

It was raining hard outside now. It stung his eyes as he looked up the old iron drainpipe to the light in the window that corresponded to the Ladies in the plans. The pipe was freezing cold and wet beneath his hands. He looked down. Dodge stood beneath him, watching nervously, trying to guide him to the vital first footholds that would allow him to gain the momentum he would need to monkey up to the first floor where he would try somehow to get the replacement fob to Red.

'Hello? Are you all right in there?'

It was Losberne. He was knocking at the bathroom door and Red ducked lower behind the desk.

Do something! He's not going away, she texted.

'What's going on in there?' Losberne asked, speaking through the closed door of the women's lavatory.

She thought he was about to go in and would see immediately that she wasn't in there but her message to Dodge paid dividends and the telephone on the desk above her head started to ring.

'I'm coming!' Losberne shouted.

She heard footsteps then the phone being lifted from its cradle.

'Package? Now? I'm afraid there's been … OK. Sure. I'll come outside now.'

She heard Losberne replace the phone and reach into his pocket. There was a jangle of keys, more footsteps and then a click as he unlocked the front door and stepped outside onto the street.

Red wasted no time. She sprang up and ran across the gallery to the stairs, taking them three at a time. Dodge's text message said that she was to go to the upstairs bathroom.

She crossed a mirrored bedroom with a shagpile carpet, entered a compact white bathroom and ran to the porthole window, catching sight of the silhouette of a body, clinging to the drainpipe and a hand reaching out towards her in the rain.

She flipped open the window and squeezed her hand through the gap but was unable to rotate her arm. She felt her elbow graze against the brick as she strained to get her hand further to meet the outstretched hand outside. She heard a grunt from the drainpipe as the climber strained to reach her. His position was precarious, perched on a wet wall fifteen feet above a row of sharp metal railings.

She turned, and edged her bottom into the sink. It gave her an extra six inches' reach. She felt the key fob touch her fingertips and then, when she had it, pulled her hand away slowly so as not to risk dropping it.

With the fob in her hand Red ran back to the top of the stairwell and crouched there, trying to see if Losberne had returned to his office.

'I wouldn't use that loo for a bit,' she said from the top of the stairs but no one answered. She came down the stairwell fast and stopped, peering out through the doorway at Losberne who was talking into his mobile. He looked agitated and kept turning round and peering back through the glass into the gallery.

Then the doors of the van across the street opened and Dodge came out carrying a box in his arms. She watched as Losberne lowered his mobile momentarily and then began shouting at Dodge.

It was all Red needed. She burst across the gallery and skidded to a halt on her knees at the foot of the server stack, then ducked beneath the desk to bind the scanner to the new key fob. There was a beep and then it was in her hand, pressed tight up against the electronic reader on the server that opened with a click, allowing her in, taking out a second conventional hard drive that she fire-wired into the main drive in the stack.

One thousand ... two thousand ... three thousand ... She counted silently, listening as the door opened then slammed shut as Losberne stormed back into the gallery towards his office and she waited, listening to his footsteps before standing up and dashing in the direction of the ground floor toilet, straightening her dress as she ran.

Losberne must have heard something because he spun round on his heels, puce faced, and glared at her.

'I wouldn't go in there for a bit if I were you,' Red said, feeling the hard drive in her hand.

'The cleaners will be in first thing,' Losberne replied, coolly observing her suspiciously from the doorway.

'I'm sorry,' he went on, 'I didn't mean to leave you alone in here just now but I had some joker on the telephone. But since I did, I'm afraid you're going to have to wait a moment.'

She watched as he buzzed the intercom by the door to his office.

'Could you come up here please, Brittles?'

She stood open-mouthed, her head scrambling as the steel bolts that held the strong room door fast slid undone and heavy footsteps came marching along the rear wall of the gallery's main space towards Losberne's office. Brittles had an emotionless oblong face and long arms that extended ape-like by his sides. She watched him lift his hands, his movements robotic, like Frankenstein's monster as he stepped closer looking to place his hands on her shoulders and pin her to the spot.

'Search her,' Losberne said, standing back, his arms folded as Brittles lumbered over to Red lifting his own arms to indicate that he was about to frisk her.

'If this is the way you treat your interns, you can stuff your work experience up your arse ...' she said, pushing past Brittles and flouncing out across the main gallery to stand fuming by the front door with her phone to her ear.

'Yes, the police please. I'm being held against my will. That's right, the Losberne gallery. I think I've been drugged ... yes by a pervert!' she spoke urgently into the mouthpiece.

Brittles followed her to the door, looking anxiously at Losberne who, preferring to have as little to do with the police as possible, motioned to his hulk to let her out.

Sikes was stood outside the van, shielded by the rear doors which were open. He watched as Red strode away from the gallery and Losberne stepped out after her, waving his security guard back into the gallery as he strode off in pursuit.

'Now!' he said, slamming the van doors shut and screeching across the road to pick her up.

32

Fagin was sat in the kitchen peeling potatoes when they got back. He was in his dressing gown and he wiped his hands on it before greeting each of them in turn, holding them at arm's length to admire them before pulling them close and kissing them on both cheeks.

Twist was the last to be kissed. Fagin's breath smelt of pickled cabbage and *tuică*, and when he pulled back from the clinch he held onto Twist's head, turning it to show it to each of the others.

'Have I ever been wrong? he asked them. 'Did I ever pick a dud?'

'Flattery won't cut it,' said Dodge, holding his palm out, 'respect me!'

Twist watched Fagin's smile curdle as his hands reached into the pockets of his dressing gown. He winced as he pulled out a fat red bundle and began peeling off fifty pound notes.

'You did well today but phase two begins tomorrow. Until then, you've earned yourselves a night off.'

He peeled ten fifties from the wad and handed them to Dodge.

'Go out and have some fun,' he said, handing the same amount to each of them in turn.

'Yay! Here we go,' said Batesy.

'But not too much fun. I need you back here at six a.m. clean and sober.'

'Six!?' Dodge complained.

'We've got to be ready to move the minute the call comes through. I'll stay tuned to Losberne,' Fagin said, 'so don't worry your pretty little heads about it.'

'What if he's into heavy phone sex? You could be in for a steamy night, boss!' Batesy said, laughing as Dodge grabbed him and Twist by the arms and started pulling them both with him towards for the door.

'You're coming with us, Twist. It's time we got you laid,' Dodge said.

Twist didn't fight him. He knew it was pointless to resist but he saw an opportunity and he took it, turning to catch Red's eye, thinking maybe, just maybe …

'You coming, Red?' he asked.

'We got plans,' Sikes said.

Twist felt Dodge yank him hard, like he was sending him a message as Sikes walked past them and put his arm round Red.

'You did good, girl,' he said, kissing her long and hard on the lips.

Twist didn't need to see any more. He let go of his grip on the door frame and let Dodge pull him out into the corridor where, out of sight of the others, Dodge pushed him against the wall and gave him a quick slap round the face before placing his finger on the tip of Twist's nose.

'Come on, Twist,' he said, pressing the finger harder, until Twist's nose flattened. 'Let's get out of here.'

The party was like a bad dream. Nothing made any sense. It was in a basement lit by fake electric candles. A hellish subterranean hole in which two unlikely tribes were fighting for control, engaged in a form of highly ritualised combat. On one side of the room there were breakdancing drag queens and on the other Japanese body-poppers who kept calling one another out onto the floor to dance off, mano a mano. Dodge and Batesy had of course become wrapped up init, starting out as would-be compères but soon finding themselves cut off in no-man's land, back to back, taking all comers. It was hysterical, the stuff of nightmares.

There were chequered red and white tablecloths on the tables that hugged the walls forming an arena-like dance floor, and there were people at the tables drinking carafes of Bulgarian wine sealed with silver foil. The wine had a bitter chemical aftertaste and Twist was onto his second bottle when Dodge sat down and put two warm pints of Stella on the table, pushing one at him until he picked it up and started to drink.

'We all love her,' Dodge said, 'but it's like Fagin says, we're family. It's my fault. No, really. I'm sorry. I should have given you the heads-up before you got ideas.'

He pushed his pint against Twist's but Twist didn't move.

'Come and have a dance, mate. You'll feel better. Plenty of other chicks out there … well, one or two. Look at 'em, gorgeous. You're spoilt for choice,' Dodge cajoled, trying to avoid eye contact with a six foot three unnatural blonde in a leopard-skin leotard who had been stalking him all night.

'I'm better off on my own,' Twist said.

'You're better off with cash in your pocket, a roof over your head and dinner on the table. Don't go pissing in the soup.'

Twist took a long drink from his pint and smiled, watching Batesy do a double backflip and crash-land in the arms of the leopard woman.

'Why do you think Red came after you in the first place? Do you think you've got the Lynx effect or something?' Dodge asked, staring at Twist who didn't respond.

'Well it was FBoss who sent her. He needed you in. That's why. Not coz she fancied you. Come on! Wake up. You've got to see that,' Dodge went on, chewing his bottom lip.

'Fuck off,' Twist said.

'Time to grow up,' Dodge said, standing up and shaking his head.

Twist looked at the pint, then picked it up and downed it, watching over the rim as Dodge reached Batesy who was being systematically ripped apart by a pair of Japanese death droids. He stood up, walked up the stairs and began to climb wearily up to the first floor where there was a kind of chill-out room and a balcony overlooking the city.

It was already late. Past three and there weren't many lights on in the Square Mile. He tipped back the bottle of gut-rot wine and was just about to tell himself it was the last one when a hand reached out and took it off him. He looked to his right but the thief had vanished so he spun one eighty and saw that Red had painted her fingernails a different colour on each hand. The ones on her right hand pink as she tipped up the wine and took a long, hard swig.

'How did I guess you'd be up here?' she said.

Twist reached out and took the bottle back from her, turning away and resuming his position, leaning on the railing, looking out at the city.

'Are you running errands for FBoss again or is it Bill this time?' he said without looking back.

'Shut up,' she said. 'How was I to know you had *feelings*?'

'Wasn't it obvious?' Twist said, turning to confront her.

'Do you know the difference between a man and a boy, Oliver?' she said, staring him straight in the eyes. 'A man tells you what he wants, looks you in the eye, stands up for it. A boy? He's gonna sit there with a faraway look in his eye, hoping Father Christmas brings him what he's dreaming of.'

'So what are you doing here?' Twist asked, watching as she stared straight back at him.

'I came to tell you something. When I was in with Losberne, showing him your stuff, he was into it. And I'm not just saying that. You must have heard him talking, right. When you were in the van. He really thought it was good.'

'I missed that bit,' Twist said.

'Why?' Red replied.

'Because I was up a drainpipe handing you the right key fob. Besides, he thought it was your work. Not mine.'

'So?'

'So he was just trying to fuck you.'

'No, Oliver,' she said, flatly, telling it straight. 'I've been around a lot of blokes. When he put his hand on my knee, I thought I was going to puke ... but it wasn't just that. I could tell he was really surprised when I showed him the photos of your stuff on the walls. I mean it. He was shocked. At how good it was.'

Twist felt himself torn. His mind telling him to ignore her, that she had been sent again, by Fagin, to check on him, while his heart felt like it was swelling, working harder, pumping arterial blood to places in him that had never been touched before.

'You played it so cool in there ...' he said, watching Red glow, 'you always do.'

'I'm with Bill, Oliver.'

Twist watched her turn and lean against the railing, reaching out to the wine and taking a good long drink. He had nothing to say to that apart from the truth. And that was that he'd never been in love with anyone before her and that he had absolutely no idea how he was going to tell her or survive without her if she rejected him.

'Yeah, I got the message,' he said, 'but I never imagined you with a guy like him, that's all. He's cool, sure. He's just so ... old.'

'He's twenty-eight!'

'Yeah. Ancient.'

Red gave him a long hard look.

'You know what it's like when you're a kid? Anything a grown-up promises – social worker, foster parent – don't mean shit. It's all just talk.'

'Tell me about it.'

'Well Bill's not like that. He's there for me. He says something, he does it. Like, there's this dance school in Berlin. Soon as this job's out of the way, he's gonna pay for me to ...'

'So that's why you're with him?' Twist shot back.

'Fuck off!'

Twist watched as she turned to go.

'And if he ever … wasn't there …'

'Stop it, Oliver!'

He watched as she turned at the top of the stairs but she was smiling. Not angry or upset like he thought she would be. She walked back to him.

'If Bill wasn't in my life, I'd be out dancing every night. He's hopeless …'

He watched her turn back to the stairs and the dance floor below.

'Come on, we're wasting time …'

'What happened to his leg?'

'He used to run, too. Taught me everything I know. Got cocky one day …'

'I thought you wanted to be a dancer?'

'Yeah, but Bill said …'

He watched the smile fade from her lips.

'We agreed, running first. Just till we get ahead. Then it's gonna be dance dance dance. Ain't no stopping us now though …'

Downstairs the breakdancing had turned ugly. One of the robots had been groped by one of the drag queens and the two sides were facing one another across the packed dance floor. Twist watched as Red wove her way through them into the heart of the impending clash. She started to move and immediately the two factions gave her space as she slid into the rhythm, drawing all eyes to her.

He watched her see something in the crowd and start to laugh. It was Dodge and Batesy. Dodge was breakdancing like a drag queen and Batesy had become a death droid. A circle had formed around them which she forced her way into, spinning again, weaving a circle around them like a sorceress keeping demons at bay.

Twist watched the three of them moving around one another. They looked good together. Batesy chopping at Dodge who was gyrating with his hand on his hip unimpressed, while Red spun faster, beckoning Twist to come to them, to let his mind go and to simply dance and forget about everything for just one night.

It may have been an hour but it could have been three that he danced with them until the crowd had thinned out on the dance floor and Dodge was telling him about an after-hours place that kept the music going all the next day, forgetting what Fagin had told him about the six a.m. curfew. But Twist was watching Red, who kept looking at him, giving nothing away, not rejecting or inviting him, just neutral, her intentions unknown.

'You up for it?' Batesy said, lurching in at them, Twist's heart falling as Red shook her head.

'Nah, I need to cool down,' she said, turning to Twist, 'but you should go ...'

33

Twist didn't know how it happened. One minute he was outside with Dodge and Batesy who were fighting a rearguard action against drag queens all trying to pile into the same mini cab to the after-party in Bow, the next he was running after Red who had bet him a hundred she could get up onto the roof of an apartment made of mirrored glass about half a mile away before he could.

It was clear and cold and the stars were out. He was faster than her on the flat but he wasn't thinking straight. His tendency was still to go round obstacles whereas she would go over them and shout 'cheat' down at him as he ran, until the challenge changed and was less a race and more like the game they had played the first day of training. She led and he tried to follow.

Two steps up onto the roof of a Range Rover, three onto the brick gatepost of a cemetery and four down into the graveyard, full tilt over tombstones like they were hurdles in a steeplechase until she slowed, veering to the right on the path, running up an eight-foot church wall and pulling herself up onto it, looking down, no helping hand for Twist as he tried and failed to follow.

The top of the wall wasn't flat. Two triangular tiles met in the middle, forming a ridge. He tried to do it his way. Stand upright and tightrope it like any self-respecting bipedal hominid, but his feet slipped out from under him and he hit the ridge hard, falling to his right, hooking his left calf in tight to stop himself from falling.

Pulling himself back onto the wall he could see her disappearing fifty feet away, her arse in the air as she ran, monkey-like, using her hands and feet. He got down, gripping the ridge with his hands and starting to walk them forwards, faster, slowly getting the hang of it, feeling the burn in his deltoids and his shoulders.

He stopped and looked up. She was a long way from him now. Beginning to climb a four-storey whitewashed apartment block, pulling herself up from one balcony to the next. Never once looking down or looking back.

'Hey!' he shouted after her, winded by five pints of Stella and the gut-rot red that sloshed around inside him, the pain of the stitch biting through the numbness of the alcohol, the endorphins and the cold.

The climb was easier and the balconies were like a climbing frame. He pulled himself up with his arm strength, using his feet to guide him and reach up above him to get purchase in the gaps between the balcony railings and the apartment walls. By the time he reached the roof he felt less fucked up but he was too late to catch her.

She was one hundred feet ahead of him now, vaulting railings from one roof terrace to the next. The building made of mirrors rose up above her at the end of the row of terraces, maybe ten or eleven storeys, some four hundred feet tall, reflecting the streets of Bethnal Green below.

From a distance a lot of things looked impossible but up close you could always find a way. Just as Red was doing now, finding handholds on window ledges, using the secure, modern drainage pipes and cable TV lines to climb swiftly up the vast mirrored edifice.

He remembered watching an old climbing movie. About a free climber who scaled without ropes up overhangs that people said couldn't be climbed. The film was called *Les Pointules Du Mort*. All the time people would be saying to him that it couldn't be done but he'd always be philosophical. That nothing was impossible until the moment you fell.

And Twist was trying not to fall now. Trying to get close to Red as she climbed effortlessly up the mirrored glass that reflected the headlights of a late-night minicab dropping off on Cambridge Heath Road below them, losing sight of her as she reached the roof, climbed up a trellis and over a wall onto a lavish roof terrace at the very top of the building where a pool lay steaming in front of a glass-fronted penthouse.

It was incongruous, Twist thought, having a penthouse in a neighbourhood like this but that was just one of a bag full of questions that would keep until the morning. He looked up as the last of his breath deserted him to see that she was stepping out of her clothes and walking to the pool and smiling to herself as she reached up her arms to dive in.

The water was warm. Magically warm in the night air around them that was now below freezing.

'How d'you know about this place?' Twist asked, sculling a few strokes away from her on his back after she surfaced, too close for comfort.

'Bill brought me here once,' she said. 'We used the lift.'

Twist looked around. It was impressive.

'Who lives here?'

'A man called Rodchenko. Arkady Rodchenko.'

Twist took a moment to register before it hit him. He gulped a mouthful of water and started coughing and had to raise his head to stop himself from choking.

'Don't worry, Twist. He's probably fast asleep.'

He lunged towards her until he was close enough to grab her wrist and turn her to face him, feeling her place her fingertip on his lips to silence him.

He looked at her, up close like that, thinking she fitted right in here, like the mirrors on the walls. Revealing only what was on the surface. Nothing of what was inside.

'You know Fagin's a liar, don't you?' she began, breaking his grip and pulling away from him, sculling backwards across the pool.

'And that all that stuff he told you at the beginning about working for insurance companies ...' she said, smiling, '... that it's all nonsense?'

Twist could see the outline of her body, visible but shrouded by the dark water as she swept her hand around in a tight arc showing him the pool and the penthouse belonging to Rodchenko.

'This is who Fagin's working for now,' she said.

And so Twist listened, resisting the urge to move closer and touch her out of sympathy as she recounted the story of her capture the night after Sikes had come home without Harry. How Sikes had come to get her and done a deal with the Russian gangster at his club. A deal in which he would 'buy' her back by delivering the first three paintings in Hogarth's series, *A Harlot's Progress* to Rodchenko here at his penthouse and then secure his fee by taking the remaining three paintings while they were out of the safe on display during a high-profile auction a week or so later.

Twist blinked and looked nervously up at the low-lit penthouse lounge.

'Bill has sworn some kind of oath to Rodchenko,' she said. 'I wanted you to come here. In case anything happens to me.'

Twist drew back as Red slid through the water towards him, trying to get his head around the information she'd just laid on him before she reached him and he lost the capacity for rational thought altogether.

'Sorry?' he managed. 'So Sikes has sworn an oath to this bloke Rodchenko and you wanted me to come here and swim in his pool in case anything *happens* to you?'

He felt the lip of the swimming pool tap him gently on the back of the head and the tiles of the wall behind him press against his shoulder blades. He raised his arms but she took his biceps in her hands and drew herself quickly into him until she was close enough to pincer his chest with her knees, then hook her feet around the small of his back as he pushed forwards off the wall, struggling to free himself.

'No ... Red ... talk ...' he started but it was no good. She had her thighs wrapped tight around his diaphragm and she only had to squeeze gently to silence him and freeze him there. He was powerless to break away from her as she leaned forward and bit his lip, releasing the pressure with her thighs so that he could breathe, drawing air from her lungs as she closed her mouth on his.

Twist did not know how long they hung like that in the water. But it was the most complete happiness he had ever known and it obliterated everything, reducing his field of awareness to a single sensory stimulus, the feeling of her body, pressed tightly against his so that he didn't see the moon falling in the sky and the halo of dawn rising up on the skyline, or the electric light flicker on inside the penthouse.

But Red was faster than Twist. She saw it before we did. Not that Twist was capable of responding. He was watching hers. Wondering if he would ever touch her again.

The terrace was freezing as he ran across to his clothes, struggling to get into his jeans and feeling his T-shirt wet against his back, then running to the edge and lowering himself until he was hanging, looking back into the pent-house. There, through the French windows, was a shirtless Russian standing staring at the sun which was rising in the east, a pair of black eyes, deep-set in a long face sitting atop a bull neck and barrel chest.

'Come on!' Red whispered from beneath him but Twist held on. He was looking at the Russian's back as he turned and squatted, drawing up a steel bar with two hundred pounds on each end in a dead lift, the lateral muscles framing a sword-carrying angel whose ink wings had been carefully grafted onto his massive shoulder blades. And then, when the man turned, Twist saw more tattoos on his vast, white, hairless chest. He found himself staring at a picture of the Madonna and Child and there were steeples and church spires.

And then Twist relaxed his grip and fell to the deck to find that she had gone.

'This never happened, right? We were at the club all night,' she said, looking up at him, seeing that he understood, before lowering herself onto the wall and dropping off into the church grounds.

He watched her sprint across the churchyard, vault the iron railing on the far side then land with both feet on the pavement and look back at him before turning to jog on.

The sun had already been glinting off the mirrors as they'd sprinted past the entrance to the Russian's block. He'd caught her pretty quickly, faster than her on the flat, and stolen a kiss, and then suggested they follow the canal, out of sight to his tower in Newham to get some more sleep.

They'd covered the ground fast, following Old Ford Road then bearing due south on Parnell and Fairfield roads before hitting the hard shoulder of the A13 which took them all the way towards the East India Dock and the broken land east of the Blackwall Tunnel approach road.

After crossing the Limehouse Cut and Bow Creek they dropped down off a brick wall into a railway siding then crawled through a hole in the fence and out onto Twelvetrees Crescent. It was here that Twist, turning sideways, caught Red's flinch but missed the fist which came out of nowhere and slammed straight into his face and took his legs clean out from under him.

'Got you!'

Twist could hear the words but he was blind. There was just the pavement, cold and hard beneath him as stars danced in the half light above his face and he tasted blood in the back of his throat where it was flooding down from inside his nose.

'Call the police, young lady!' Bumbola boomed, his voice familiar but distant as Twist struggled to push himself up off his back.

'I will. You're a psycho!'

Red's voice sounded real enough. Aggressive and in Bumbola's face, as she stood over Twist, protecting him from the hands that were reaching down to take him.

'Vandalising council property. It's a serious offence,' Bumbola boomed.

Twist winced at the pain as he lifted his head from the pavement and opened his eyes to see Red still standing above him, preparing to fight a man who was over twice her weight.

'Go on! Try it!' Bumbola shouted, as Twist blinked and kept his eyes closed, listening to the sound of a car approaching, and pull to a stop as hands took his arms and hoiked him to his feet.

34

The sun was shining low across the building site as she skirted it behind the corrugated iron fence to its left. Down there the day was just beginning. An engineer in a hard hat briefing his foreman and his crane operator, wolf whistles greeting the catering lady arriving on her bicycle as the apprentices sloped in past the security guard on the gate.

Prising back a piece of fence she took a steep path down through thick undergrowth to what would once have been the sun deck on the south-facing side of the old hotel. An ash tree had fallen across it perhaps ten years ago and a wilderness had sprung up around it, complete with a den of foxes, buried deep below the roots of the upended tree.

The fire escape was still covered in frost and it stuck to her hands as she pulled the ladder down to climb up, rehearsing the whole time what she would say to them when they asked her where she had been and where she had last seen Twist. And she wondered, despite all her practice, how effectively she would be able to lie to them, because something had changed up on the roof looking down, watching the police-woman leaning next to him as he lay on the pavement bleeding.

And she still felt guilty. Knowing that it should have been her by his side.

The guilt had eaten her up as she'd run from the scene knowing that she could not present herself as a witness, telling herself she had to go back, as her feet had carried her left behind a row of shops to a fire escape behind a kebab house, which she had climbed, out onto a frosty, slate roof.

And from up there she'd watched as the fat traffic warden accused Twist of trying to mug him. Watched him play the victim, miming each action and hearing those lies. She'd look around her, but there were no tiles she could have thrown at the liar, just concrete beneath her fingertips.

So she'd been forced to watch silently from the roof. The policeman calming down the traffic warden, swallowing his lies as the policewoman had cuffed Twist and placed him in the back of the car, radioing in shortwave, letting Red know where they had taken him.

'You're late,' Bill said.

They were all there. Fagin, Bill and Dodge, gathered in a semicircle round Batesy who was backtracking through the email logs on the hard drive she'd bagged at Losberne's gallery. They were looking to correlate a text from Losberne to his PA telling her to arrange for the paintings to be moved to a second vault before the auction, with one giving the password for his Securicor account.

'Of course he's going to move them after Red barged in there the other night. Yes, go on! Down a bit, Batesy ...

Yes. That one … Where have you been?' Fagin asked as Red crept into the room.

'Yeah, sorry, I fell asleep …' she said.

'Where's Twist?' Bill said, keeping his eyes on her as the others turned to look back at the screen and Fagin punched the desktop as Batesy opened an email from Securicor detailing the exact time and date they would pick up Losberne's Hogarths.

'He left with you, right, Dodge?' she said, catching Dodge's eye as he turned.

Back me up on this, please God, back me up …

'They went off to this after-hours party. I was knackered. That whole thing with Losberne. I had to crash …'

'Why didn't you come back here, like FBoss told you?' Bill said.

'One too many, I guess,' she replied, willing someone to step in and save her as Bill stared into her without blinking. She felt a wave of relief as Fagin finally raised his left hand and spoke.

'Bill, I gave them the night off,' he said, eyes still glued to the screen, 'the paintings weren't going anywhere until morning. There's no harm done.'

She watched Bill's face, his dead eyes holding her gaze for just a second too long before turning back to join Fagin with the question that she could not answer.

'It is morning. So where is he?'

35

DS Charlie Brownlow sat alone in the back of the bar thinking maybe he hadn't in fact seen it all. He was fifty-nine now. In 1989 he had reopened Scotland Yard's Art and Antiquities Squad and his career had seen many successes. Even conservative estimates suggested he might have saved the insurance companies over one billion pounds.

He'd recovered a Rubens, a Vermeer and a Goya from the Provisional IRA's most feared criminal organiser, and uncovered a plot to smuggle the head of Amenhotep III out of Egypt dipped in plastic to disguise it as a knick-knack from an airport shop. But he had never, as far as he could remember, ever attempted to break open a gang of wannabe ninjas whose members could, according to several eyewitness police reports, fly.

His mobile rang. The theme from *The Godfather*. Taxpayers' money every Friday at three, or a tip-off to the rival you were supposed to be fingering. An offer no self-respecting snitch could refuse.

And it was most likely one of these informants who was calling him now. A criminal who might be at any level of the trade from knocker to organiser, drug to diamond dealer, or perhaps one of his captains of organised crime who might be seeking a plea-bargain having been offered a stolen painting as collateral on a loan.

He put down his pint of Guinness and picked up the phone. A glimmer in his eye as he saw that the caller was a good person, his partner, forty-year-old DS Olivia Bedwin, overeducated and currently in possession of a parole-breaking graffiti artist called Twist who she claimed had recently decorated the back wall of the National Gallery with an exact replica of Blake's *The Simoniac Pope*.

'So what's the connection?' Brownlow asked, listening to the silence on the end of the line.

'A young homeless vandal who climbs buildings and likes art ...'

Brownlow rubbed his eyes. He felt tired and old and wondered if anything would change the shell game. A game in which gallery curators and the auction houses where the gods of art and money ran down underground channels to the 'dark' auctions where the global elite could buy stolen art, anonymously and tax free.

He heard Bedwin's theory. It reminded him of a time when he was young and ambitious.

'A would-be Banksy who was fallen in with a gang of acrobatic thieves who have been systematically stealing contemporary and modern art works, apparently freelance for the past twelve months ...?'

'Quite a shiner,' the lady detective said to him, courting sympathy as he looked up at her nice teeth which became visible when she smiled.

They were the only white thing in the airless interview room in Newham's police station. Everything else was a dull matt grey, including the stationery. Twist looked beyond his interviewers to the door where a single foot-square panel had been cut into it. He saw the visitors to the police station coming and going. Twist looked up at the lady cop. He could see she didn't want to be here any more than he did.

'Oliver, don't mind if I call you Oliver, do you?' she went on. 'Can't keep saying "Twist". I'll sound like I'm in a—'

'Casino. I've heard that one before,' Twist replied, watching as the old man Brownlow looked down at the photo of Bumbola's van covered in his tag which he'd been having trouble convincing them he'd had absolutely no hand in.

'Personally I think it's an improvement,' she went on. 'Well, in any case, judging from the state of your face, I'd say the punishment already rather exceeds the crime.'

'So let me go,' Twist said.

'Metropolis Parking Solutions, the contractors whose property you vandalised take a very different view, as does your parole officer, who understandably feels very let down after securing you the work experience with the undertaker ...'

Twist stared at her, bracing himself for the slap which he knew was coming but which stung nonetheless.

'To be honest, Oliver,' Brownlow began, 'a bit of graffiti doesn't really concern us in the Art and Antiquities Squad. Except when someone walks off with a chunk of Banksy. Your run-in with Warden Bumbola was just a happy accident that brought you to our attention. What we really want to talk to you about is this gentleman.'

Twist looked down as Bedwin opened her matt grey folder and pulled out a mugshot, turning it so that there could be absolutely no mistaking Fagin's face, twenty years younger, his hair in a ponytail, a skinny, gypsy thief.

'Almost a cliché, isn't he?' Brownlow began. 'Cornelius Faginesc, FBoss, Fagin …?' He started out running gangs of London dippers on the underground – kids he found at Simon shelters, on the streets. He moved up a gear in August 2011, using his gang to orchestrate large-scale looting. But the weird thing about him and the reason he's come up on my radar is that during these raids on warehouses, high-ticket luxury goods and boutiques in the last two years, he's developed a taste for art … So far he's avoided what we call "headache art", stuff above the hundred thousand mark that he can't fence quickly, but we have it on good authority that he's aiming a little higher now. Possibly stealing to order …'

Twist didn't flinch.

'Now, how about this chap?'

Twist looked down. It was a surveillance shot taken on the street. It showed Sikes with another man.

'William Sikes, alias Bulldog, born Peckham 1984. An orphan, like you. Graduate of the Fagin academy. Now also moving in higher circles including …'

Twist watched the lady cop's finger slide across the glossy surface of the photograph to a man with a bowling ball for a head. A bull of a man in a black puffar jacket.

'Archangel, born Arkhangelsk, 1972.'

He rubbed his eyes and tried to look bored but it was a struggle. It was the Russian. From the penthouse, the one Red called Rodchenko with the paintings on his wall.

'How am I supposed to know these guys?' he asked, watching as Bedwin pulled a third photograph from her folder and turned it as she pushed it over towards him.

He bit his lip. It was a CCTV grab of him and Red going into the Tate. He was fiddling with his iPad as she strode ahead confidently.

'Nancy Lee, alias Red. Known associate of Sikes and Fagin ...'

Twist gulped. Brownlow clocked it.

'Pretty girl, isn't she?' he went on.

Twist looked up at him. He had wrinkles around his eyes which were brown. There was real concern in them.

'I could get you out of this, you know. If you gave me something to go on,' he said.

'I don't have anything.' Twist shrugged.

He knew in situations like this it was better to say nothing. Not act up. Dumb insolence would get you nowhere. Just act like you weren't bothered. That you were on top of it, had done nothing wrong and so had nothing to account for.

'That's not what I was hoping you were going to tell me. You see, when someone's been used by Sikes, they've got a nasty habit of ending up like this ...'

Twist looked down at the next photograph that came spiralling out of the file. There was a boy on it. He was lying facing the sky. His legs one side of a fence, his arms the other so that his body formed an inverted U, bent against the natural curve of his spine had been broken by the spike which had punched up through his back emerging from his sternum.

'His name was Harry. Harry O'Neill, born 1996. Died last month,' Bedwin said. 'Red's last running partner. Take a good look.'

She held up the photograph for him to take but Twist did not take it. He was afraid his hands would shake uncontrollably if he lifted them up off the table top.

'So you don't know Sikes?' Brownlow said.

'No,' Twist replied.

'I'll trust you on that.'

Bedwin glanced across at Brownlow. Twist could see that she didn't trust it at all.

'So there's no reason you wouldn't want to help us catch him,' Brownlow said.

Twist squirmed in his seat. They must know they had him now.

'He wouldn't do that to Red. She's his girlfriend,' he said, listening to Bedwin who had begun to chuckle darkly to herself.

'Don't mind DS Bedwin. Used to work in Domestic Violence,' Brownlow went on.

'I could tell you some stories,' she said, daring Twist to ask her.

'You all right, son?' Brownlow asked, pulling his hand from his pocket and placing some loose change on the table. 'Go and get yourself a drink from the machine out there. I'll have a coffee, black, one sugar and Bedwin here likes tea, milk, no sugar.'

Twist stood up. His head was spinning. He reached down for the coins and saw that Bedwin was putting the photographs back in the file as Brownlow studied the space between his thumbs which were lying flat on the table either side of Harry's corpse.

Outside the room the world began again. Saturday morning and Newham's underclass were beginning to lay siege to the station. There was a drunk outside the revolving security doors banging on them, crying to be let in.

Twist put a one pound coin into the slot and found the code for black coffee with sugar. There was a whirring sound as the cup was rotated into place and he stood up and glanced back inside the room where he could see Brownlow and Bedwin locked in a heated discussion.

Then he glanced up at the clock which read nine a.m., the second hand ticking away, and he realised that he needed to get out. He looked over at the heavy security door locking him and the police inside the station. They had the same kind of doors in Beltham, the kind that could only be opened with a key fob from the outside or from the security staff behind bullet-proof glass inside the station itself.

He pulled the coffee from the machine and put in the money for the tea, watching the clock tick round. Then he walked round the partition so he could look out into the street. There was a woman wearing a blanket out there. She had wild scarecrow hair and she was clutching a two litre bottle of White Lightning cider. Twist stuck his middle finger up at her through the glass.

It took her a second to focus, then her chin jutted out and she freaked. The cider bottle exploded against the security door and she followed quickly after it, snatching at it, bending at the hips, sweeping the floor with her hands until she had it clutched tight to her chest but the other drunk, the guy with the nose, had seen it too. He grabbed her face and she started screaming. A light went on above the door and Twist saw two policemen leave their plexiglass cage and run across the space he was in to break up the ruckus.

He watched as the security door opened and they stepped out to deal with the fracas and Twist smiled, watching the door slowly close behind them, two feet, one foot then slow as the piston on the hinge filled with compressed air.

'You are planning on letting him go, right?' Bedwin asked Brownlow, whose back was still to the small window in the door to the interview room.

'I want to give him another chance. There's something about him ...' Brownlow replied, nodding to himself.

'That's lucky ...' Bedwin replied, pointing out through the glass.

Brownlow stood and turned round, following Bedwin's finger out across reception in time to see Twist vault the partition and catch hold of the top right-hand corner of the security door.

36

He ran from the police station with the theme of an old film playing in his head. It took him about ten seconds and eighty yards before he realised it wasn't in his head but in his pocket. And the theme music was from *The Godfather*. It had sounded way better coming out of the speakers in the Prince Charles cinema off Leicester Square than it did coming out of the mobile phone he now had in his hand.

'Who is this?' he asked.

'DS Brownlow. Nice stunt back there, Oliver. I just wanted to make sure you've got my number. In case you remember anything about our Mr Sikes.'

'I won't,' Twist replied, and hung up.

He walked across the road to an open storm drain that would take Brownlow's concern down into the sewers of Newham just as he was about to drop the phone.

'Oliver!'

Twist looked up and saw Red jogging down the street towards him. He slipped the mobile phone back in his pocket as she approached him, looking surprised.

'They let you out?' she asked, hands on her knees, regaining her breath.

'I escaped,' Twist replied, burying his face inside his hood, trying to figure out where they stood now and why she had returned.

'Oh yeah?'

'Seven care homes. Beltham Young Offenders Institute. I can get out of anywhere.'

Red started laughing. Then he looked up at her and she caught sight of his two black eyes and the strip holding his nose together.

'Your poor nose ...'

He saw her staring at him. Shock registering at his mess of a face and something else, something new that hadn't been there before. Something she was quick to conceal. Twist knew that what had happened between them was over. In the past. And there could be no going back. But what upset him more was that he could now see that Red had taken him up there for a reason. And that, between the Godfather in his pocket and the Devil in the penthouse, he was stuck between a rock and a very hard place.

'Better get back,' Red said. 'Bill's been asking questions. I told him you went to the club with Dodge and Batesy.'

'What d'you do that for?'

'I can't tell him I was coming home with you at six a.m.! He'd *kill* me ...'

Twist winced. He knew now it was true. It was what he feared most and he would do anything to stop it happening.

He watched as Red turned to run back the way she had come. Back to her so-called family.

'We don't have to go back, Red. We could go anywhere in the world. Anywhere … Berlin …'

It sounded dumb. Like a little boy telling a little girl that he was going to take her up in a hot air balloon to a place where there were no lessons, just playtime and beautiful happy children who never had to do any homework.

'And what are we going to do for money?' Red said.

'You could get a job as a dancer …'

'We're this close to payday, Oliver. This close …' she said, holding her finger and thumb close together and peering through the gap at him. 'I'm not backing out now. You want out, I can't make you come with me. But if you don't come they're going to know you peached.'

It was a funny expression but he knew what it meant and it made his blood boil.

'I didn't!'

'Only one way to prove it,' Red said.

It was her last word as she turned and walked, then broke into a slow run. Slow enough that he could catch her but fast enough to force him to make a decision. Go back and finish the job or walk away now and risk never seeing her again.

37

Fagin, Bill and Dodge turned as one when Red walked back in with Twist. Only Batesy stayed where he was, headphones on, staring into a single monitor, watching as Losberne appeared in shot in the cobbled mews behind his gallery and giving urgent hand signals to a van driver who was backing slowly into the loading bay.

'You've got some explaining to do, boy,' Sikes began.

Twist didn't like being called 'boy' any more than Dodge was going to enjoy being roped into his lie.

'I went to a party. A club with Dodge and Batesy ... ask them, go on.'

'What club? What's its name?' Sikes asked.

'Man, I was wasted. I dunno ... it was a pop-up club, look, Dodge,' he said, appealing to Dodge who had turned back towards the monitor, 'help me out here ... Batesy?'

'They both got back hours ago. So what kept you? And what the fuck happened to your face?' Sikes rammed his question home like a fist.

Dodge and Batesy turned now to look at him. Fagin scrutinising him and Sikes staring, leading the case for the prosecution as Red stood back, knowing better than to say a word, staying well out of it.

'I, er ... got arrested.'

Bill exchanged a look with Fagin who shook his head.

'Been having a quiet word, have you?' Sikes went on.

'It wasn't like that! It was this traffic warden, see? I wrote on his van, I mean, they say I wrote on his van but I didn't. It was a set-up but anyway, he got a bit ...' Twist paused, picking his words carefully, '... vexed.'

He watched as Sikes took the information in, Fagin wrinkling his beak, like he had smelt something bad.

'You wrote on his van last night?' Sikes asked.

'Nah, last week. I just ran into him today when I was on my way back here wi—'

Twist stopped himself just in time, risked a desperate glance at Red who mouthed 'no' imperceptibly.

No! On no account can I say I was with you, that I knew you were at the police station ...

Sikes pushed back his chair. It made a short screeching noise as he pushed himself up on his good leg, then, with a single fluid action, gripped the chair back and hurled it across the room at Twist who was forced to put his arms up to prevent it smashing into his face.

It gave Sikes the time he needed. To reach Twist and plant his hand across the span of his face, gripping his cheekbones, the flat of his palm just touching the hairline fracture on the bridge of his nose.

'Cops give you this, did they?' Sikes asked, eyeballing Twist through his outstretched fingers.

'It was the traffic warden ...'

'You need a better story, man!' Dodge spoke at last.

'And what did you give them, eh? To make them let you out?' Sikes whispered in Twist's ear.

'Nothing.'

A silence descended, broken only by a growl from beneath the desks that held the bank of monitors.

'If he'd peached, Bill, why would he come back here?' Red finally asked, stepping forwards towards them.

'Who asked you?' Sikes spat back at her.

'I'm just saying,' Red replied, stepping back again.

'Shhhhh!'

It was Batesy. He was craning forwards, both hands on his headset, trying to hear what Losberne was saying into his mobile phone.

'He's on the phone to Securicor. Confirming the pick-up ...' Batesy said.

In an instant, the mood changed. Fagin began to rub his hands together and Sikes let go of Twist's face.

'Round three,' Fagin said, as Sikes turned back from the monitor and gave Twist a lethal stare.

'You better pray this one goes like clockwork, Twist,' he said.

38

The lock-up was behind King's Cross Station. It wasn't the wasteland it used to be. There were tidy warehouses and shops and cafés backing off from the old red brick arches where solitary car mechanics and storage facilities still existed, throwbacks to the post-industrial decay that Fagin told Twist he'd hidden in after he'd escaped from the holding camp on Bexley Hill and made his raggedy arsed way across country, sleeping in barns, sometimes in ditches, in the summer of 1983.

There was a yard around the entrance to the lock-up and a tall wooden fence that sheltered them from prying eyes but Twist could tell Fagin was on edge. He watched him stroke his beard as he stared down at the wooden crate beneath the half-closed shutters of the lock-up. The plywood box was plastered in labels now, the paint not yet dry that read, *Artworks. This Way Up.*

Twist had sprayed the labels using cans and stencils which he'd pre-cut back at the hotel. He reckoned he'd done a bang-up job but nobody else seemed too impressed. He stood up and took a step back to admire his handiwork, then looked up at Batesy who was stood on the far side of the box looking sour-faced.

'Why's it always gotta be me?' Batesy asked, glowering at Fagin.

'You're the lightest. We could put Bill in there, but we'd need a forklift,' Fagin replied.

Dodge started to laugh. He sounded like a hyena, circling behind Batesy who was gripping the edge of the box straight-armed, refusing to climb in. Twist couldn't help but feel sorry for him. If anything went wrong he would be trapped in the back of a sealed high-security van. He was staring into the crate with an expression on his face like it was full of rats.

'Stop whingeing, Batesy!' Fagin snapped, motioning to Dodge to use force if necessary.

Twist watched as Batesy sidestepped Dodge and took the silver art tube which Fagin had somehow concealed inside his three-quarter-length green coat. As he ducked his head down into the box Dodge stepped forwards and knocked three times.

'Anyone tries to open the crate without doing that first, you set off one of these in their face,' he said, holding up what looked like sticks of dynamite.

'And keep this on at all times,' he added, passing Batesy a bunched up latex mask. Batesy looked up at them out of the box like a dog that sensed it was about to be abandoned.

Fagin stepped forwards and pushed his head down, taking the lid from Twist and sliding it closed, holding it down with one hand while motioning for Twist to fetch the hammer from the lock-up and nail it shut.

'Losberne's arranged the pick-up for eleven thirty,' Fagin said, turning to Twist. 'How's that sign coming on?'

Twist stopped hammering and walked into the lock-up. He picked up a plywood sign about ten foot by two foot. It read *St Pancras Fine Arts*.

Then they waited. About twenty minutes later an armoured Securicor van backed up towards the steel shutter of the lock-up above which Twist's sign, *St Pancras Fine Arts*, now hung.

Twist walked to the steel shutter and banged on it twice. It rolled up, revealing Dodge in overalls and the crate on a cart which he wheeled over to the rear doors of the van as they were being opened by one of the van's guards.

Together, Dodge, Twist and the guard slid the crate down a steel ramp into the back of the van. Then the guard went back to the cab and came back with a clipboard which he held up for Dodge to sign.

'Straight to our gallery in W1,' Dodge said, Twist watching as the guard checked his itinerary.

'Should be there in twenty,' he said, adding, 'Just the one pick up on the way' as he slammed the doors shut, sliding a hinged metal plate across them which he padlocked, before returning to the front, climbing in and signalling to the driver to start the engine.

Dodge waved as the van pulled away, watching it until it had disappeared round the corner before pulling down the steel shutters and climbing up a stepladder to rip down the St Pancras Fine Arts sign.

Ten minutes later Twist was stepping up the same ladder to put the finishing touches on a painted sign above a rented garage door in a mews behind New Burlington Gardens. This

time the sign read *St Pancras West*. He looked down nervously as he heard the door being unlocked from the inside,
watching it open slowly, then breathing a sigh of relief as
Fagin's nose emerged from within. Twist craned his neck and
stared down into the empty space. There were bare concrete
walls where there should have been paintings.

'Don't worry,' Fagin said, 'they're here to pick up a bronze
statue of the Trojan horse. Not buy the Mona Lisa.'

39

Less than a quarter of a mile away, the Securicor van was parked outside the Losberne Gallery where men in overalls and white gloves were carefully removing the three Hogarths from the wall, supervised by an anxious-looking Losberne as they were placed, one at a time, into a padded packing crate which was then slid onto a trolley and wheeled out to the vehicle.

'Little bitch,' Losberne muttered to the guard, 'she was up to something. I tell you that's the last time I interview an intern who hasn't come personally recommended.'

He winced as Brittles and the Securicor guard lifted the crate marked 'H' into the back of the armoured van then reached out to hold the arm of the guard just as he was about to close and lock the rear doors.

'Excuse me,' he said, staring in at the other crate, 'I thought you were just taking ours?'

'We had another drop-off nearby,' the guard said, checking his clipboard, 'St Pancras West ring a bell?'

Losberne shook his head.

'Never heard of it,' he said, as he took the guard's clipboard and signed the paperwork, watching as the guard locked the rear doors, climbed into the cab and told the driver to get under way.

He watched as the van pulled slowly out into the middle of the road and shook his head as he walked back into his gallery, pausing by force of habit to check his reflection in the mirror, then pausing again by his receptionist's desk to ask her to check his schedule. It was a daily request that gave him just long enough to stare down her cleavage as she clicked onto his weekly calendar.

'You ever heard of St Pancras Fine Arts, Rosie?' he asked when she looked up.

'I'll Google it,' she said.

It was the first time he'd sat in the armchair facing her desk and he turned, feeling strangely vacant, looking out in the direction the van disappeared in, wondering how many small-time dealers there were in London, like St Pancras Fine Arts, struggling to make an honest living.

He watched as she scanned down the results, then turned and looked back at the road as a black BMW 5 series pulled out from where it had been parked across the street. He felt a sharp pain in his chest as he saw the girl in the passenger seat. She was sat next to a late-twenties male with a livid scar that ran down from his hairline to his right cheekbone.

Then he was up but unsteady on his feet, running for the door as the colour drained from his cheeks.

'Get me Securicor on the phone. Now!' he shouted, startling his receptionist as the BMW disappeared out of sight.

'Sir! They're on the line,' she said, holding up the phone and watching as he put it up to his ear.

'Hello, yes, yes, this is Dr Losberne ... Yes, your men just picked it up. No, everything is not fucking OK,' he said, shaking his head. 'I think I'm being robbed.'

40

There were pinpricks of light in the darkness. Tiny holes drilled deliberately in the top right-hand corner of each side of the crate. They were about three millimetres in diameter. Not enough to see in or out through, but wide enough for Batesy to suck fresh air into his mouth as he fumbled with his mask. It wasn't easy. His palms were clammy and the sweat ran down his fingertips which he was running across the mask face, like a blind man getting acquainted with a stranger.

When the mask was on it became even harder to breathe and he groped in each corner until he found the catch and gently pushed the lid to one side, feeling the cold air on his face as his in-breath drew it through the mouth of the mask. He could hear sounds now. Bryan Adams' 'Summer of '69' playing on the radio in the cab. He climbed out of the crate as they banked into a corner, and he cursed as he felt himself slip, fall and knock the lid against the quarter-inch-thick steel wall of the van.

BAM!

It sounded like a bass drum. He froze momentarily, thinking that if he could hear the radio in the cab then odds on the security guards in there could hear large bangs coming from the rear of the van. So he didn't have time to waste. The van appeared to be slowing down but that had to be because they were in traffic. Any moment now they'd take the next exit, slow down and stick a shotgun in his face.

The crowbar felt reassuring in his hand as he prised open the six foot by four foot crate containing the Hogarths. Pulling the three paintings from the box he pushed out the blade of his craft knife and sliced each carefully where it met its frame then rolled them up together until all three fitted snugly inside his silver art tube. It was almost too easy. Like taking art from the walls of a kindergarten ... until the van braked at the worst moment imaginable.

He was half in the crate fishing for the smoke bombs as the van lurched off the road and he was thrown forwards against the cab wall, forcing him to use his hands to protect himself from the impact. Hands which contained two smoke bombs which he heard smack the rear wall, then feeling the cold outrush of CO_2 a millisecond before a toxic cloud of purple gas hit him in the face, stinging his eyes and forcing him to the floor, choking, trying to catch his breath.

Red clocked the van first. Pulling into the slow lane before braking hard and sideswiping off the road into a police observation lay-by.

'They've stopped, shit, they're getting out,' she said, watching as the cab doors opened and steel toecapped boots hit the tarmac. The two big men, who looked to be former military, stepped out of the van brandishing a pair of pump-action twelve-gauge shotguns. She looked across at Sikes who was sizing them up. The one six four and broad, the other touching five ten but with a kind of compressed energy and a look in his eyes, like he was enjoying himself, willing there to be a robbery so he could hurt someone.

Sikes slowed to almost a crawl, a car horn blasting behind him as he pulled into the slow lane, buying more time to figure out his next move as purple smoke spilled out of the back of the van, engulfing the guards who had their shotguns at their hips, taking no chances, unable to see Batesy. Red just hoped, for his sake, he'd made it out of the crate, knowing full well that if the smoke bombs had gone off then the chances were he was most likely choking to death.

She looked across at Sikes. His eyes had turned black. She could see his knuckles through his leather driving gloves where he was gripping the steering wheel, pulling the car in now, tight behind the van, the guards too busy waiting for the smoke to clear to see what was going on behind them – then backing up a couple of paces as a figure in a Prince Harry mask stumbled out of the back and collapsed face down at their feet.

'Bollocks to this!'

She felt Sikes's arm brush past her knees as he reached for the glove compartment, pulling out his own mask and cocking his Beretta.

'Tell him I'm going in. Plan B,' he said.

'Bill, no …' she managed, but it was too late. He was already out of the car, a black shadow disappearing into the purple haze.

The tall guard didn't know what hit him. The pistol caught him hard round the right side of his face and knocked him cold. Sikes didn't wait to see him hit the floor but stepped over to the second guard who had just torn off Batesy's mask and was trying to drag him by the hair back into the van to lock him up.

Red was out of the car now, running towards Sikes as he stabbed the barrel of the Beretta into the side of the second guard's face, holding it there, angling down into his body through his skull so the bullet couldn't miss. She watched as the guard let go of Batesy's hair and dropped his shotgun and Sikes turned him around, forcing him to his knees while reaching down to pick up Batesy's mask, shouting at him to 'man the fuck up' and put it back on.

She saw all this because of the wind which was blowing in gusts, lifting the purple smoke just long enough for her to see Sikes, turning towards her, pointing to his face and shouting at her too.

'Get your fucking mask on!'

And then she saw him take aim up at the red brick wall on the side of the road and open fire. Once, twice, three times, the bullets ricocheted up off the brick until there was a smash and the fourth bullet penetrated the lens of the CCTV camera. The volley lasting no more than two seconds from beginning to end. Just long enough for the big man on his knees to pivot on his right foot and slam his fist into Sike's ribcage right over his heart.

Red watched Sikes step sideways, reeling from the blow, then cock the pistol and shove it in the guard's face, forcing him to lie flat on the floor as she heard a siren wailing behind her.

'Police!' she yelled, watching Sikes look beyond her then look back down and shift his aim from the base of the man's skull to the back of his right knee.

'Tube!' Sikes yelled at Batesy, who was back on his feet, unsteady but holding out the artwork doing exactly what he was told.

'Now run,' Sikes said, gesturing with the gun, but as she turned, Red saw the first cop was already out of the car and taking up a firing position behind the passenger door, some fifty yards behind them.

She watched as Batesy stared at Sikes through the mask in disbelief then put his hands up as Sikes lifted the gun and pointed it at his chest.

'Bill no!' she heard herself scream but the moment had passed and she stepped back as Batesy brushed past her, his arms still up in the air, jogging back to where the cops were standing, aiming at him, telling him to walk not run as he closed the gap between them.

And then she heard the shot. It rang in her ears and she heard a man screaming in pain. She turned to see a pool of blood spreading out on the ground and the guard squirming in agony, blinking in disbelief at the fragments of his kneecap which were lying on the tarmac next to his face.

She crouched, worried the cops were going to open fire but saw they were keeping their sights on Batesy. He streaked past them to their left but they held their fire, instead returning their aim to the chaos in the smoke that now blanketed the road, four feet deep from side to side.

She looked at Sikes, his gimlet eyes shining through the slits in his mask, and she wondered if this was the moment when he felt his existence made sense.

'You good? Watch what I do,' he said, holding the tube parallel with his leg and letting it fall gently to the ground rolling towards her, then winking at her and stepping back into the van as the cop by the right door fired a volley of three warning shots and his friend started with the loud hailer.

'Drop your weapons and raise your hands above your heads and you will not be harmed,' he said, as she crawled out of sight, groping for the silver tube until she had it and pulled the strap over her shoulder.

She heard a volley of fire behind her. The sharp percussion of the Beretta as Sikes fired a controlled burst at each door of the cop car, the bullets slamming home, silencing them as he rushed forwards into the smoke towards the BMW. There was only one way out and she watched him take it, gunning the engine then reversing at speed at the police car, the cop on the left getting off a single round before the BMW smashed into the front of the squad car and accelerated away.

It was now, she thought, it was now or never as she crouched, keeping low, moving past the Securicor van in the opposite direction to the police, upping her speed to a comfortable fifteen hundred metre pace, wondering how in hell they were going to get away with it this time.

'He said twenty minutes. Where are they?' Dodge shouted, skidding his BMX in a perfect left turn to a stop in front of Fagin and Twist. Fagin had his phone to his ear.

'Nancy's coming on foot,' Fagin replied, clicking his mobile off.

'Time for a diversion. Twist?' Dodge said, meeting Twist's eye.

'Bill said the boy must stay where I can see him,' Fagin replied.

'He's faster than me though,' Dodge said, watching Fagin think about this, then nod and reach inside the folds of his green overcoat for two identical silver art tubes.

'Go!' he shouted, slapping them on the back as they pulled on their Prince Harry masks and snatched a tube each.

41

They had a call for a black 5 series and they came off Park Lane, sharp left at the BMW dealers, Bedwin accelerating east on Aldford Street then north on South Audley Street before taking a hard right on Mount Street as the controller on the radio told them that there were two suspects; one male in the car, armed and dangerous, and the other a male juvenile on foot heading south-east.

'Losberne said a girl ...' said Brownlow, staring through the windscreen at the redhead running in the opposite direction, past them, her face wrapped in a headscarf, making like she was out exercising, on her way to Hyde Park, as opposed to scarpering with $20 million of art strapped to her back.

'Looter chic,' Brownlow said, 'slow down. Yes ... yes! That's her. Look at the tube. She's got the art! Pull in! That's got to be her!'

Bedwin mounted the pavement fifty yards behind her as she headed west along Mount Street. Brownlow got out, keeping a respectful distance, breathing steadily, putting other pedestrians between her and him and slowing to a walk when she looked behind her, scanning the pavement to see if anyone had picked up her trail.

'Suspect, female, heading west,' he said, speaking into the radio in the front pocket of his herringbone tweed as two masked and hooded figures burst out of the street in front of him and accelerated towards the girl, one running, the other on a BMX, and both of them carrying identical silver art tubes.

He started to run as the one on the BMX pulled what looked a red stick from his backpack, about ten inches long, smacked the base of it on the crossbars of his bike then tossed it behind him, red smoke billowing out behind. It sent the pedestrians in front of Brownlow into a panic and made it hard for him to maintain his pace, as the smoke blocked his line of sight with the boy who appeared to be taking the tube from the girl.

He spoke urgently into his radio, telling Bedwin to loop back around in the car and hit them before they crossed Park Lane into Hyde Park where it would be much harder to reach them, particularly if they headed to the eight-exit subway beneath the roundabout in the park's south-western corner.

But then the second male, the runner, made it harder again, this time green smoke billowing up, shrouding the movement of the tubes which the little bastards were shuffling between them like cups in a shell game. It forced him to run faster, something he couldn't recall having done in the last ten years.

'Er, heading west …' he said, watching as the runner and the BMX peeled away from the girl. 'Er, heading west, south and …'

He looked up as Bedwin sped past him and pulled hard left, and watched in disbelief as the kid on the BMX hopped up onto the bonnet, rode across it, and dropped off the far side, as the runner and the girl split, forcing him to play their game and pick one tube, hoping his colleagues recovered the other two.

He watched as the runner slowed, crossed the road then doubled back on the pavement on the far side.

'East,' he coughed into the radio, checking back for cars then making his mind up and turning and sprinting after the boy coming at him fast and low from behind a row of parked four by fours, watching him sidestep a man in a blue overcoat and accelerate holding the tube under his left arm.

The gap appeared from nowhere. Four feet between a Land Rover and a white van. And Browmlow launched himself horizontally at the boy as he reached it, finding himself clutching at air as the boy leapt, both feet in the air. He felt the top of his head graze the sole of the runner's shoe, turning his head just before he hit the railings to see the kid use the impact to tuck into a ball then stretch out, his back arched and his feet outstretched to land back on the pavement, feet forward, soaking up the impact in his knees before springing back into his run without missing a beat.

He was flat on his back now, staring up at the sky. Maybe he wasn't concussed. Maybe there *was* a police helicopter above the park. There was only one thing he could say for sure.

He was getting too old for this shit.

42

Twist was running south down the one-way street making for the maze of subterranean walkways beneath the round-about. He looked across the four lanes to his right that fed the roundabout from the conurbation of Hyde Park Corner. It gave him a view of a giant bronze man in the park. A warrior of some kind about twenty feet tall holding a sword and a shield but otherwise naked. Twist could almost hear him, defiant, calm, saying, *Come on, if you think you're hard enough* to whoever or whatever was coming at him, which as far as Twist could see was a crowd heading towards a Christmas-themed fairground about three weeks too late.

It was called the Winter Wonderland but there wasn't very much wonderful about it. The punters looked retarded, panning out like zombies looking to sink their teeth into something. They reminded him of the cow people he saw in the Newham retail park when he went to steal fresh cans, staring in through the windows of the superstores. Dull-eyed, bovine creatures, out grazing, looking for something to take home and chew on.

He cut right, bursting across the traffic which streamed down four lanes, looking up as a helicopter crossed heading south-east, the direction Dodge had gone in. He saw the first cop a second after, running south and approaching the naked warrior from the north side of the park. He put on the pace and cut into the herd, pulling off his mask and handing it to a small boy before slowing to a walk and ducking under a cordon and into Santa's Grotto, guessing correctly that the fat guy must have packed up and gone home already.

Dodge heard the helicopter before he saw it pass over Leicester Square. He had to avoid it or he'd never lose the police car on his tail. He reached the pedestrian zone and veered between two bollards down a narrow passage to the right of the square, using the downhill slope to build his speed, standing on the pedals, looking back as the squad car skidded then wedged itself hard between the concrete posts.

He pedalled out of the alleyway, rode blind across the street and nearly got flattened by a police motorcyclist on a BMW 1150 GS. It was a heavy bike. Not good for off-road but that didn't help Dodge much. He was on the road now and the GS came down on him like a great bird, swooping in at him from the right.

When the road curved left to Trafalgar Square he cut in front of a bus, hopped up onto the kerb and, through a series of swift cuts, made his way through the throng to a left turn that would take him to some steps on the Mall.

He swerved far out across the road, around a statue of an old general on a horse then came up fast to the top of the steps. There were about twenty, then a platform then another twenty. He scattered a group of skaters whose curses turned to a cheer when the police motorbike appeared out of the side street behind him.

Racing to the edge of the terrace he took off, landing on the walkway and bouncing once, hitting down a second time then drawing the handlebars up into his chest and pushing down hard on the pedals, lifting the bike up.

There was no way the cop was following him and he heard the screech as the two hundred and fifty kilo motorbike skidded to a stop at the top of the steps. He turned to see the guy looking down, furious, as Dodge bowed to the skaters before turning and accelerating away.

Sikes was driving more slowly now. He must have aimed his shots well because there were no police cars in pursuit. It was hard to catch a thief in a BMW when your front tyres were blown out. He'd driven hard at the police, sending them scattering, then taken a series of right turns that had led him around the scene of the stand-off and back north up to the point where he guessed he'd find Batesy.

Batesy had called in from the south side of the Telecom tower having first made for cover, losing his pursuers among the crowds of tourists on Oxford Street before moving up to hide in the private garden in the centre of Portman Square. Three minutes had passed since Sikes had taken his call and told him to head south to the north end of Fitzroy Street where there was an underground NCP car park.

Which is where Sikes was approaching now, watching Batesy, shoulders hunched like the weight of the world was upon them, hurrying along, relief in his eyes as the car slowed to a stop and the passenger door popped open.

'Oi, mate, we're clear,' Sikes said.

'You sure?'

'Sure I'm sure. Hop in.'

Batesy got in and shut the door after him, the car pulling slowly out.

'Sorry about the mask, Bill,' Batesy said, looking nervously at Sikes as he turned out onto the Marylebone Road heading east towards King's Cross.

'Nothing to worry about mate, nothing to worry about at all,' Sikes said, watching the lights go green outside Madame Tussauds.

CCTV footage of the Securicor van played on the monitor. It showed the guards shrouded in smoke opening the back of the van as Sikes stepped into the frame, smashed the shorter guard in the face with the butt of his pistol then yanked Batesy up off the floor by his arm.

'I've been over the tapes – all the escape routes, nothing but Prince Harry every which way.'

The CCTV operator looked up at Bedwin and Brownlow who were stood behind him, back in the basement of New Scotland Yard.

'Go back a second, when he pulls the guy up off the floor ...' Bedwin said.

Brownlow looked down at the monitor as the technician paused, rewound, then froze the image of the thief in the mask tumbling out of the back of the van, gasping for air.

With all the smoke it was hard to see what was going on but Bedwin was nothing if not determined.

'Can you zoom in? There's something wrong with the angle of the mask,' she said.

The technician zoomed in on the mask itself and then it became clear. It was actually sat on the top of his head.

'Look, he's pushed it back,' Bedwin said, leaning forwards to touch it, watching Brownlow thinking …

Hmmm, and who have we here?

43

There were two discarded Prince Harry masks on the floor. Twist, Dodge and Red were stood watching Fagin. He was wearing a pair of cotton gloves and he was standing in the corner of the room he called his laboratory but to Twist's mind it looked more like an operating room. A cold steel table top with the three Hogarths unfurled on it.

Fagin had already checked the edges where Batesy had cut them free and now he was poring over them with an electronic magnascope, humming, occasionally rising an octave when he found further evidence of their authenticity.

'Good work. Some imperfections but what is perfect after all? There is no such thing,' he mused, turning to face them, 'in art … or in crime.'

He looked behind them as footsteps approached down the corridor.

'Maybe that's Batesy now,' he said.

But it wasn't. It was a man and his dog. A dog that went everywhere the man went.

'Got them?' Sikes said, a leather leash taut round his left hand as he strained to maintain balance and keep Bullseye from running amok.

Fagin cast his hand behind him and nodded.

'Sorted,' Sikes said, letting Bullseye pull him across the room towards Fagin who often fed him out-of-date sausages to stay on his sweet side.

'You seen Batesy, mate?' Dodge asked as Sikes passed him, then watched in horror as the punch came from nowhere.

It was a straight right across the body, slamming into Twist's jaw, knocking him to the ground. Fagin, Dodge and Red all turned and stared at Sikes. Stunned silence as Twist spat blood and reached up to check that his jaw wasn't broken.

'Bill?!' Red said, looking down at Twist, thinking it was the second time he'd been punched and she'd been unable to help him.

'He's a grass!' Sikes replied, watching Fagin who was shaking his head in disbelief.

'We got the paintings Bill ...' Fagin said.

'Right. So the van just suddenly stops. The guards pile out. They knew what was going down. Same morning he's popped round the station for a little chat.'

Dodge was kneeling by Twist, trying to help him up but Sikes pushed past him and grabbed Twist by the hair.

'I didn't tell them anything!' Twist said.

'Worked you over good, didn't they?' Sikes said, pushing his palm against the bridge of Twist's nose.

It brought water to Twist's eyes but he didn't scream. He wasn't going to give Sikes the satisfaction.

'It was the traffic warden—' he began.

'The traffic warden? You can't even come up with a decent lie!'

'It's true!'

Red opened her mouth to say something but stopped herself. Twist could see that she was completely torn. He turned away from her, appealing to Fagin.

'What I need to know, Twist, is how you hold up under a beating,' Sikes continued. 'Bet you fall to pieces, eh? Tell them anything to make them stop ...'

'Easy, Bill ...' warned Fagin.

'Only one way to find out. You want some more, boy?'

Sikes released Twist's hair but simultaneously whipped the chain holding Bullseye against the dog's face catching it on its nose. Its jaws snapped an inch from Twist's face but as he drew back he felt a weight bearing down on him and he looked up to see Sikes kneeling on his shoulders as he tried to scramble away, then snatching him by the lapels, hoisting him to his feet and hurling him into one of the two straight-backed chairs facing Fagin's desk.

'Take off his hoodie,' Sikes said, turning to Dodge who stared back reluctantly, looking at Twist then back at Sikes, before pulling it from Twist's back, leaving him in his sweat-soaked T-shirt.

'Hold him,' Sikes said.

Twist felt Dodge's hands grip his wrists, pulling them behind the chair. He didn't struggle. He still felt sick from the punch. There was no way he would make it out of the room before the dog caught him.

'Bill, please ...' Red began, Twist looking up and seeing genuine fear in her eyes as Sikes rounded on her.

'Are you soft on him?'

'No!'

'Then not. Another. Word.'

He turned to Dodge whose grip had relaxed.

'Mate ...' Dodge said, appealing to Sikes.

'I said hold him!' Sikes snapped. 'Do it or you're next.'

Twist felt Dodge's grip on his wrists tighten.

'Which hand d'ya do your writing with? All those pretty pictures ... I'd have clocked it if you were a lefty.'

Bill took the free chair and pulled it up alongside Twist. Then he grabbed his right hand by the thumb, twisting it back so that Twist had to follow his lead and lay his right arm flat on the chair.

'You make a sound through any of this, we're gonna know you squealed.'

'We need him, Bill,' Fagin said, finally.

'Nance can do anything he does,' Sikes replied, looking at her, challenging her.

Twist looked from Sikes to Red. She looked desperate. Torn in half.

'He's faster than me. Better climber too ...' she said.

'I told you to shut up!' Sikes shouted back at her, turning to Dodge.

'You got him?'

Twist stared straight up into Sikes's eyes, maintaining contact as he drew his right fist up, psyching himself up, ready to take the blow and swallow the pain. But the punch wasn't for him. It was for the dog. A rabbit punch to the nose.

It went crazy. Its backbone kinked as it lurched up at Sikes's hand but he held it tight by the collar as it writhed and tugged, its jaws opening and closing, making a high, keening sound, a mixture of rage and pain.

'Right, Bullseye, when I say the word …'

Red stepped forwards. She couldn't bear it any more. Twist looked at Sikes's face. It was the first time he'd seen him look surprised.

'What are you doing?'

'You're making a mistake.' Red said it like a warning.

'A mistake?'

'The traffic warden hit him. It's true!'

Twist couldn't believe what he was hearing and he felt his fear shift. From what was about to happen to him to what Sikes might do to her if she said what he thought she was about to say.

'And how would you know?'

'I was there!' she said, steel in her voice.

'What?'

'We were on our way home. The traffic warden decked him, just like he said.'

'On your way home from where?'

'We … spent the night together.'

She gulped, wondering how the hell she was going to survive the next five minutes.

For a moment Bill was open-mouthed, incapable of speech. Then he pulled a gun and Twist saw Red flinch as he handed Bullseye's leash to Fagin and then passed him the gun. Fagin cast Twist a look of complete confusion, then an apology as he raised the gun, tottering as the beast pulled him off balance.

'He moves, shoot him,' Sikes said to the old man, then turned, grabbed Red by the hair and dragged her struggling out of Fagin's laboratory.

The door slammed shut behind them. Fagin held onto the gun but Twist felt Dodge release his grip on his wrists. They exchanged a horrified look as they heard another door, further down the corridor open, slam shut and lock from the inside.

An early morning jogger had called the fire brigade on his mobile at first light. It was still smouldering when the police called it in half an hour later. The windows were black from the smoke that was billowing out through the window on the driver's door. The oxygen had ensured that the fire had raged inside the car. The leather seats had burnt up right down to the springs. All the plastic fittings had melted and one small flame still flickered, feeding on what was left of the sponge cushioning of the front passenger seat.

Brownlow stepped out of the passenger side of his vehicle and nodded to Bedwin. They walked over to the burning wreck together, winding their way through weeds and rubble, the local bobby turning to them, stepping back, deferring to their authority.

'You check the boot yet?' Brownlow asked him.

The cop shook his head and Brownlow stepped up to the back of the vehicle, the BMW badge blackened on the boot above the lock. Brownlow turned to the cop who handed him a crowbar and took a step back as he wedged it in by the lock and began to work it hard against the mechanism.

There was a pop and a hiss of fetid air. Like pork burnt and left to rot. Brownlow covered his mouth and pushed down on the crowbar, his whole weight on it. The boot swung open and Brownlow took a step back as the cop put his hand up to his mouth.

The shape of a boy's body was visible immediately. It had carbonised and the arms had shrunk. They were stick thin and had hooked claws for hands. The flesh was gone from the skull. It was shining and black and the mouth was open in a scream.

He had been roasted alive.

Dodge was pacing up and down, phone clamped to his ear, desperately trying to reach his friend, Fagin still holding the gun on Twist.

'This isn't like him – he gets withdrawal symptoms if he's not plugged in,' Dodge said.

'Maybe he's lost his phone,' Fagin replied.

'Not all of them! I've got to go back and look for him.'

The three of them turned towards the door as it opened.

'Nobody's going anywhere,' Sikes said, walking into the room, his arm tight around Red's waist, her eyes downcast, staring at the floor.

'You bastard ...' Twist stood up but felt Dodge's hands on his shoulders, pushing him back into the chair.

'Don't do it ...' Dodge warned him.

Sikes ignored Twist and walked calmly over to the paintings, rolled them up and slotted them back into the art tube. Twist struggled to get past Dodge who was in front of him now, blocking him from reaching Sikes, as Fagin shook his head, lowered the gun and placed it on the desk.

'Look at me, you son of a bitch!' Twist shouted across at Sikes.

'Twist, no ...' Dodge said.

'Stop, everyone!' Fagin shouted, raising his arms. 'Let's keep this in perspective. We've got the first three Hogarths. Result. But the job's not finished. When Batesy turns up we'll need to regroup and work out how we're going to pinch the remaining three from wherever Sotheby's decide to put them up for auction.'

Sikes ignored the hubbub from the boys and spoke directly to Fagin.

'Sotheby's aren't deciding anything,' he said, calmly. 'Rodchenko has had a conversation with the owner of the remaining three pictures. He's been clear with him. The auction isn't going to take place in the auction house itself. The vault and the security is too slick. Rodchenko has leant on him. The auction is going to take place in the hotel in the Shard. As for the first three, he wants them tonight. Just to be safe.'

'When do we get paid?' Fagin asked.

'Half when he gets these,' Sikes said, holding out his hand for the gun as Fagin passed it to him, 'and half when he's got the other three.'

Fagin didn't respond.

'Show's over, Twist,' Sikes said, pointing it at his chest.

'The Shard, Bill. Think!' Fagin interjected. 'With five runners it's possible. Not with four.'

He stepped up, not between them but to the side, careful to stay out of the firing line, but it was Dodge who Twist was watching.

'Five? What about Bate—' Dodge began, staring at Sikes then at Fagin.

'Batesy didn't make it,' Sikes said.

Twist watched Dodge's face move from shock to horror to blind rage as he took a step forwards, shook his head then launched himself at Sikes.

'You …'

But Sikes raised the gun. He pointed it at Dodge's face.

'We do the job. Exactly like we planned it. OK?' Sikes said, pointing the gun back at Twist. 'You step out of line again, I'll kill you.'

Twist looked at him. He couldn't think of anyone in his life he'd hated more.

'You can't kill all of us,' he said, watching as Sikes hugged Red closer to his side then raised the gun and pointed it at her head.

'I'll kill you. And then I'll kill her,' he replied.

Twist watched him turn and hustle Red out of the door. Then, as soon as he was gone, Fagin looked from Dodge to Twist and sighed.

'Better listen to what the man says, boys,' Fagin said. 'Big day tomorrow ...'

Twist stood to follow Dodge out. He was shaking. When he reached the door he felt an arm on his shoulder.

'Twist,' Fagin said, 'I've been reviewing the situation and I think you and I ought to have a little chat.'

44

There were two men in suits stood outside the building. They were talking into their mobiles and one of them was smoking. They were just ten yards apart, talking to one another on the phones and nobody noticed both of them watching as the security guard stepped out of the glass tower and crossed the road, whistling to himself, telling himself that today was going to be different with the pretty girl who ran the van where he bought his coffee each morning.

The Suits watched him as he took a left into a cobbled pedestrian zone demarcated by black cast-iron bollards. The van was nestled against the railings which protected an old Elizabethan era church. It was a shining aluminium van built around a 200cc Vespa. It had *Forza* written on the side. The security guard thought it meant 'Strength'.

The two Suits stayed ten metres apart from one another the whole way. The one in front reached the van first and joined the queue, stepping in close behind the guard. Close enough to hear him ask for his usual.

'Two sugars with that …' he said, fingering his ID which hung on a yellow ribbon around his neck, trying to summon up the courage, telling himself that this Italian girl stirring his latte didn't want a condo in St Tropez or heli-skiing in Klosters. She wasn't interested in marrying Tim, the captain of industry, or Ralph, the Derivatives whizz. She wanted a salt of the earth Englishman. She wanted him.

But then something poked him hard in the left kidney. Hard enough to be deliberate, not a mistake. And certainly hard enough for him to forget about asking for her number and focus instead upon turning around, eyes blazing to confront the nearest suspect.

Who, by the cut of his jib, was most likely a trader from one of the private equity funds high up in the sky above his work station. A suit who right now was staring at his girl, smiling, pushing to the front of the queue.

'Excuse me, do you mind if I …?' said the suit.

The guard stood his ground but he didn't want to be a dick about it. Not in front of the girl whose Cake Of The Day the Suit was eyeing wolfishly, set out so prettily on the little fold-out table at the front of her stall.

'All right, gorge?' the Suit said.

He said it loud and it in an accent that made the guard resent him even more. Loud enough to muffle a faint beep that came from the breast pocket of his jacket as the suit pushed past him towards the girl who was laughing, looking at the interloper like he was something special, something she hadn't seen before.

Twist took off the suit jacket and hung it on the back of his chair and took a sip of his tea. He'd only worn a suit once before and that had been during his appeal. He'd borrowed it from a mate who was three inches shorter than him. It had made him look stupid and he was sure the jury had held that against him, the big kid who'd grown up too fast and turned into a bully and needed to be taught a lesson.

But this one felt different. It fitted him better around his chest and across his shoulders and right down to the polished black boots. And it was made in a fine, black wool and had no shiny patches on the knees or the elbows. It was the kind of suit he could get used to wearing. The kind of suit he could see that Red would like. No fancy stuff. Sharp but understated.

He looked up from his tea and saw Dodge sit down opposite him. He was grinning like a jackal, sliding something across the café table towards him covered by his right hand. Twist looked down and saw a packet of red Marlboros next to his teacup.

He shook his head but Dodge insisted so he took the packet and opened it. The seal had already been broken and there were only four cigarettes left in it. Which left plenty of space for a flat black metal device, the size of a bank card but fatter, about the width of his index finger.

He pushed the pack back at Dodge, then pulled a pair of sunglasses from his jacket pocket, put them on then stood up and walked to the Gents to change.

The guard took his time getting back. They watched him cross the street from the café. He looked beaten and he frowned when he saw the tourist in the T-shirt and shades posing for a portrait slap bang in the middle of the entrance it was his job to police.

'Scuse, mate,' he muttered, reaching for the ID card which hung round his neck, drawing it through the swipe point and reaching for the keypad to punch in his four digit password.

*

They watched the man take his clothes off. First his jacket, then his tie, unfastening it and unbuttoning his shirt, turning it to pull it off his muscular shoulders and up from out of his belt where his abs had run to fat.

It had taken ten minutes from the foot of the Shard to reach the basement changing room of the Fitness First off Chancery Lane. They had raced the entire route. On strict starter's orders, a flat run, no fancy footwork but at a pace, a little over a mile through the City, through pedestrians and drivers moving impatiently towards lunch.

They watched as the man stood up, turned and took the bait, looking around him to see if anyone else had seen it. They watched as he looked their way, at two young men sat leaning forwards, breathing heavily, wearing running shorts and T-shirts drenched in sweat.

'Nope,' Dodge replied, looking across at Twist who was similarly attired.

'You must have dropped it,' Twist shrugged, as he stood up and walked past the man across the changing room.

By the time the twenty pound note was in the man's wallet Twist had switched the padlock on his locker for an identical one and was halfway to the lavatory.

Dodge watched the man put the wallet in the locker, turn the key of the new padlock then walk towards the stairs and up to his workout in the gym.

When Twist came out of the lavatory cubicle he took watch at the foot of the stairs as Dodge unlocked the padlock, took out the police uniform inside, folded it carefully and slid it into his rucksack.

Dodge allowed himself a smile but paused before closing the locker fully. Twist watched, quietly amused as he reached back inside, pulled out the man's wallet, took back his twenty pound note then snapped the padlock shut.

The sun was hovering like an apparition above the jagged tip of the Shard as Twist and Dodge clambered up onto the roof of the red-bricked warehouse from the fire escape, Dodge telling him they had to get off the street and lie up until FBoss gave them the signal.

Twist looked around at the rooftops, tracing its line across the horizon as if he was drawing it. It had been his idea to come back this way. To take the left-hand fork through Shoreditch past the warehouse and the wild party to the Russian's penthouse which rose like an eagle's eyerie above the streets of Bethnal Green below.

'Strip.'

Twist turned and saw that Dodge was ahead of him again. Somehow more focused and alert even now that they had completed the tasks allotted to them. He was stood in his boxers, pulling on a pair of jeans, wasting no time to beat the winter wind that blew against his back.

Twist knew what he was looking for but in the daylight the grey sky sucked the colour out of buildings so that it was hard to see the shining half dome which had guided Red as she'd led him, illuminated, across the graveyard and along the church wall to begin the climb up to the penthouse and the pool a week ago.

He stepped forwards, staring out to the north-east, and saw what looked like a dome on the horizon and strained his eyes until he was sure that it was their dome, in profile, calling him back again.

'Where are you going?' Dodge said, breaking the spell.

Twist looked down at his feet. They had carried him twenty feet towards the penthouse across the flat roof.

'Can you give me an hour?' he said, looking back at Dodge, looking him straight in the eye.

Dodge shook his head.

'We've got to get back,' he said. 'You heard what Sikes said. Trust me, he's serious …'

'There's something I need to do,' Twist went on, crossing his fingers behind his back. Hoping that Dodge would have more sense than to ask and implicate himself but realising too late, when Dodge didn't respond, that he had misjudged his friend.

'You never …' Dodge began, narrowing his eyes, battling to keep the lid on the ugly idea that now presented itself.

Twist watched him freeze, his whole body tensing up, staring back, searching for some kind of reassurance that he would not be able to give him without endangering him.

'What?' Twist asked, but knew the question and began to answer it, in the hope that his response would bring them closer, show that they were two minds, thinking alike.

'No—' Twist began.

But Dodge cut him off. He just had to ask the question out loud. Twist could see that.

'You been talkin' to the pigs?'

'No! I wouldn't do that. Let's call it – a gamble …'

Twist watched Dodge's brow furrow.

'A gamble?'

'A spot of Russian roulette.'

Dodge now looked completely mystified.

'Please, mate. Wait for me here. Please. We'll tell FBoss the guard took his break late.'

But Dodge didn't like it.

'Listen! You got me into this, man,' Twist started, pointing his finger at Dodge who was shaking his head. 'Red's in trouble. More trouble than you know. You've got to let me go. It's the only chance she's got.'

Dodge weighed this information. He prided himself on knowing everything, passing on his wisdom to newcomers, and this revelation hurt his pride.

'Half an hour, tops,' Twist went on, not waiting for approval but turning on his heel and racing back across the rooftop, retracing the way that Red had led him, the night she had wanted him to see and to understand the tie that Sikes had made and the promise that must be broken.

The drop was still perilous as Twist climbed up the glass wall of the apartment block and clambered over the trellis to drop down and land by the side of the pool. He used his hands to cat-walk in the half darkness towards the French windows, then stopped, peering in through the glass at Moll Hackabout, whose sad timeless story now hung on the low-lit walls inside.

They had left her alone tonight. Moll, who had been sold short, seduced, molested, maligned, impregnated and infected in a story that was as old as the profession she had fallen into. First the mistress of a wealthy London Jew caught in bed with her aristocratic lover, then the brothel worker staring alluringly out, make-up hiding the small black spots, the sure signs of syphilis that left her swathed in sweating blankets as crow-like quacks profited from her final demise.

He took a step back from the window and scratched his head, thinking, trying to figure out a way inside, but he was afraid. Afraid of the things that Red had told him that night, about the men who wanted the pictures, of her first encounter with them and the things they would do to her – that Sikes would let them do to her if they failed to deliver on time.

He looked up, one storey up, where there was a crack, an opening in the narrowest of bathroom windows and he reached inside his kitbag and felt the cold rubber of the mask touch the skin of his face. There was a sunlounger beside the pool and he took the cushion from it then upended it and began to climb the mahogany cross struts until his fingers found the crack and pushed the window open.

45

The guard standing outside the Shard saw the van arrive. It was early on account of the two police outriders who had muscled through the City traffic and were now forcing a TV truck from the delivery bay outside the service entrance.

He turned as his supervisor came marching out from the service entrance, flanked by two more guards. The four of them split into pairs and formed a corridor along which the two men from the vault strode to be met by the gallery's guards who were unlocking the bar across the van's rear doors.

There was a satisfying sucking noise as the hydraulic ramp reached the floor. Then the men in the overalls lifted each crate in turn, sliding it into its own row on their trolley and wheeling it back towards the service entrance, up a ramp, along a corridor, down in a lift, along another corridor to a solid steel door.

The guards stopped at intervals along the way, sealing doors behind them and positioning themselves along the route, bristling like pimps protecting Moll from the attention of suitors who could not afford her.

The first guard listened to the sound of a click and the turn of a six-inch-wide screw deep inside the foot-thick circular steel door. He turned and stared back down the corridor, his hand resting on the leather holster at his side.

He didn't need to understand why the manager of the tallest building in the City had decided to host an auction of eighteenth-century art. It was way above his pay grade. All he needed to do was be extra vigilant in response to Scotland Yard who had confirmed the report of the robbery from the gallery that had held the missing three Hogarths.

He stepped into the vault. There was a steel grille dividing an outer room filled with stocks and bonds from an inner room where several large safes stood at intervals around the walls.

One of the men in white coats unlocked this door and motioned to his colleague to push the trolley inside. Then he turned and walked back out again, locking the grille and ushering him out so that he could turn and pull the solid steel door closed with a thunk.

Fagin had tried on sixteen suits before he had found 'the one'. To his mind it was the perfect expression of the high point of 1980s power dressing in a colour consistent with the taste of a Russian oligarch hailing from the Siberian city of Krasnoyarsk. It was dark crimson and double-breasted with shoulder pads so wide that the Emperor Ming might at any point order the invasion of Earth to recapture them. He turned, throwing his hands out to the sides like a peacock raising its fan, and stifled his irritation as Dodge smirked.

Then he turned and took a good long look at himself in
the full-length mirror at the far end of the dressing room.
The Stalin moustache was a nice touch. It nestled beneath his
nose like a forest at the foot of a mountain. Theatrical, no
doubt, but authoritative and with his scar-faced bodyguard
dressed in a black, tailored Armani suit behind him, it would
be a fool who stared at it too long.

Reminding himself to watch for viscous canapés that might
get caught up in it, he heard the door open behind him and
he looked up the aisle to see Sikes. Deathly quiet since the
showdown and staring at Red, as Bullseye sometimes stared
at him when the mutt couldn't understand why he was being
punished.

And it wasn't enough that Sikes was in the coldest
doghouse in the world. Fagin knew Red's moods and he had
never seen her as silent and self-composed as she was now,
so he worried as she stood there in a figure-hugging gold
chiffon dress with faux diamonds glittering on a carapace of
silver around her neck. Would she stick with the programme
or deviate from it? He looked at her and she met his eye
and nodded back at him. Concentrated and lethal beneath
the Eurotrash veneer, she would sit on his arm like dazzle
camouflage, drawing attention away from the play until it
was her turn to shine.

They stood for a moment looking at one another in
silence. It was as if they were off to perform in the opening
night of a play. Except that no one was smiling. And Red
looked ghostly, ashen-faced. And it bothered Fagin deeply.
That something was at stake, beyond the obvious. Something
he was not party to and prayed now would not raise its ugly
head until after the score had gone down.

Dodge had waited for Twist in a greasy spoon that serviced the workers on the building site that surrounded the old hotel. From there they'd run back together, opening the door to Fagin's room late but with their mission accomplished.

'Don't even look at her.'

Sikes glowered at Twist, certain he had caught him trying to catch Red's eye from across Fagin's office.

'Purple Sergei', as Dodge was now calling Fagin, was busy with his printer. Twist watched as the old man shielded the screen on his laptop from him and Dodge who were stood behind his left shoulder.

'Sightseeing for you today, boys,' he said, reaching for a pair of e-tickets which read *The View From The Shard*.

In other circumstances Twist would have taken his camera, taken some photographs of the art hanging on the walls in the observatory. But times had changed. Fagin turned back to face Sikes and Red, and clapped his hands.

'Round four,' he said.

46

The approach road was blocked all the way back to London Bridge Street as the cars of the good and the great descended slowly into the underground beneath the tower. Maseratis, Bentleys and Porsches, all turning in a multimillion-pound corkscrew of steel, plastic and glass four floors below the red carpet where those with chauffeurs were met with the cameras of the paparazzi and the screams of adoring fans.

'I am Renzo Piano and this was my vision, I foresaw it not as a tower but as a vertical city for thousands of people to work in and for millions of people to take to their heart and enjoy.'

Fagin was reading the blurb in the programme. He felt strung out and bereft of the milk of human kindness as his gang warred silently with each other around him. Sleep had not come easily for three nights. It was the same exhaustion he'd felt stumbling along the jagged ridges of the Carpathian Alps. Hunted like an animal by the tyrant's mountain troops, lying up in barns and beneath hayricks, too frightened to knock on the doors of strangers who might already be in thrall to the vampire Ceauşescu.

The authority always haunted him on these nights before a job and as sleep came he returned, his long hands reaching out from the foot of his bed, scrabbling crab-like up his body as he lay prone in the darkness walking through each of the team members' roles in turn.

Dawn had seen him bleary-eyed at his desk, staring at a Russian phrase book while trying and failing to glue on his moustache, the day passing in final drills with the crew, each repeating in sequence the actions he or she would take as he clicked on his stopwatch like a track coach clocking laps.

Exhaustion had dogged him all afternoon, finally sinking its fangs in at a quarter past six. With just forty-five minutes left to zero hour he had slipped on an empty crisp packet and fallen hard on the floor of his office. It was getting to be a habit, he thought, lying there, his head resting on a 1994 edition of *Lyle Antiques*, until Red had come in looking ten million dollars and scooped him off the floor and propped him up with his back to the wall facing his desk.

From there he'd instructed her to take the secret key from around his neck and open the bottom drawer and bring him his ziplock bag that contained his medication, so that just ten minutes – two modafinils, a Dexedrine and a beta blocker – later he'd been back on his feet, suited and booted, and marshalling the troops into the back of the Bedford which had taken them across town to the lock-up where, beneath the shadow of the sheltering wall, Sikes had sat waiting.

He looked from behind the tinted glass at liveried servants straight from the pages of *Barry Lyndon* who stood bowing as they offered the glitterati a glass of wine as they stepped from their chauffeur-driven cars into a blizzard of camera flashes and the din as celebrities were recognised and fêted by the crowd penned in by steel bars on either side of the red carpet.

He sat up and looked at Red as she wrapped her white ermine tighter round her neck, preparing to meet the night air. She was more than Sikes deserved and that is why he would lose her. He was no longer the precociously talented young gymnast Fagin had taken under his wing. He was unrecognizable, having chosen the wrong path. And Fagin wondered if he'd even had a choice at all. If his path hadn't been predetermined, the damage done long before the fall, during his childhood. So that when misfortune had happened, he'd had no reserves to fall back on, deciding to take by force what life had never given him, to be a hammer not a nail, a wise guy not a mug.

Fagin watched the black fabric stretch tight across Sikes's shoulders as he stepped out from the passenger door, the crowd murmuring as Red emerged and turned her back on him. She was Cinderella come late to the ball and the paparazzi knew it. The flash of their cameras dazzled Fagin as he stepped out to take her arm and lead her up the red carpet, believing what Sikes never would: that she belonged to no one and that her only commitment was to the score.

'Stay, Bullseye,' Sikes snapped at the dog as it turned and whined in the footwell in front of the passenger seat. He slammed the door and the limousine pulled away with Cribb in his cap behind the wheel.

But Fagin could see that was not going to stop Sikes from trying to hold on. To the one good thing he had left, stepping forwards to whisper in Red's ear, oblivious to Dodge and Twist who were working their way against the steady flow of caterers, brandishing their e-tickets along with the ID tags that identified them as card-carrying gentlemen of the press.

47

The reception was taking place in the open plan Gŏng bar of the Shangri-La hotel on the fifty-second floor of the tower. A chosen few had been invited to spend the night after the launch party, of which the auction was a part, in one of the luxuriously appointed suites.

Red let herself be led by Fagin. Her fears about his purple suit and Borat moustache soon disappeared as they rubbed shoulders with dissipated artists, B-list celebrities, rock stars and the Qatari sheik who had financed the construction of the tower.

Sotheby's, who were running the auction, tipped him to lead the bidding but there were other speculations, most notably about the identity of the gang who had stolen the missing three paintings in broad daylight in transit from the Losberne Gallery.

There were rumours that the infamous Kosovan jewel thieves, the Pink Panthers, were at work while others suggested that the theft had been an inside job, deliberately designed to drive up the price of the three paintings that were about to go under the hammer. A sensational PR stunt which could well be followed with an equally audacious tower heist.

'Of course, there is no knowing what these ninjas will try next ...' Red heard a grizzled art hag opine to her Chinese collector friend who nodded his agreement.

Red turned to Fagin and nodded to the ladies loo, but when she started walking towards it she felt herself held fast around the upper arm. She didn't have to turn round to know whose fingers were bruising her as she kept smiling sweetly at the hag.

'I need the toilet,' she whispered, recoiling as his breath entered her ear.

She felt him kiss her ear then her cheek and then down her neck to her halter line.

'I'm coming with you,' he said, and she felt herself being pushed against her will away from the crowd and the Ladies into a corridor.

There was the overwhelming urge to scream out loud. Not just because the points of his fingers were digging into the pressure points in her deltoids, sending electric bursts of pain up her arm and into her neck. She knew it was irrational not to fear him. He knew now that he was losing her and this made him more dangerous than ever. But his behaviour, dragging her around, unable to leave her alone, demeaned him. It was pathetic.

It was an angry scream. It wanted to escape from her. Not born of fear but rage that this man had killed two boys and would kill again. That was a fact. And it jarred with the scene. These silly people, high up in their glass tower, staring at life and death and saying it was beautiful.

But Fagin reached her as she opened her mouth and wrapped his arm around them, embracing them both. He hissed something quietly in Romanian as he drew them into the disabled toilet and stared into Sikes like a publican reasoning with a drunk.

'Bill, don't make a scene, you're supposed to be a body-guard,' he said.

She felt Fagin's hand on her bare shoulders as he tried to prise Sikes off her but the strength remained and the pressure increased, drawing her closer as he stared blankly back at Fagin like he was a stranger whose face he had never seen before.

'You think I can trust her to stick around?' he asked, at last.

They slipped away from the tourists and slid over a railing to a secure door that was marked *No Entry* and Twist watched as Dodge pulled the counterfeit fob from his sleeve, the tip of his tongue edging from the corner of his mouth as he punched in the four digit code and the door clicked open.

As they raced down the service stairs they peeled off their thick clothes, transforming themselves in one-footed hops, pausing only briefly on landings until Twist was wearing a harness and rope coiled round his midriff and Dodge was wearing the policeman's uniform and they were standing next to the service elevator on the twentieth floor.

A red light began flashing when Dodge swiped the card. It was indicating that there was no elevator on the far side of the steel doors, just a chasm that dropped some three hundred feet beneath them into the bowels of the earth.

Twist stuck his neck out and looked down into the abyss.

'Rather you than me, mate,' Dodge said.

48

Inside there was a buzz of anticipation as the crowd filed into the hotel's dining room. The auctioneers had covered the three hundred and sixty degree windows with red cloth to keep the focus on the paintings which were stood, covered, on three stands on a small stage at one end of the room.

There were probably twenty rows and there were twenty chairs in each row, divided by a central aisle. The first five rows were all reserved but Fagin, true to form, had managed to secure himself a seat in the third row where he could cover both the exit and the action on the raised podium at the front.

As they'd agreed in the plan, Red was seated behind him in the cheap seats, again close to the end of the row and partially obscured by a pillar from where she was still able to see Fagin as he turned and winked back at her. She then glanced over to where Bill was using the cover of the crowd milling in through the entrance to reach behind the red fabric

to its left to ensure that the fire alarm was also exactly where
it was supposed to be.

Two porters in lab coats pushed a trolley from the service
elevator to the right of the stage. They lifted its protective
cloth to reveal the three paintings. There was a hush, rever-
ential, as the auctioneer appeared, a neat, unremarkable man
in a grey suit distinguishable only by his wooden hammer
and the reading spectacles that he pushed onto his nose as
he stepped up to the lectern and began.

'Lot 146. Three paintings, numbers four through to
six from William Hogarth's six painting series *A Harlot's
Progress*. Oil on canvas. 1731. Hogarth was the greatest
satirical artist of the early Georgian period and these paintings have attracted interest today due to the controversy
surrounding the alleged reappearance and theft of the first
three in the sequence from a well-respected central London
gallery two weeks ago.'

Red looked at the pictures standing on the trestles at the
front and shivered. They showed the descent of the girl,
Moll Hackabout. Red knew the pictures they had stolen
from Losberne by memory and so could pick up the narra-
tive without listening to the auctioneer who began the story
from the top with the assistance of a projector operated by
a colleague at the rear of the circular auditorium:

'After arriving in London from the provinces the pretty
but gullible girl Moll is met by Mrs Needham, the pock-
ridden madam who procures her for the wealthy Jewish
merchant who in turn casts her out for cuckolding him with
a second lover, forcing her to become a common prostitute.
She finds herself arrested in the third picture by Sir John
Gonson, who stands staring at the wig box of the notorious

highwayman, James Dalton, possibly one of Moll's lovers, which hangs above her only piece of furniture, her bed.'

Red turned and saw Sikes's eyes, blank and emotionless staring back at her, refusing to answer the question, implicit in her glance at this moment as the auctioneer switched the audience's attention to the pictures that were on sale.

'The fourth plate on display here today shows Moll inside Bridewell prison, beating hemp for hangman's nooses while the sadistic jailer steals clothes from her, who stands next to a card sharp, a Down syndrome child, a pregnant African lady and Moll's servant who appears to be wearing Moll's shoes.'

The auctioneer paused while the spotlight shifted to the second in the series, picture five.

'In plate five Moll lies dying of syphilis as Dr Richard Rock and Dr Jean Misaubin bicker over the relative benefits of bleeding versus cupping the patient while the heroine's addled infant son picks lice or fleas out of his hair as Moll's clothes hang down from her, almost like ghosts drawing her into the afterlife.'

Red glanced up at the security guards who were positioned at each of the six pillars. The pillars formed a circle, within which the chairs formed a square. It was like a holding pen, containing the high rollers, but it was still hard for them to keep track of the partygoers who weren't going to bid and who were standing alongside her, hugging pillars, sipping their drinks.

'The sixth and final plate shows Moll at her own wake, dead aged just twenty-three years of age, surrounded by scavengers. Here, the parson spills his brandy and has his hand up the skirt of the girl next to him, who appears pleased. Here, Moll's madam drunkenly mourns on the right with a jug of "Nants" brandy, appearing to be the only one upset by the treatment of the dead girl whose coffin is being used as a tavern bar. And here Moll's former colleague, a mourning young whore, steals a handkerchief while another checks her appearance even though she too shows signs of a syphilitic sore ...'

Red watched the guards scan the crowd and turn as one, their eyes refocussing upon the tip of a pink newspaper in the third row. The auctioneer's voice rose in tone, expressing his surprise at the speed with which the bidding had begun.

'Two million pounds ...' he said, pointing at the man in the revolting purple suit who leapt up, bang on cue.

'I can smell burning!' Fagin yelled.

She watched the high rollers raise their noses to sniff the air, turning impatiently to look around them, some looking to the security guards who were doing the same.

'Sit down!' a dark-haired man in the second row snapped.

But Fagin didn't. Instead he found inspiration.

'I won't sit down! I am a nose. A professional perfumer and I tell you this is an emergency ...'

And that was a claim no one could deny and the sign that she had been waiting for. Her fingers prised open the clasp of her handbag and reached inside for the ring of the smoke bomb which she pulled inside the bag, half closed and let drop to the floor.

'Sir, if you could kindly just ...'

But the auctioneer could not compete with her scream, the one that had been building in her all afternoon but which she could now release full force at the top of her voice.

'Fire!' she cried, her hands clamped to her mouth watching as people jumped to their feet and Bill calmly elbowed the fire alarm and the stampede began.

'The fire's in the lobby. Not this way!' Bill shouted.

The voice of authority, cool in a crisis and in full possession of the latest information, standing arms outstretched in the doorway. Pandemonium broke out. The front runners, the cowards and the most able-bodied turned back into the room, colliding with those who came behind them as the auctioneer gestured desperately to the porters to get the paintings to safety.

'Get them back to the vault!' he shouted.

The two porters were quick. One took the paintings from the stands while the other unfurled the covers and dropped them over each picture. It was something they had practised before many times at Sotheby's. But they were nervous now, working in a strange environment, wondering how wise it was to go down in the lift when the fire on the ground floor would be drawing the oxygen down the shaft like a vampire sucking on a carotid artery. Red watched a buyer shout across at them as they ensured the paintings were ready for moving downstairs.

'You sure you want to do that?'

It was the same guy, the dark-haired one with the big mouth. Either he still didn't buy there was a fire or he was just saying what the porters were thinking. But hearing their thoughts stopped them and they looked to the auctioneer to take the tough call and shoulder the responsibility.

'The vault's completely fireproof, I can assure you. Nowhere safer ...'

The porters wheeled the Hogarths out along a corridor towards the service lift which would take them all the way to the basement if it wasn't already being used to evacuate human beings. Swiping their card, they punched the code into the keypad and when the lift doors opened they pushed the trolley ahead of them into the elevator sniffing the air like a pair of beagles.

'Wait!'

They turned to see a young policeman running along the corridor after them.

'I'm coming with you,' he said.

'No one goes down there but us,' the older porter said.

'We've had a tip-off,' the policeman said. 'Robbery in progress ...'

The porters stopped and thought about it, looking around for the auctioneer, but he was long gone, panting up the stairs to the roof, speed-dialling his investment-banker friend who knew a guy that rented out helicopters.

'We have our procedures ...' the younger porter said.

'And I've got orders. Those paintings aren't going anywhere without me,' the policeman replied.

Only the policeman had anticipated this impasse. He knew only too well what their procedures were and why they had them. They were in place to prevent thieves wearing Prince Harry masks abseiling down lift shafts, opening hatches and stealing the paintings from under their noses.

The doors slid shut behind the porters who turned gobsmacked to see the light on the panel pointing down. The young porter lunged for the closing door like a striking fencer but was too slow. They shut with a clunk and when they turned to look for support from the policeman they saw that he was already running for the stairs.

49

As the lift began its descent, Twist was still dangling from the hatch inside, his rope still fastened to the rung of the service ladder one floor above. His back hit the roof at the speed the lift was going down and he was dragged back out through the hatch, bent double at the hips like a puppet on a string.

But he had reflexes faster than a marionette's and he used them to catch hold of the edges of the hatch as his feet disappeared above his head and the rope began to whip through the karabiner at his waist.

He could feel the friction through the harness as the lift pulled him down and the rope spooled out in a straight line above him. He watched as the length at his waist shrank to nothing and then felt gravity take control once again and he fell back down through the hatch to the floor of the lift.

He hit the emergency stop button and the lift ground to a halt between the eighteenth and nineteenth floors, the light flickering as he reached inside his rucksack and pulled out a can and shook it three times, always three, for good luck. Then he took aim, depressed the nozzle and covered the CCTV camera with matt black paint.

He yanked his mask off and took a deep breath. Then he reached inside the rucksack for his craft knife, pulled the cloth cover from the paintings and went to work, cutting the canvases from their frames with the respect they deserved.

The buyers were streaming out of the reception and onto the street, like rats scurrying to the tune that Fagin had piped for them. Red would have joined them but there was no chance. Bill might as well have handcuffed himself to her as he pushed her down the rear fire stairwell until they'd reached street level, followed by Fagin. And then there was Oliver to think about. If he succeeded and returned with the paintings and she was not there, Bill would kill him and take them without a second thought.

She looked across at Fagin. His moustache was hanging loose on one side and she watched him reach up and cover it with his hand. The plan was working. Cribb, their getaway driver, had the easiest job of the entire team. He was parked in a limousine fifty yards along the road. She could see its bonnet visible at the end of a slip road as it nudged forwards, the engine idling, Cribb in the driving seat still wearing the chauffeur's hat.

Fagin raised his hand to his face and tore off the moustache. He was smiling. Then she looked at the bonnet of the limousine. It was disappearing. Cribb had put it in reverse. There was a single blast of a siren and an unmarked police car braked hard as it passed the alleyway and came to a stop, blocking their path to Cribb and safety.

The male detective was older, reaching retirement age and he was calm and unsurprised in the face of the chaos emerging from the Shard. He looked for a moment at the entrance then up at the hotel and then back down at the road in front of him, turning a full circle, scanning the cars that were pulling away, focusing on each one, missing nothing. It was obvious he was not here to put out the fire.

She heard coughing and she looked over to see Fagin leaning forwards to hide his face. She watched as the second detective, a woman, younger, maybe forty, appeared from the car behind him, talking into a phone, coordinating the squad cars which had blocked both entrances to the feeder road.

She felt Bill release his grip on her wrist and slide his hand down to clutch her own, pulling her forwards and turning to face Fagin, playing the concerned friend, and she followed his lead in a half-skip backwards as they moved towards the two cops.

But the damage had already been done. The old cop was staring down at Bill's hand as it turned her own, exerting just enough force to spin her outwards so that she gave him partial cover as the cop turned back towards Fagin and they strode past him. But his partner was more certain and Red watched her keep her eyes on Bill as a second wave of buyers spilled out at them from a side street. She was speaking urgently into her hands-free mic, pushing the crowd out of her way, reaching inside her jacket with her right hand for what could only be a gun.

Red felt a sharp tug on her wrist and within a second they had turned and then they were sprinting, bursting through the crowd against the flow, stepping up off the road onto the pavement where there were fewer people. Bill pulled her low as they ran, slowing to the pace of the surrounding crowd as they passed the policemen at the end of the street who were standing on the inside of their car's door frames surveying the crowd from above.

And by some miracle they got past them, reaching the corner of the main road that led to Tower Bridge Tube station and spotting a Rolls-Royce which was parked up, its driver hidden by his newspaper, blissfully unaware that just two hundred yards away the tallest building in London was supposedly going up in flames.

She watched Bill motioning downward with his hand and the Rolls' electric window whirred down in response.

'Finish early?' the driver asked.

Bill leant in and smashed the driver hard across the side of the face with his telescopic cosh. It stunned the man. He looked up at Bill as the cosh hit him on the temple, this time knocking him cold.

Fagin got in the rear door and Bill pushed Red in alongside him then pulled the driver out of the car, got in and hit the accelerator, swerving out across the street into oncoming traffic, sideswiping a Ferrari and scattering socialites as he went.

50

DS Brownlow could see now that the auctioneer's relief at not having to explain the expense of a helicopter flight while the building didn't burn must have been short-lived. For the fact remained that there had been smoke without fire and that left a single question hanging tantalisingly in the air as the guards prised open the elevator doors with a crowbar.

Was this just an elaborately planned hoax or a full-blown, balls-out heist?

Brownlow had run down into the basement as soon as they'd identified Fagin in the crowd, leaving Bedwin outside to orchestrate the pursuit. He had not communicated this information to the auctioneer yet but he didn't have to. The guy was old enough and smart enough to know that he'd been comprehensively mugged. His career hung in the balance and he was going to pieces.

'Come on, come on ...'

The tension was killing Brownlow too. Standing here, peering into the darkness of the lift as the guards pulled back the doors and the auctioneer buckled under the strain.

'Thank God,' he gasped.

Brownlow watched as the porters wheeled the trolley out of the lift and along the corridor to the vault.

'Wait!'

The sound of his own voice surprised him. Like something had leapt out of his mouth, a part of him that still cared and was inside the lift now staring at the floor. Forcing him down onto his knees, scrubbing in the dirt, placing faith in his hands, using them to pick up any differential in texture and temperature, something he should tell Bedwin. That when your eyes and ears played tricks on you, place your hands on the object and to hell with forensics.

He looked up at the CCTV camera above him then turned towards the paintings and lifted the cover, listening to the sound the cloth made as it brushed over the corners of the frames. The auctioneer saw them first; Moll shredding rope, Moll dying of syphilis and finally Moll in her coffin, nothing untoward there. His relief was palpable. 'Thank God. Get them back to the vault n—'

'Hang on,' Brownlow interrupted, leaning in closer, scrutinising the paintings. He was getting slow but his instincts were still sharp and he had seen the three tiny marks that the auctioneer had missed. The paintings were perfect in every way except one; where William Hogarth's spidery signature should have been there was another sign-off, one that he recognised.

TWIST

Stepping back with his hands on his hips, wheezing for breath, Brownlow began to laugh. Twist had pulled the blinkers over the experts. The signatures on the originals were tiny and so were Twist's graffiti tags, each located in the exact same spot as Hogarth's were on the original paintings.

He stepped past the fakes into half light, looking up at the ceiling and a tiny gap where the service hatch had not been fully shut. He pulled the trolley across the lift floor until it was directly beneath it and reached up to push the hatch open as one of the guards stepped forward to give him a leg up.

It was dark in the elevator shaft and it took his eyes a few seconds to adapt, during which his gaze followed a service ladder which climbed its entire length, disappearing into the darkness hundreds of feet above him.

'Torch,' he said, hearing his knees crack in the silence as he knelt down to take one from the guard inside the lift.

It was a powerful torch and its beam shot up the shaft, reaching a point of light one hundred metres up. He trained it on the ladder and began to ascend, gradually at first, then faster, as he sensed movement and zeroed in on a spider-like figure climbing fast with a silver tube strapped to his back and what looked like the back of a latex mask on his head.

As if sensing that he was being watched the figure stopped and looked down, and Brownlow locked eyes with the boy called Twist and felt the mild elation sour into something like disappointment. He had given the boy the benefit of the doubt and released him but he had read him wrong. Shaking his head, watching the boy begin to climb fast up the ladder, he reached for his radio.

'He's in the lift shaft,' he said.

51

He could not climb any faster. He was taking two rungs at a time, each footstep sending a hollow metallic clang ringing up into the void to return a half-second later as an echo. Like the bells ringing in the ears of a hunchback scaling a bell tower as the mob bayed for his blood in the streets below.

He told himself not to panic. That Fagin's assumption would prove to be correct. That the police would guess he would use the lift doors and then head down, not up, using one of the three stairwells which they would be watching like hawks, evacuating the building before working their way back up it, methodically, floor by floor.

In the darkness the sound of the echo was intensified, carpeting the sound of steel twisting behind his back. The lift had already begun its ascent when he turned and saw the cables moving in opposing directions and he realised that Fagin had not counted on the man who was stood on top of the lift holding up the torch.

It was the detective called Brownlow and he was shaking his head from side to side. He didn't look angry or bitter, just tired and old and sad. Twist broke eye contact first and turned back to the ladder, scrabbling now, up towards the next set of elevator doors. It was clear that Brownlow intended to take him now. That he would not shout down and tell the guy operating the lift to take his hand off the handle.

Fifty metres, forty metres, thirty ... the spotlight growing wider as Twist worked his jimmy hard into the crack between the doors. They didn't budge and Twist could hear Brownlow's voice now, clear, growing louder by the second.

'It's over, Oliver. Tell me to stop the lift.'

Twist's field of vision shrank. The torchlight in his eyes deliberate, trying to blind him. He got the fingers of his right hand into the crack but there was no sign of an automatic mechanism that would open or shut them once pressure was applied. Instead the doors held his fingers like a vice. Twenty, ten ...

Twist looked down at Brownlow.

'My hand!' he shouted down.

But Brownlow didn't flinch. He would not be fooled again. Twist looked back at the door and tried to get the jimmy back in. It slipped from his hand. He looked back and saw a look of fear spread across Brownlow's face, then light flooding in through the gap between the doors and a pair of hands emerging, seizing him by the straps of his rucksack and pulling him through the foot-wide gap and out onto the fourteenth floor.

Hands, Twist realised, that belonged to a uniformed policeman who now had him by the lapels as they tumbled backwards and hit the ground. Twist swept his own hands up and out to break his grip but the man was too strong and held him fast and Twist drew back his head to butt him, but froze. It was Dodge.

Twist fell sideways off Dodge then pulled him to his feet and they ran together down the corridor to a right-hand bend. They tore round the corner and saw a policeman sprinting towards them and turned, then saw the lift doors open and two security guards waiting like sprinters in the blocks inside.

Twist felt Dodge tug his rucksack back towards the policeman and they ran again, full tilt, straight at him and Twist saw at once what Dodge was doing. There was a pair of antique chairs halfway along the corridor and they hit them together, planting their inside feet on the chairs to get lift and sliding, their backs to the walls past the policeman.

And then they were in the service stairs, taking four at a time, climbing higher up the tower in a race against the lift.

Bill spun the Rolls-Royce into a hard right on to Tooley Street, gunning the V12 engine to outstrip the police car on his tail. It was a Phantom, with an extended wheelbase and a kerb weight of over two and a half tons but he was throwing it about like a dodgem at a fairground.

Red stared horrified as a black cab braked, swerving off and mounting the pavement as he pushed the Phantom blind round the outside of a number 47 bus. She looked back at Fagin, who was struggling to lock his seat belt.

'What are you doing?!' he yelled from the back seat. 'This was never Plan B or even Plan C! It is imbecilic. Stop! Before you get us all killed!'

But Bill was silent, focusing grimly on the rear end of a Golf, and Red closed her eyes as he accelerated into the back of it, nudging it once, twice, before the driver lost control, over-corrected, fishtailed then spun out, slamming sideways into an oncoming van.

The lights of City Hall and Tower Bridge flashed past them on their left as they lurched onto the dual carriageway of Jamaica Road, heading for the Rotherhithe Tunnel. She turned and looked at Fagin. His face was chalk-white and he was trying to stop himself being flung around. He had one hand pushed against the central armrest and the other wedged up where the door met the roof.

A second police car joined the first, pulling out suddenly from a side road, forcing Bill to slew wide out to his left. He burned rubber to correct his line then, spotting a gap in the central reservation, released the steering wheel, allowing the car's momentum to carry them through it.

The mouth of the tunnel appeared and she saw the orange glow of the ceiling lights and the sirens dropped to nothing as Bill roared into it, swerving violently to avoid oncoming traffic. She watched as he swerved too late, clipping a BMW 3 series which smacked into the side wall, flipped over and got hit twice by the two cars behind it.

And then he put his foot down and they burst from the tunnel and the sirens were to their right as the police cars appeared once again. Red felt a huge pressure on her chest as Bill slammed on the brakes and she was squashed into the seat in front. As time slowed down she saw Bill smile for the first time, his head way back, fighting the G-force as the huge car dropped from seventy to thirty and he yanked on the handbrake and spun it in a perfect one-eighty, slamming into the side of an oncoming bus which stopped them dead.

And then he hit the accelerator, so hard this time that she was thrown back against the seat and followed Fagin's lead with the seat belt as Bill gave the cops the finger and re-entered the tunnel heading in the right direction.

'Are you fucking crazy?!'

It was the driver of the second car to hit the BMW. He was stood, trying to pull open the BMW's passenger door. It had been squashed to half its original width by the twin impacts and there was a guy in the front seat looking bad. He was slumped forwards and he had blood running from a head wound.

Bill slammed on the brakes and the great car skidded to a halt, turning thirty degrees. Red watched him get out of the car, march towards the guy and point his pistol at his face, forcing the guy to put his hands up and back away until he was on his knees facing the wall.

Sikes then turned and motioned for them to get into the guy's car, an old Passat, which only seemed to have a crushed bumper. She climbed into the back seat as Fagin got in beside her and then they were off again, leaving the carnage and the police cars behind them.

Twist and Dodge scrambled out onto the roof and raced along the edge of the building. Ninety-five storeys up, London was laid out beneath them like a circuit board. The ledge was not wide. Maybe about three feet and Twist was wondering where it was going to get them when Dodge climbed over the side and jumped out into mid-air.

Twist heard a smashing sound behind him and he turned to see a fist in a black Kevlar glove punch out the remaining glass in a window. He ran forwards to the point where Dodge had jumped and looked down at his friend who was stood impatiently in a window cleaner's cradle.

Twist shook his head and climbed over the edge and jumped. It was a ten-foot drop and the cradle swung out wildly when he hit it, then lurched down as Dodge hit the button. He looked up to see the guard staring down off the edge of the roof at them.

'Stop the cradle!' the guard shouted. 'Kill the power.'

Twist watched the shadow of a second guard retreat from the glass inside as their descent continued until, five storeys lower, they stopped, a distance of at least two hundred metres above street level.

'What now?' Twist said, looking past Dodge to the policeman they had jumped over, smiling smugly at them through the glass.

But Dodge was reaching into his rucksack, pulling out a smaller fabric pack which he handed to Twist.

'Put it on,' he said as he pulled out a second, drew out some straps and harnessed a parachute to his back.

Twist felt the cradle beginning to wind back up again. It focused his mind, which had temporarily stopped at *I don't know how to do this*. Then he looked over at Dodge who was grinning.

'Sorry for getting you into this,' he said, climbing up onto the edge of the cradle which tilted forwards as he stood upright, holding onto the cradle's cord to steady himself.

Twist pulled the pack onto his back and fastened the straps across his shoulders to another strap which fastened around his waist, then climbed up onto the edge and looked across at Dodge.

'It's easy,' Dodge said, drawing out a toggle at the front of his pack. 'You just pull this.'

Twist found his own toggle and gripped it hard in his hand. 'Can't go through life trusting no one,' he said.

Then, as one, they stepped off the cradle and jumped.

Twist saw the dome of the nineteenth-century wharf-turned-shopping-emporium loom up at him. He looked down and saw fairy lights climbing the cast-iron pillars that supported the rectangular glass panels of the roof. He was descending too fast and had no control, trying to remember what instructions, apart from 'pull this', Dodge had given him, but losing his thoughts to the cold air and the fear.

There was a flat stretch of roof before the dome about five metres across and he tugged hard on both handles and felt the parachute crumple above him and the roof rush up at him. He hit the ground hard and rolled, feeling the nylon cords of the parachute entangle him as the fabric caught the wind and lifted up like a kite, pulling him onto the glass panels.

Snatching up the cord with his hands as the parachute began to drag him up the dome, he heard laughter from above him and he turned to see Dodge, tugging gently on his own handles, executing the perfect textbook landing, collapsing his chute with a quick flick of the forearms before it dragged him out onto the glass.

'Well done, mate,' Dodge said, reaching out with a knife to cut the cords so that his chute lofted up, caught the estuarine wind and sailed out across the river.

Twist watched Dodge beckon him, then take off, gaining speed to a flat sprint to plant his foot and jump the gap to the next building but he didn't follow him. He had his own move to make.

52

They parked in the shopping centre car park then walked up the ramp to the street. Fagin looked pale, crumpled but determined in his purple suit, leading them into the shadows on the dark side of the street to the steel ladder that climbed four storeys to the rendezvous.

Red looked up at the gap between the buildings each time they reached the outer edge of the stairwell, wondering if she would see a pair of dark-clad figures leap across above them. But they were met by no one when they reached the roof and crouched, flattened against the back of a forty-eight-sheet advertising hoarding.

Her nerves were wrecked after the car chase but she was still thinking straight and she saw now, for the first time, the pain Bill was in and the danger his death wish posed for them all.

'They're late,' he spat.

'You drive fast, Bill,' Fagin replied, pushing back with his feet so his back slid up the smooth weather-beaten plywood of the hoarding until he was upright and visible to the single dark figure who was running towards them.

'About time,' Bill growled.

'Where's Oliver?' Red asked, not even trying to disguise her concern.

'We got split up,' Dodge replied.

Red watched him shuffle back on his feet, alert and out of reach as Bill stepped forwards.

'Who's got the paintings?' Bill said.

'He has. You think we switched in mid-air?'

Bill stayed within the shadow of the hoarding, his expression invisible to Dodge.

'Where is he?'

'He was right behind me and then ...' Dodge protested, throwing up his arms.

Red watched Bill reach slowly inside his jacket pocket and pull out his Beretta and aim it at Dodge's chest. There was nothing to be done. He was fast and he was holding a gun.

'He's telling the truth,' said a voice from above and behind them.

Red knew it was Twist and she turned, searching for him until she saw the outline of his body, dark against the dull glow of the night sky on the far edge of the roof. He had his right arm hooked over his shoulder and he drew the silver tube up from his back and held it skyward like a sword.

'You want them?' he said. 'Then she comes with me.' He pointed the tube directly at Red.

She moved too slow and felt Bill's fingers snatch her and pull her hard against him, pressing the cold hard metal of the gun barrel into her right cheek.

'You really think she's worth it?' Bill asked, and she saw Twist lower the art tube and hold it back off the far edge of the building where the river ran below.

'Try me,' he replied.

'Do what he says, Bill,' Fagin cautioned, stepping forwards so that he was behind Bill was was also moving, step by step, towards Twist with the barrel of his gun pushing into Red's right ear.

'Meet you halfway, boy,' he said, watching Twist step down from the raised platform, cross the roof and rejoin the edge, walking along it with the tube extended fully in his left hand above the drop.

53

'You got more stones than I gave you credit for,' Sikes said, messing Red's hair with the barrel of the Beretta.

Twist was close enough to see the scratches on the butt of the gun where the serial number had been filed off. He shuffled a half-step closer to the edge, watching Fagin cross silently behind Sikes and stick his neck out over the precipice.

'Helicopters,' he said, craning one ear in the air as he peered down at the street below. 'We can't hang about.'

It was a busy street. There were late-night shoppers leaving the Galleria, laden with bags in the darkness, a bus stop with a queue filled with exhausted grandmothers clutching their bargains, a pair of Spanish au pairs and a drunk who kept getting up from his perch in the doorway of the cinema exit to grovel.

For a moment there was silence. Twist met Sikes's steady gaze and the pair of them stayed like that, eyeballing one another, waiting for the other to blink. But the growl from the stairwell surprised everyone. It was Bullseye with Cribb following.

'I got the text,' Cribb said to Fagin, pointing at the dog. 'I'm sorry. I couldn't hold him …'

Twist tensed, watching the dog pad across the roof, its head low to the ground, stalking closer, uncertain why it had been left alone, making its way back to the heel of its master. It was an ugly brute and stupid, even by dog standards.

'Sick,' Sikes muttered, and Twist looked down and saw an ugly snarl split the dog's punched-in face, drawing the folds of flesh back to reveal its canines as it crept towards him across the rooftop, keeping low so that Twist could not watch dog and master simultaneously.

He heard its growl two feet from his groin and he fought the urge to look down at the threat, failed, and that was all it took. A hand flashed beneath his eyes and he felt himself caught by the front of his jacket and pulled down hard onto the roof. He was rolled over, flat on his back, a gun in his face, pushing its way past his teeth into his mouth.

'I'm still faster than you,' Sikes said, taking the tube from Twist and passing it back to Fagin who went to work immediately, his hands moving fast, pulling off the lid.

'It's them, Bill. Let him go,' Fagin said.

Sikes forced the gun further into Twist's mouth until it was pressing down into his throat so hard he couldn't swallow.

'Can't do it, FBoss. Little runt thinks he'll step into my shoes.'

Twist heard the hammer of the pistol being cocked, then felt the barrel scrape against his lips as Sikes pulled it out of his mouth.

'Come here,' Sikes said, pulling Red close to him.

It was below zero and the wind chilled the sweat in Twist's clothes. He knew it was the end of the line. The game he was playing now was for everything and he was playing against a psychopath with a gun held to the head of the girl he was in love with. And even if the card he was about to play trumped Skies and they got away with the money, they still had to outrun the law.

It was a pretty hopeless situation and he had walked right into it with his eyes open but it was like Red said; the difference between a man and a boy was that a man stands up, looks you in the eye and asks for what he wants. And he'd made the decision to change the moment she had put it out there, but in one respect only. His imagination was his best friend. The only one who'd stuck around. And if he did get out of this alive he wasn't going to compromise again.

He stared into Sikes's eyes.

'You'll get more for them as a set,' he said, watching Sikes's eyes widen as he reached inside his rucksack.

'Don't you move.' Sikes pointed the gun at Twist again.

'Easy,' Twist replied. 'Just going for my phone.'

Twist watched as Fagin craned sideways, holding his head at an angle so he could see round Sikes's back.

'Go on,' Sikes said.

Twist brushed the screen with his fingertips, spinning through the media, until the one marked '+3' appeared and he saw Fagin pull on his beard and Red bite her lip and Sikes flick the gun barrel, telling him to start.

So he hit play and the grainy video began, shaky and indistinct, the screen filled with the red brick of a wall, the black metal of a pipe and the hand that gripped it. Then a shot of a section of a white wooden window frame and the room behind it, a bathroom, cobalt black tiles to the ceiling and an antique bath.

And then back to the window and a hand reaching up to unhitch the latch, and the worn sole of a red Converse gripping the glass from the inside. Then the camera readjusting to take in the room inside, a bathroom, and Twist looked up and saw recognition seep into Sikes's eyes as he saw the polished gold taps in the cobalt-tiled wet room in the penthouse suite that belonged to the Russian, Arkady Rodchenko.

And the memory was not his alone. He watched Red's eyes as the camera moved unsteadily down the hall from the bathroom onto a mezzanine level, then turn and look back suddenly to capture a twelve-foot-tall painting of an angel brandishing a broad sword.

Red risked a glance at Twist. She saw now what he had done. She looked back at Fagin, who stood poker-faced behind her, and wondered if he'd had anything to do with this deception. He watched over her shoulder as the camera entered the living room and panned round until it picked out three paintings hanging, uplit, in plain view on the living-room wall.

Their details were indistinct in the shadow but as the camera got closer it was clear to make out the first of the Losberne Hogarths, allegedly lost in a fire over two hundred and fifty years ago before resurfacing in the hands of a lecherous art dealer in the second decade of the twenty-first century.

A jump cut followed and then the camera was steady, propped up on the same table, capturing a pair of nimble hands reflected in a mirror, working quickly, rolling the third of the Losberne Hogarths up tight so that it slotted neatly into a tubular silver case.

Twist watched each of their expressions in turn as he appeared in frame, lifting his mask and raising his thumb to the camera.

He felt a hand slap him on the back and he dropped the phone. Twist watched as Dodge came round from behind him to pick it up but came up short as Sikes zeroed the Beretta's sights on his left eyeball.

'Where are they?' Sikes said.

'I walk out of here, with Red. I'll call you, tell you where you can find them,' Twist replied.

'No way.'

'We need the paintings, Bill … They'll have helicopters up in the sky by now,' Fagin said, twisting his hand up into the air as he entered the exchange on the right side of the gunman.

'Helicopters should be the least of your worries right now,' Twist added, watching Sikes's expression.

'Rodchenko?'

Twist nodded.

'What's he going to do when he finds out you double-crossed him?' Twist said.

'What?'

'I sent him the video, told him where the rendezvous was. He'll be here any minute now.'

Twist watched Sikes's face as it hit him in the stone-cold silence that followed. The most powerful crime syndicate west of Moscow now wanted him dead. He was recalling the circular chamber and the oath. The night he'd bargained for Red's freedom. Repeating the words, parrot-fashion, stood stripped down in the surreal luminous half-light cast by the jellyfish propelling themselves through the glass tubes of Rodchenko's aquarium.

It had been the first of the eighteen *vory* codes that
Rodchenko had spoken in Russian and Sikes recalled his
frustration at being forced to wait, a full second, sensing
Rodchenko's sadistic pleasure, before the Russian translated
the oath into English so that Sikes could understand it. It
was, Sikes had since discovered, a ritual that now spanned
continents but which dated back to a specific time and place,
deep inside the ice fields of Siberia where the dark brother-
hood had been forged in the frozen hell of Stalin's gulags in
defiance of the state.

He'd known that night that he was signing his life away
but he'd had no choice but to comply. He had loved Red
then and there had been no other way to save her than to
accept the offer that Rodchenko had made him. To swear
fealty to a higher criminal order which was the sickest joke
of all considering his long-held wish to abandon Fagin and
his two-bit schemes and move up to the bigger leagues.

Sikes had read the codes many times since the night he'd
sworn to uphold them. He'd weighed up each oath in turn,
playing through the kinds of situations that he might find
himself in when he would have to abide by them or face the
consequences. But he had never expected this and he smiled
now, his eyes blinking as he stared at Twist, steeling himself
to uphold the first oath he had sworn, that he would never,
as a thief 'under the law', show his emotions.

'Time's running out, Bill,' Twist said. 'What's it going to be?'

54

Sikes was smart but not like Fagin. His idea of a Plan B involved smashing a two and a half ton Phantom the wrong way up a one-way street and Twist watched as he struggled to assimilate all the facts. Fact one, he couldn't do Twist like he had done Harry and then Batesy. Fact two, he was going to have to let Twist take his girl. Fact three, if he didn't do what Twist wanted in the next five minutes he was going to die a horrible prolonged death at the hands of hardened Russian criminals.

Twist watched him turn to Fagin. It was a revelation to Twist, like watching the hands of a clock rewind ten years in five seconds. To a time before the gang, when Sikes had been running, wanted for attempted murder on top of two previous for aggravated assault. Red had told him all about it. How he'd caught up with Little Ricky, his younger sister's dealer, in a truck stop café in Romford and stuck a screwdriver through the side of his skull. His sister, who had been sixteen when she'd OD'd. The only family he'd ever had.

Fagin nodded back at him and Sikes lowered the gun and released his grip on Red. She stepped away into the space between him and Twist. She looked at Twist and then turned and looked back at Sikes and at Fagin behind him.

'I'll find you,' Sikes said.

But Red shook her head and took Twist's hand when he reached forward for her and then they turned and they were running, building momentum, their hands separating as they approached the gap. A single shot rang out and Twist felt Red react, following her as she dug in her heels, skidding and dropping beside her, the gravel flying above their heads as they slowed to a stop.

He felt the gravel embedded in his hands where he had used to them as brakes, and turned to see Dodge wrestling with Sikes. He had deflected the first shot and now he was fighting for his life. It was a close contest. They were on the floor, grappling. Dodge had his thighs around Sikes's chest and he was trying to choke him but Sikes was fighting back, using what little oxygen he had available to strike Dodge repeatedly in the face with the butt of the Beretta.

'Oliver! Oliver! Come now!'

It was Red. She was up and screaming his name. Begging him to come with her before it was too late. Twist saw blood spurt from Dodge's nose as Sikes broke it and Fagin running for the fire escape shouting at Sikes to stop but doing nothing to help the boy.

He turned to look at Red. He was torn. For all the trouble Dodge had got him into he'd been a good mate but now he had Red to think about, and she was screaming something about Russians and pointing down into the street below.

Two of them, getting out of the back doors of a Mercedes, one big and bear-like in a fur hat and the other angular and emotionless in a green puffa jacket and both of them light on their feet and moving fast towards the fire escape.

'Argh!'

Twist heard the scream and turned. It was Dodge. Sikes had shot him and he was down. He was lying on the floor squirming in agony. His face was a bloody pulp and he was holding his left thigh and Fagin was waving his hands in the air, calling out to Sikes as he went to pull Bullseye off the stricken Dodge.

'Run, Oliver! Run!' Fagin shouted, as Sikes raised his gun and fired. Twist scrambled to his feet, following Red who was running for the shelter of the lift engine room halfway along the hundred metre roof. A fourth gunshot followed. It ricocheted off the engine room a fraction of a second after Red took cover behind it.

Twist sprinted wide, hoping the lights of the adjoining buildings would make it harder for Sikes to focus, getting as much distance between him and the bullets as possible, then turning sharply into a tight left-hander and running for the engine room and Red.

Two more shots rang out and Twist looked left to see Sikes hobbling towards him firing wildly. He signalled to Red to run for the furthest edge of the roof as the two Russians came storming up from the fire escape, moving together, the one in the puffa jacket covering the first from a kneeling position as the Bear reached the top and drew what looked like a machine pistol from a holster concealed inside his leather bomber jacket.

Twist was sprinting and Red's hand was in his as they ran for the far edge of the roof not knowing what lay ahead. As they ran Twist thought of Dodge, left wounded, and Fagin and the paintings in the tube as the pistol shots sent gravel fizzing up from the flat tarmac to their right.

The edge of the roof came fast and they both dived flat. The rapid drilling of the machine pistols and the return fire of the Beretta sounded close on the roof behind them as sirens whined in the streets below. Twist followed Red as she turned her stomach to the edge and lowered her hands until they were hanging side by side, then they exchanged a look before dropping the twenty feet to the flat roof below.

This roof was on the third storey of the building. Sixty-plus feet to the ground but they weren't alone and they watched, turning as they ran, as Sikes dropped off the edge, rolled backwards and sprang up on his feet.

'Here I come!' he yelled, limping, fishing for a fresh clip in his jacket pocket as Red and Twist zigzagged across the roof, vaulting air conditioning units and ducking for cover as a bullet smashed into a steel satellite dish and zipped out past them into the night air. But then the Beretta stopped and Twist realised that the drilling sound had stopped too. Which meant the Russians must have legged it, with or without their paintings, when they first heard the sirens. But it left one question: had Sikes stopped firing because he was conserving bullets or because he had run out of them?

Twist reached the edge first and looked down. There was a building below but it was too far to make from a standing jump and Sikes was closing fast.

'You can do this!' Red said and Twist looked up to see herdancing backwards, half skipping. His mind burned as he weighed up the risk.

A couple of bullets left in Sikes's gun versus a twenty-foot-long jump with a vertical drop of twenty feet from a limited run-up. It took him about a millisecond.

'You go first!' he shouted at Red as he sprinted to her, fifteen feet back from the edge.

She didn't budge. With Sikes just thirty feet behind her she didn't move an inch. Not until Twist got to her and then they turned together, took a deep breath and sprinted for the edge. The floor dropped out from under him as he soared across the canyon looking down at the crowd staring open-mouthed from the street below.

And then the roof rose up at him and he hit it harder than anything he'd ever hit before. His left ankle buckled and he slipped out with it on that side, bouncing once, then spinning and turning to hit the roof again, this time face down, the gravel being driven deeper into his flesh as he used his hands like brake pads in his desperation, turning as he travelled, to see if Red was still with him.

But he could see nothing apart from a solitary figure standing on the rooftop opposite. He pulled himself up onto his feet, pain shooting up through his left ankle, and began to hobble back towards the edge. There was no sign of her, just Sikes standing training his pistol on him as he ran.

But Twist ignored the gun. It seemed irrelevant and he heard the crack as Sikes pulled the trigger. He kept running. He was only alive for one reason; Sikes had not been aiming at him, he'd been aiming low, aiming at Red.

He saw the tips of her fingers first, knuckles white as they gripped the plastic guttering. He skidded to a stop on his knees, then dropped flat and reached down and grabbed her by her collar, offering her his right hand. He saw the determination in her eyes and the muscles in her neck tighten as she let go with her right hand and snatched hold of his wrist.

He spread his legs, imagining his toes digging into its impermeable tar, and started to draw her to him, closer so that her breath was in his neck and he was able to reach lower, wrapping the waistband of her cargo pants around his clenched fist.

And then he heard a thud a couple of feet away and he felt Red shift her weight away from the point of impact. He heard the sound of hands scraping on the roof surface and he looked up, past his left shoulder and saw Sikes slipping back, winded, until he was forced to take hold of the plastic guttering.

And there he hung, suspended, staring at the wall, gulping for breath then turning sideways to look at Red, using his brute strength to pull himself up but then, once again, finding nothing on the flat roof surface that he could hold on to.

And as Twist redoubled his effort, trying desperately to pull Red up, he felt her panic, scrabbling with her feet as Sikes began to laugh as the absurdity of his position dawned on him. He was the victim of a tragic cliché.

He simply could not make it without her.

Twist watched Sikes slide his left hand along the guttering, six inches closer, then follow with the same arm. Twist tried to pull Red but they were too bound up in the mechanics of getting her up onto the roof now to attempt to move her sideways along its edge. And as Sikes slid his hands a second time, Twist saw they could not avoid him.

'Hold on!' Twist whispered in Red's ear, as he felt Sikes's fingers claw into the tendons of his left arm where the bicep met the bone.

'I've got you now, boy,' he said.

He felt Red slip, her right hand sliding back towards the edge as Twist took half of Sikes's weight on top of hers.

'No!'

He said it emphatically as he strained to hold on, feeling his feet slipping forwards an inch at a time towards the edge, knowing that if he released the fist from Red's waist and struck at Sikes's face Sikes would snatch for Red and he would lose her forever.

But then Red kicked out at Sikes's groin and Twist saw the pain in the older man's eyes, forcing him to let go of Twist's arm and turn sideways to deflect her second kick onto his thigh.

Free of his weight, Twist pulled and Red ran her feet in small steps at the wall until her entire arms were on the roof and Twist was squirming, half on his feet, trying to stand so that he could pull her the rest of the way.

And then he saw fear flash in her eyes and he felt her weight almost treble and heard Sikes's hollow laughter. His muscles burnt in his thighs and in his shoulders as he tugged and Red twisted and fought, until, slowly, Sikes's grasp began to slip and with a horrifying cry he fell, hurtling down to the asphalt below.

55

Bermondsey took Brownlow back to the beginning. To a man called Barker who had drugged Brownlow's grandmother's Rizla, then drilled a hole in her bay window and passed a thin hollow tube through the hole, allowing him to open a wire noose and lasso then pull open the window latch.

Barker had been a specialist. It later emerged he'd cased the house two weeks before the robbery using a knocker whose day job involved checking out-of-warranty boilers for British Gas. While his grandmother was in the kitchen putting the kettle on, the nice man who'd jammed her boiler was upstairs photographing the silver which Barker then ran by his fence who confirmed that it was indeed a gilt silver cup commissioned by George IV to commemorate the opening of the Brighton Pavilion.

Barker's mistake had been to carry out the robbery on a Thursday. Brownlow had spotted the logic immediately, based on his visits to Bermondsey Market as a child. In order to escape from his overbearing Rear Admiral father,

Brownlow's dad had taken him on long walks from his grandparents' house in Greenwich, one mile west along the riverbank, to scour the market. Walks which, he'd recalled the Thursday night his mother had phoned to tell him his grandmother had been burgled, had only ever taken place on a Friday morning. The only day of the week the market opened.

So with his instincts bristling he had called in sick, arriving at H. T. Speyer's superior silver antiques emporium when it had opened at nine the morning after the robbery. And there, after asking if Speyer had anything 'special', he was taken into a storeroom where Speyer had unlocked a mahogany cabinet and pulled out his grandmother's gilt silver cup, offering him a 'distressed purchase' of just ten thousand pounds.

Brownlow smiled at the memory of the circular questions he'd asked Speyer regarding the cup's provenance until, finally, he'd skinned his hand, shown his badge and watched Speyer buckle and confess to receiving it from a mysterious buyer at eleven p.m. in the car park of the Ferryman the night before.

It had taken minimal persuasion to lure Barker back with the offer of a second job and Brownlow recalled his disappointment when a grubby little man, as far from David Niven's Pink Panther as could humanly be possible, had blown into his hanky, examined the contents then stepped into Speyer's shop.

The rest of that Friday had been spent riding shotgun as Barker, who was a cabbie by day, had driven him around the hundreds of homes he'd burgled in a twenty-year career. It had been a glorious day. Recalled more fondly now than his wedding a year later, contradicting his parents' concern that he had not followed his father to the Bar and culminating in the confession that got Barker seven years in Belmarsh and Brownlow a watching brief on Bermondsey.

And he was watching still, thirty years on, taking his 'constitutional' whenever he needed a boost. Which, he reflected, he needed more than ever this dark January morning after his ailing career had slipped on a hunch, fallen badly and broken its hip.

He had grown to know them all. The snipes, the fences and the Lovejoys who handed their trades down like a curse to the next generation, all nodding, smiling as they texted blindly beneath their covers to warn their accomplices that 'The Godfather' was doing his rounds. And prevention not cure had been his sermon this morning, preached sideways to Bedwin whose only vice was loyalty after the gamble on the boy had backfired and left their budget vulnerable.

It was to Bedwin Brownlow turned now as she tugged at his sleeve. He had no idea how long his phone had been ringing. It was only a matter of time before one of the bully boys in CID caught wind of his slight deafness and used it to scalp him and steal his job.

He raised the device to his ear without checking the screen to see who was calling, but he recognised it immediately. It was the boy called Twist who was the subject of a nationwide manhunt for his part in a string of successful art heists. Hunted not only by the police but by his crew's former paymaster and every two-bit Russian hood this side of Vladivostok who had, like the recently deceased William Sikes, sworn fealty to one Arkady Rodchenko, known by his friends in Interpol as 'The Archangel'.

'I guess you heard about the reward?' Brownlow asked, listening carefully to what the boy was telling him before making his proposal.

There was a pause as the boy Twist took time to reflect upon the practicalities of Brownlow's suggestion that the busy thoroughfare of St Pancras International was as good a place as any for an old-school switcheroo.

'Is there anything in particular you're going to need?' Brownlow asked, waiting for what must have been a minute before Twist said:

'One million pounds and a brown Adidas bag.'

56

It was brown and it was in a retro style. Brownlow hadn't wanted to get into semantics with the stallholder. It had a big Adidas sign on both sides and it had been stitched well enough. The only problem he was having was with the strap. The bag weighed about twenty pounds and it cut into his shoulder blade as he came up out of the Tube station.

That was the second thing, after the bag. He'd get the word ten minutes before the RV and he'd be able to reach it in ten minutes from his 'home base' which he'd taken to mean Scotland Yard. The rest had sounded a lot like all the shows the boy must have seen on TV. Any sign of company and the deal would be off. He'd travel overseas with the paintings.

Where? Brownlow had wanted to ask. And what kind of price would he expect to get for them with Interpol and the Russian mob breathing down his neck?

He fished in his pocket as he crossed the concourse to the men's toilet. There was a sign where the coin slot should have been. It read *Out Of Order* but there was a stumpy Latin

American-looking woman with red blotches around her eyes sat on a stool behind the turnstile chewing on something, staring blankly down into a wicker basket in front of her which had some coins in it.

Brownlow raised his hand but she didn't look up. He tapped the flat steel top of the turnstile a few times but still no response. He sighed, turning to look at the clock in the middle of the concourse. It was quarter to three. He had fifteen minutes to get into the café on the far side of the barrier where the ramp led down to the Eurostar. Not enough time to be playing games with this old bag.

'Special Branch,' he said, stepping up to the turnstile. 'Open this gate or I'll have you deported.'

The woman looked up and opened her mouth. She had something in there that had maybe once been alive. She stood up and Brownlow kept his eyes on her as he passed to her left into the men's toilet. At least she kept the place empty, he thought, pushing open the first cubicle door he came to.

The money was in fifties, stacked in thousand-pound bundles. Two hundred bundles, just like the reward said, payable by the insurance company to anyone with information that led to the recovery of the three Hogarths stolen during the Shard heist.

He was back on the concourse within sixty seconds and in the queue for the Eurostar within a hundred and twenty. He had to hand it to the boy, it was a high-stakes game and he'd played a pretty cool hand. But to run he needed money. And that made him vulnerable, which was why Brownlow had to catch him now, before someone else did.

He put the Adidas bag on the roller pins and watched the man in front's black satchel disappear along the conveyor belt. He was wearing a Homburg and square-framed glasses and Brownlow thought he might be Elvis Costello but then a blonde woman pushed in front of him and he turned to complain and Brownlow saw that he was a rabbi.

'I'm going to miss my train. Do you mind? Thank you,' she said, no apology, as if everyone else in the queue wasn't also rushing for the 15:10.

He watched as she kicked off her heels and placed them in a grey box on the conveyor belt, then put her folded beige mackintosh into a separate box and stepped through the body scanner. Brownlow thought she must be a looker. The security guard gave her a double take when she walked past him to collect her stuff.

Brownlow looked back at his bag, telling himself not to lose sight of the money. He'd called ahead to each of the main stations' heads of security to ensure there was no time lost accounting for the money and he smiled at the X-ray operator as his bag sailed through without issue.

But an alarm was still ringing. He looked up at the body scanner as he struggled with the laces on his left shoe. It was the rabbi. He was complaining as the gate guard raised his hands in the air telling him it was standard procedure at all international crossings now, land, sea or air.

A moment passed. Brownlow checked the time on his mobile. He was still good. Five minutes to the RV. The gate guard touched the rabbi's pocket and he watched the rabbi look pleasantly surprised to find some small change in his jacket. Then it was Brownlow's turn. He had planned ahead and was wearing the slightly too tight corduroys that didn't need a belt and he sailed through without so much as a whisper.

He bought himself a coffee, in position at last, in the faux French café halfway down the walkway to the 15:10 train with sixty seconds still on the clock to the initial RV at 15:00 hours.

'See anyone you recognise?'

It was Bedwin in his right ear.

'Not yet ...' he replied, checking, scanning to his left and spotting the plain-clothes 'help' HR had sent them. He was in W.H.Smith pretending to read but kept looking up, moving his head from bag to bag then returning to the book, flicking through the pages like he was cross-referencing rare tropical birds. Obvious but OK if he'd actually seen the bag he was looking for.

A brown Adidas bag which was identical to Brownlow's, travelling down the concourse beneath the arm of an emo kid wearing Ray-Ban aviators and dyed black shoulder-length hair tucked in beneath a baseball cap.

Brownlow stood up and clutched his identical bag, spilling coffee across the table as the emo kid turned and smiled, tilting his shades forwards, to reveal his true identity but also to send a message, by staring past Brownlow, at the café walls behind him.

Brownlow felt the first flush of an anxiety attack. He pushed himself up and out of the chair again and turned to see a sign which read: *Support HTO – Exhibition Of Work By Local Artists.*

Terrible pictures were interspersed with those of the Eiffel Tower. The first was right above his head. It was a picture of a woman with red rings round her eyes sitting on a stool behind a pair of turnstiles with what looked like an ice cream whip for hair ...

He moved along the wall, walking his hands above the heads of a couple dining, past a black and white photograph shot from the top of the Eiffel Tower, until he reached the corner and then turned left … and saw Moll Hackabout arriving in London, fresh-faced, for the first time.

And then Brownlow was moving faster, walking his hands from one picture to the next, knocking a bottle of Coke to the floor and bumping into a waitress, until he found the second and then the third and then he turned and looked back for Twist.

But the boy had vanished into the rush of passengers who were surging down the concourse to make the 15:10. He checked his wrist and watched five seconds tick away to the moment of departure, his mind racing as the answer hit like someone had hurled a sweat-soaked sock across the café at him.

The bag!

His face contorted in anguish as he fumbled with the zipper until his hand was inside clutching a wad of newspaper sheets cut perfectly to size.

Brownlow felt his knees give way and the waitress put her arm on his and helped him into a chair. He had to think but first he had to square away what must look like dementia. He looked up and saw the manager staring suspiciously from behind the counter, enjoying the look of surprise then apology as he held up his police badge. He was using it too much today and he didn't like it. It was a sign he was losing his edge.

He crossed his hands together, closed his eyes and let his mind go to work reconstructing the details of his walk from the toilet to the café, like a sceptic groping in the dark to expose the magic trick that had just humiliated him.

But he had a trick of his own, a way of reconstructing a crime scene after he had left it, stepping into it, exploring all its dimensions like a movie director stepping onto the set he had worked with his art director to create. Except this time it was different. He wasn't just the dispassionate observer revisiting the crime after the fact but the victim, and it took an act of will to step out of the role and see the big picture.

To see the face of the unfeasibly blonde woman from the front as she pushed past the rabbi in the Homburg. And recognise it as the face of Nancy. The girl in the gang, listening to her apologise again, in a half-arsed way to the rabbi as she slid past him, her right hand tracing the contours of his stomach, dropping some coins into his pocket as he puffed up in protest.

And then he pulled back from the scene, watching her step through the metal detector and look back and wait for her coat as it rolled down off the rollers on the far side of the X-ray. Then the camera was up on a crane, looking down from above as, at that exact same moment his Adidas bag full of money was passing beneath the X-ray and the rabbi was stepping into the body scanner and triggering the alarm.

And then the camera returned to its original position, in her face, up close and personal, capturing the intensity of her eyes as she tried to act casual, delaying just two seconds until his bag rolled out from the X-ray before picking up her coat, to reveal an identical Adidas bag beneath it, then reaching to the left, picking up his and turning to walk quickly away towards the 15:10 with a fat grin on her face.

'Any sign of the paintings?' Bedwin asked.

Brownlow looked up, blinking. She was stood in front of him, following his finger which he raised and pointed over his shoulder at the wall of the café behind him.

57

The laptop screen was catching the sunlight that was flooding in through the window, over the tops of the buildings across the street and bouncing off the mirror on the wall behind the bar. Pausing for thought, she watched as he picked up two menus and used them to shield the screen on both sides.

'Shh,' he told her. 'It's starting.'

She leant into him, her hand reaching into the space between his thighs, ducking beneath his left arm to occupy the space between his arms.

'The tale of the three Hogarths stolen last week in an audacious raid on Sotheby's first auction in the Shard took a bizarre twist yesterday when a tip-off led detectives from Scotland Yard's Art and Antiquities Squad to St Pancras Station, where three paintings were recovered.'

The BBC reporter was different to the ones who had reported on the thefts before. He was older and had been investigating the possibility of links between the gang and organised crime. She reached to her right and pushed up his arm a couple of inches, intensifying the shadow on the screen so there was just enough contrast to see the paintings on the wall of the café as the camera panned across them to alight on the old detective called Brownlow whose warning Twist had ignored.

'The surprise was, these turned out to be three different Hogarths, not those taken from the auction but ones stolen in an earlier heist from the Losberne Gallery in London's Mayfair. Paintings that had been missing since they were first stolen over two hundred and fifty years ago ...'

They watched as the camera cut to Brownlow. He looked comfortable answering the questions he was taking from the ladies and gentlemen of the press with his younger partner standing tight-lipped by his side.

'Well, I suppose the message this sends out to criminals is very simple: stolen artworks will be recovered,' he was saying, 'no matter how long it takes.'

She laughed and the sound rang out across the café like a bell. It was on the Oderstrasse in a down-at-heel neighbourhood called Friedrichshain in Berlin which they had chosen because it had no police station and they would not be conspicuous amongst the other artists and bohemians huddling for warmth inside the café.

The reporter appeared once again on the screen and Red put her ear to the speaker, straining to hear him above the coffee grinder. She caught only snatches of what he was saying, fighting to keep her position as Twist's wire-like fingers bored into her side trying to prise her away from the speaker so he could hear too.

So she only caught snatches of the reporter's speculation about the whereabouts of the three Sotheby's Hogarths which were still missing after their theft from the Shard and which, given the rumoured involvement of a major Russian crime syndicate, looked likely to remain a mystery for a good time to come.

58

He'd forgotten how dangerous geese were. Vicious fowl with recidivist reptilian brains that dated back to the nightmare late Jurassic Age. He'd also forgotten how cold the Fagaras mountains became in winter as he trudged the frozen rutted track back up to his half-constructed villa where work on the pool had been delayed until the spring when the ground would thaw out enough to dig once again.

Fagin pushed the door and it creaked open. Then he lit a candle with great solemnity, shielding its flickering flame from the draughts as he strolled through a maze of crates, most still unopened, until he reached the snug he had dug out of the haystack at the far end of the barn. Then he stopped, surveyed his surroundings and pulled the cord that turned on the fan heater that hung suspended from the rafters above him.

The blast of hot air was glorious and he raised his frozen fingers, let out a satisfied groan and slumped back into a battered armchair to stare at the mud-caked wall of his palace and feast his eyes, once again, on Moll, the love of his life.

There had been a time when he thought he'd never find someone he'd want to be with always, and who would always be there for him, his match and his equal. Inconstant, avaricious and vain, they could almost have been brother and sister had she not been conceived over two hundred and fifty years before him.

He was still grateful that Twist had confided in him when he had and that he had been able to give him timely counsel. There was no doubt in Fagin's mind now that stealing back the paintings from Rodchenko had been the trump card without which Sikes would most likely have killed them all.

He lifted the receiver and dialled the black Bakelite phone from memory. Ring. Ring. Ring. But Dodge didn't answer. He spoke to Twist from time to time but he was keen to hear Dodge's news. To find out if his and Cribb's beach bar was working or if they had burnt through the money Twist had sent them and were back to their old tricks.

He smiled to himself, drawing his hand through his beard. It was only to be expected, he supposed. For after all, boys will be boys and he hated to think of them changing. But at times he missed them terribly. So much so that once he had even climbed the narrow track up the mountain side to kneel at the shrine of St Nicholas of Myra who had worked tirelessly during his lifetime to convert thieves into honest men.

But he had not prayed for that. Only that they were happy, fending for themselves and developing their innate talents to their utmost in a life that afforded them scope.

About the Author

Tom Grass was responsible for creative development at TV production company Pure Grass Films when he first began work on *Twist*, his first novel.

Tom believes in the power of storytelling to bring about change and has co-created interactive stories with young people in Haiti and Africa that encourage them to think for themselves and challenge social norms.